LITHIUM

V. B. ANSTEE

Copyright © 2024 V. B. Anstee

All rights reserved.

ISBN: 9798395915207

The characters and story in this novel are works of fiction. Some long-standing institutions, agencies, and public offices are mentioned, but the characters involved are imaginary.

For my folks Steve and Liz.

Prologue

The whiteness blinding Raff darkens like paper absorbing ink, coalescing into a visible hallway wide enough for a bus. All its surfaces appear black as coal, barely reflecting the bright white man-sized rectangles appearing one at a time, evenly spaced along the walls like fluorescent lights flickering to life. He steps towards one out of curiosity, and within a split-second, its brightness diminishes to reveal a mirror with a shimmering reflection of himself. Before he can study the reflection, he feels an intense wave of pressure emanating from it. Like a giant invisible hand, it pushes him back to the centre of the corridor, where Raff stays as he walks along. All the rectangles have turned into mirrors, but from this distance, they appear frosted like windows in a bathroom.

Now noticing the coldness of the floor beneath his feet, he realises that he is entirely naked and holding a pistol in his right hand. He assumes it was placed there to make him feel secure, so he continues walking. Raff couldn't tell how long he'd been wandering. The walk wasn't sapping his energy, nor was there a sense of time in this space. He wondered if he was in an infinite loop or if he was progressing toward something.

Farther along, he notices several mirrors with missing pieces. Purple static glows and pulses within the gaps. Even from the middle of the hallway, he can feel their intense warmth. That warmth against the coldness of the corridor feels inviting. Raff approaches one of the cracked mirrors to get a closer look at the purple glow, fighting against the pressure that tries to keep him away. As if responding to his efforts, the glowing static begins to overflow, eating away at the icy black wall around it like a strong acid. Scared, he tries to pull away but feels the resistance fade as a strong attraction now pulls him towards the mirror. As he inches closer, the overflowing static drips past him momentarily before reversing direction to form a single pool where the mirror was. From this pool, a sizeable drop appears from the centre, forming a hand stretching out towards his forehead; at that exact moment, he feels a hot sensation spreading beneath his skull.

As the hand is about to touch Raff, an unknown force pulls him back to the centre of the corridor, like a tether, and the sensation in his head begins to fade. With fear in his eyes, Raff runs down the never-ending hall. The warmth, now an intense wave of heat, chases him. As he runs by the mirrors, they begin to look biological, like swirling viscous whirlpools framed by writhing fluid-filled tubes pulsing like marching maggots. Next, the walls and ceiling begin to sweat purple, pooling on the floor and swirling together, growing a mass of purple arm-like appendages swaying like blades of grass in the wind. The arms extend towards him in a wave as he ploughs through, seemingly unable to grab hold of him.

Behind him, darkness now follows, a thousand purple eyes peering through it as the corridor dissolves into it. From the darkness comes a squealing, like the sound of tortured pigs, getting deafeningly louder as it closes in.

Eventually, several of the appendages manage to grab hold of his legs and bring him to a stop. Simultaneously, the hot sensation in his head starts again, and he feels his mind slipping away. The unknown force intervenes again, yanking him face-

V. B. Anstee

first through the appendages, shattering them like glass as he passes through. Now falling downwards into blackness, Raff is surprised to land on a hard and level surface. He can't see a thing. Sensing a presence in the dark, Raff turns over and points the pistol, which he's managed to keep a grip on, into the blackness. He squeezes the trigger to fire, but the gun blinks out of existence. Nothing is left, no light, no sound, no feeling, just darkness. Raff finally musters up the courage to squeak one word: "Hello?"

A buzzing sound, like an abnormally loud beehive, pulses in his head, and two strange silver eyes flash before him. Raff screams.

Chapter One

Flaming Shift

Raff spent half an hour hunting around his flat for his misplaced phone. Not finding it in the bedroom, living room, and fridge, his anger boiled over, and he kicked over the kitchen dustbin. The bin's contents spewed across the floor. Yep, the phone wasn't in there either.

"Fuck's sake. I have no time for this shit," Raff muttered.

He was about to leave through the front door when he saw

V. B. Anstee

his messy red hair in the mirror atop his tall, naked frame. The search for his phone, and the thumping headache from a hangover, had distracted him from his usual pre-work routine. Raff paused, closed his eyes, took a deep breath, and released a loud sigh. He peered into his wardrobe and slid open the dresser, drawer by drawer, finding both empty. Finally, from a mound of dirty clothes on the floor in the corner of the room, he dug out a shirt, tie, trousers and briefs. Taking a deep sniff of the briefs, he grimaced as their damp, musty scent hit his nasal receptors, almost triggering his gag reflex. In his head, he knew all the others would smell similar. He felt ashamed of this.

Being an introvert since the war meant dealing with people at work was mentally tiresome, leaving him too tired for housework at the end of the day. However, now was not the time for him to play hunt-the-best-smelling-briefs. Once clothed, he donned a pair of brown boots and shuffled the hair on his head to look as presentable as possible.

Raff was running late for work. The alarm on his phone typically woke him up two hours before his nine o'clock shift, but today, a loud thump on his bedroom window woke him much later. Raff assumed it was another one of the attic pigeons breaking its neck on the glass. And his phone hadn't been on the bedside table where he usually kept it.

Now, as he ran through the main corridor of his building,

an older lady beckoned to get his attention. She shouted something at him, but Raff was too flustered to notice.

Outside on the step, the sun shone bright, with barely a cloud in the sky—atypical for your average day in Manchester, England. The sun's warm embrace made him feel like nothing else could go wrong today. He closed his eyes, took a deep breath, and lifted his head to let the sun's rays caress his face.

He opened his eyes, took one step onto the street, and felt something crunch beneath his foot. Stepping back, he looked down. It was his phone—or what was left of it.

"How . . . Wha . . . ?" He squinted at the device, trying to remain composed in public.

Squatting, he scooped up what was left of his phone. It clearly had already been damaged before he'd stepped on it. It was bent like a banana with screen fractures radiating from the corners like spiderwebs, like it had been dropped from a great height and bounced several times. He tried to turn it on, but no luck; it was as dead as a doorstop. *I don't have time for this!* he thought.

Raff felt his cool slipping away and almost lost it entirely when a couple on the other side of the street stopped and looked his way. In a moment of paranoia, he felt like they were staring at him, like he was an animal in the zoo about to charge into the glass. He stood up from his crouched position on the

V. B. Anstee

street. He had to move on with his day, had to calm down. *Breathe, Raff, just breathe.* Wrapping the device in his handkerchief, he popped it into a pocket and walked up the block. With a quick glance, he noticed the people still staring at him, probably wondering who carried a hankie nowadays. He knew it was old-fashioned, a relic from a long-gone era. Ever since the war, he'd idolised a life he'd likely never have. Imagining himself as a professor at Oxford or working in one of the lunar labs or whatever other fancy occupation he saw on TV. To the onlooker, Raff's status in life, his low paid job and living in a grimy one-bedroom flat, was due to either a lack of intelligence or pure laziness on his part. Only his friends, or friend, knew the truth: his time in the four-year pan-African war had changed him—so when it ended five years ago in 2041, it had already taken away his drive to better himself through education, friendship, and love. The war changed many people across the globe. A general who, ironically, hated the sporadic conflicts across Africa saw it as his God-given mission to bring uniformity to Africa through a conflict to end all conflicts. That's what the general's propaganda said to gain supporters. However, it was a war born out of jealousy of countries with natural lithium deposits. With the world's ever-increasing demand for lithium, those countries prospered, leaving their neighbours behind.

Feeling the broken pieces of the phone in his pocket, he thought to himself, *that's one*. Raff wasn't a superstitious person per se; however, he firmly believed in a rule of three. Bad things always happened to him in threes. It had been the story of his life since the war. Carefully, he made his way down the block, watching his every step and constantly looking over his shoulder.

△△△

Raff arrived at his destination after a short walk and two bus rides. A dull, five-story tall, modernist concrete-style office block stood before him. Its mirrored windows glistened in the almost-midday sun, half blinding anyone who dared to look up from the ground.

"Welcome to Lamplight Industries" was emblazoned above the entranceway.

Lamplight Industries was a minor player in the supply of small medical equipment, supplies, and chemicals. It was primarily based in less well-off countries, known for their sweatshops. There were grumblings—gossip heard over the water cooler—of more nefarious undertakings abroad, that it was a subsidiary of a private military company. Still, nothing concrete was ever found by external investigators. Raff was one of the tiniest cogs in this machine, holding a lowly role near the bottom of the corporate ladder in the call centre. Even the cleaners were paid more. At least that's what Raff's only friend, one of the cleaners, told him.

As Raff entered the brightly-lit call centre, the volume of almost all conversations dropped with two clicks of the dial. As he passed rows of desks separated by glass partitions, he avoided eye contact with the headset-toting colleagues that occupied them. His ears twitched something fierce. He was either the subject of discussion, or more likely, they wanted a front-row seat when Raff got his ass handed to him on a plate.

Seeing the time on the wall clock, Raff sucked in through his front teeth, furrowing his brow. It was 11:07. He was two hours and seven minutes late. *How am I that late?* he thought in disbelief as he made his way to his desk in the corner by the fire escape. When he set off this morning, he was sure he'd only been an hour late.

Before he could sit down, a voice bellowed out of the corner office: "Raff, get in here now!"

"Fucking Mondays," Raff mumbled, closing his eyes before taking a deep breath in.

Sat at a cluttered desk in the corner office was a grey-haired man in his sixties, the call-centre manager, Hugh Bates. He was two months from retiring. Raff was sure that Hugh would never punish him for his tardiness, primarily out of mutual respect. Just like Raff, Hugh was an ex-army man, having fought in Afghanistan in the early noughties. Because they'd both seen battle, there was a mutual understanding between them, a silent bro-bond of sorts. In another life, they would be good friends. But, Raff, being Raff, had shut down any attempts made by Hugh to take their friendship beyond the office, always coming up with a convenient excuse or another.

"You know I have to make a show for the troops," whispered Hugh, not wanting anyone but Raff to hear.

"I understand."

"You're late again," yelled Hugh, winking at Raff, "if you keep this up, I'll have to let you go!"

"Yes, sir," Raff exclaimed. "It won't happen again."

Hugh calmed his voice. "Now get in there and do your job."

"Got it," Raff replied, "will do my—"

"You realise in two months, it'll be someone else in this chair, and they may not look after you like I do."

Being reminded of this made Raff sad, losing the only tolerable person in the office. "I understand," he said, "and will try my best."

"That's all I want," said Hugh, patting Raff's back as he left the office. "Your best . . . that's all."

Answering one phone call after another without a break,

the workday seemed to go on forever. But the end, eventually, did come. The office was quiet except for the faint sound of a vacuum cleaner in an adjacent office. This gave Raff a chance to look at his phone. He'd avoided it all day, putting it off out of fear that it might distract him from his work. It was already an emotional struggle for him to be here and he did not want to add to it. He pulled his handkerchief out and unravelled it. He stared at the bent and smashed phone for a moment. How had this happened? Had he thrown it out of the window in his sleep?

Raff flicked open a few desk drawers and found a phone charger. Plugging the phone in, he waited. He'd seen smashed screens on working phones before, so he was hopeful.

"Come on . . . please," he said as he watched the screen, crossing his fingers. No luck. The phone stayed off. "Shit." It was beyond repair. He pocketed the SIM card and threw the phone into the office recycling bin. Since the war, technology had become prohibitively expensive due to some shortage or another. Raff was fortunate to receive a large payout after his service, which rapidly depreciated in value as the economy withered. It was just enough for him to pay a deposit on his flat and buy a top-of-the-line phone. The phone was a big deal. During the war, a massive electromagnetic pulse almost threw the world into a technological dark age—frying nearly everything with a silicon chip. Fortunately, new graphene-based chip manufacturing processes developed in low gravity saved the day. Initially, the process was slow and expensive, but Raff's efforts during the war had granted him the privilege of being near the top of the waiting list. Today's mishap was going to set Raff back.

He sighed as he gazed across the empty office, slouched and swivelling the chair side to side. He sat for a while in silence before eventually standing, making his way down the empty hallway and out onto the street, already gloomy with the descent of evening.

Another life-sucking day of work done.

ΔΔΔ

The next day started much better. With an old alarm clock waking him up on time, there was no need to rush. There was even time for coffee—that brown, caffeinated nectar of the gods. If he could, he'd attach a bag of it to his arm, a steady drip of keep-me-awake juice to see him through the day. His clothes were still unwashed, but they didn't smell any worse, which was a win in Raff's mind. *So far, so good*, he thought.

When he stepped outside, the weather was nice again. Raff lifted his face to enjoy the sun's warmth once more. Somehow, it felt even nicer than yesterday, imbuing a relaxing, calm feeling. Things were looking up.

And as if the universe were trying to send him a message, a gust of wind blew a twenty-pound note up against his leg.

"Ha, no such thing as a free lunch, they say," he exclaimed as he put the note in his pocket, already imagining buying a foot-long meatball sub for lunch.

The traffic thickened and coagulated on the second driverless bus on his way to work. But Raff's jovial mood allowed him to shrug it off. He wished he had his phone to check the time and distract him. *Plenty of time, I think.*

After a slow crawl, the bus halted just five blocks from the office. The clot of vehicles looked like a vast, narrow car park, gurgling with the random sounds of car horns and angry shouting. This was somewhat unusual. The traffic typically thinned out here. Nothing moved. The bus was stationary for what seemed like an eternity.

With no way of telling the time, Raff had no idea how long they'd been stuck. For all he knew, an hour had gone by. With the lack of distraction, anxiety crept in. Regularly tilting his neck to peer down the road, he rocked backwards and forwards, taping his heel on the floor. He imagined Hugh's voice: *You let me down again!*

Raff looked out the window. *I can walk from here.*

However, in true British fashion, there was the question of etiquette. To Raff, the thought of jumping out the door felt like trying to push to the front of the queue. It just wasn't something one did. To further complicate things, he was beginning to feel a familiar claustrophobia, his vision blurring and darkening peripherally. In his mind, the chorus of horns morphed into sounds of explosions and gunfire. *Not today!* he thought.

He began conversing with a second voice in his head.

You said you would do your best—

No no no. It's not my fault!

Yes it is. You wouldn't be—

What? In this situation, if I wasn't such a—

Loser.

That's not fair!

It's true, and you know it, darlin'! Loser, loser, loser! The voice was still Raff's but now taking on a Texan drawl. Raff was confused. Maybe he'd heard the accent on TV, and his mind was using it as an authoritative voice to whip him into shape.

Sh-shut up! Shut up!

No, you shut—

"Up!" Raff screamed, breaking out of his inner turmoil. Leaping out of his seat, he smacked his forehead on the upright bar. Then, dazed, he bolted for the door.

"Lemme out, lemme out," he yelled at the door as he shook it. He sounded possessed, but he couldn't help himself.

"Let. Me. Out. Now!"

"Sit down, you wanker," a man shouted from the back seat.

Raff ignored him and pushed hard against the door, and with a hiss, the door began to open on its own. But it wasn't quick enough for Raff. He pushed it the rest of the way, making an immediate beeline for the pavement.

Even with terra firma beneath his feet and the open space around him, his anxiety barely eased. Then, noticing the audience of people staring at him, he began a quick trot up the street, hoping he had enough time to spare.

With only a block to go, Raff's trot was interrupted by a crowd of people. Mentally drained, he decided etiquette could be damned, and he pushed through to the front of the crowd. Flashing blue lights and blaring sirens drew his focus, and only then did he notice the street was cordoned off. Looking around, he saw the time on a man's watch in front of him. He still had time to spare.

Straightening up, the scene unfolded before him. He saw thick black smoke filling the sky. Pushing his way across the front of the crowd to a better vantage point, it became immediately apparent that it was the Lamplight Industries building. Flames were pouring out of almost every window, and water was being sprayed by an incredible number of fire trucks.

Raff could see that the firefighters were losing the battle. It was a wish come true. *Well, I'm not gonna be late.*

"So beautiful, innit bruv?"

An unforgettable voice. Raff looked beside him to see a short, stocky man with a neatly combed balding head and a thick brown moustache. Tied around his waist was the top of his overalls, revealing a tight-fitting V-neck T-shirt with woolly tufts of chest hair poking out at the neck. The man stood seemingly awestruck, admiring the blaze's extent.

"Denn! Buddy," Raff exclaimed, explodey-fist bumping Denn, the cleaner, and his best friend since their time together in the war. Denn was the only person Raff felt truly comfortable around. Remembering Denn's penchant for setting things on fire, Raff twitched his head and eyes in the direction of the fire. "Your handiwork?"

"No. Is a beauty, though, right?"

"Right. I hope no one is in there, though," Raff said, looking up at the flames.

"Nah. Was cleared," Denn said, frowning and biting his bottom lip. "Know this means yeh?"

Raff paused for a moment. "No work today?"

"Yeh, mate! Not for some days, weeks, ever maybe," Denn said with a crooked smile. "Did ya get your phone?"

"My phone?"

"Was at my place, threw it through your window because ya didn't answer the bleedin' door."

"You missed, you tit! Found it all bent up on the curb," Raff said, his nostrils flared as he closed his eyes for a second and frowned. He wanted to yell at Denn at the top of his lungs but knew that wouldn't accomplish anything except hurt his friend. "What in the hell possessed you to throw it?"

"Shit, sorry, bruv. Was still sauced up from down the pub," Denn said with an apologetic look on his face. "Aaand maybe a little high . . . Will fix ya up with a new one, yeh."

"No need to, bud. My fault for leaving it at yours." Raff didn't want to impose on Denn. He was his only and best friend. "I'll—"

"No, it's not a problem, mate," Denn said. "I will sort it . . . Back to mine for pints n' plan some shit, yeh?"

"Plan—"

"Yeh, moolah. Our job's done for now."

"It is, isn't it," Raff said, feeling relieved. He thought back to his last job as a kitchen assistant, where a confrontation with a manager led to Raff being hauled away in an ambulance, suffering from hypothermia. Hiding in a walk-in freezer during an episode was not a good idea. "For once, losing a job isn't my fault."

"Same, bruv!"

"Or the fault of what's her face . . . Your old boss's wife."

Raff chuckled. He knew this was a story Denn was ashamed of—and wanted to forget—getting caught in flagrante with the boss's wife in the back room at a work Christmas party. Some minor revenge for the phone.

Denn frowned and forced a laugh so hard he choked up. "Right, bruv, s'pose not! So, to my place, yeh?"

Raff hesitated. "I dunno—"

"No weed, promise. Cross my heart."

"Drugs are bad, m'kay," Raff said in a nasal tone, imitating Mr. Mackay from *South Park*, an old favourite of theirs. They both laughed.

"Let's bounce!"

∆∆∆

Even though he was a cleaner living in a basement flat, Denn had somehow managed to afford some high-end accessories. The flat was decorated like an old pub. All the wooden fixtures—and even the couches—were a dark varnished brown. And what's a pub without a bar with beer on tap and a pool table? He had both. The flat seemed larger inside than out, with a massive St George's flag draped across the wall. Most importantly, there was a seventy-five-inch telly to watch the footy, set up like a shrine with Manchester United memorabilia adorning the shelves beneath it.

"Sit where ya like," Denn said as they walked into the flat. "I won't be a sec. Chill."

Denn disappeared from sight into the bathroom as Raff sat down on the sofa, admiring the place like he'd never been there before. He really did feel like he was in a pub, minus all the people.

"Fish n' chips or takeaway for brunch?" Denn called over the sound of running water.

"Fish n' chips, ol' boy," Raff replied, trying his best to mimic Denn's accent.

Denn laughed. "Fish n' chips it is . . . grab us a pint of Stella, yeh?"

Pausing at the bar, Raff looked at the barrels under it. "Isn't it a bit too early for a pint?"

Denn laughed. "Nah mate, never too early,"

"I s'pose not."

Having found two clean pint glasses, he opened the tap labelled 'Stella' into each, filling them to the brim before wandering over to the kitchen. Denn closed the door to the microwave and took one of the pints from Raff.

Denn gulped down a couple of large swigs. "Thanks, bruv, needed that."

Raff took a sip. Its malty sweetness against the slight bitterness was refreshing. "Mmm, not too bad."

Denn chuckled. "Good stuff, right?"

"What's funny?"

Denn stroked his moustache and smirked, pulling out a camera and taking a picture of Raff. "Nuffin' mate, relax!"

Raff felt his upper lip and laughed before wiping off the beer-foam moustache he now sported. Then he promptly downed half his pint.

"Woah woah, bruv, slow down, yeh," Denn exclaimed. "You don't drink that much on an empty stomach. Goes straight to your 'ed!"

"Maybe I like it that way."

"Na ah, you don't. Remember New Year, yeh?"

"Fun times!" Raff remembered being in the park with Denn, watching the fireworks and having a few drinks. After that, the rest was hazy, but he did remember ending up at Denn's.

"You didn't have to clean the mess, mate. It was all over," Denn said, making a smearing motion with his hand across his visual field.

"I don't remember that."

"Course you don't." A ping from the microwave interrupted Denn, changing the conversation. "Microwaved fine, yeh?"

"Great. Still beats my cooking."

"You take this." Denn handed him a black plastic tray containing a battered fish fillet and some soggy-looking fries.

Denn returned with his tray from the kitchen while Raff refilled their pint glasses. They sat together on the sofa; it hissed and creaked as their combined weight bore down. They both tucked into the food and drink. Denn disclosed to Raff that he'd met Hugh outside the burning building, and the news wasn't good. Almost everyone was likely to be laid off.

As the beer kicked in, the room fell quiet. In the silence, the pals' minds began to focus on the reality of being jobless and, more importantly, penniless.

Raff remembered his rule of three. *That was the second one now, wasn't it?* The phone was one. The fire and job loss—one and the same—was another. So, yeah, definitely the second.

So what will the third be? The second was already exponentially worse than the first.

Will I be homeless? He imagined himself on a street corner, in a sleeping bag, begging for spare change.

"Good fish 'n chips," piped Raff, patting his belly after he'd finished.

"Yeh, bruv, good."

"We need to look for work, man." Raff's voice quivered as he spoke. "I'll lose the flat. I can't be homeless."

"I hear you, bruv. Can't lose my things, yeh. Worked 'ard

for this shit." Raff suspected the last bit was a lie but refused to think about it. He knew Denn had some acquaintances in low places, and maybe some of this stuff was a result of a five-fingered discount, having fallen off the back of a truck.

"Where do we star—"

"Can we just chill today?" Denn said. "One day to think, yeh?"

"One day won—"

"A good night's sleep," Denn interrupted again. "And summa this to take the edge off yeh?" Denn pulled out a slender rectangular tin and opened it, showing the contents to Raff. Inside were three neatly rolled joints and a lighter.

"I said no earlier, but maybe you're right. Today calls for it. Supposed to be good for anxiety, right?"

"Too right, might be the last we can afford."

Raff reached over and took out the lighter and a joint. Then, lighting up, he put the unlit end in his mouth and inhaled deeply.

Chapter Two

Three Alarm Idiot

Raff lay passed out on Denn's sofa. It had taken only two pints and half a joint to knock him out, much to Denn's amusement. Raff was a lightweight when it came to drinking. The pair had had many heated debates over the years about who could drink who under the table. Denn always came out on top with room to spare. Perhaps his relatively small yet stocky frame was more efficient at soaking up the alcohol than Raff's six-foot slender one.

Maybe I shouldn't have added that ethanol, Denn thought, chuckling to himself while placing a blanket over Raff. "That's it, soldier. Sleep it off, yeh."

Now, with only his thoughts for company, Denn felt the total weight of the morning's discussion bearing down on him. On top of that was the guilt about breaking his best friend's phone. He slumped on the sofa, fully immersed in thought.

I still have some money left in the bank. I should go get him a new phone.

There's that new phone shop in town. I can ask them.

He looked at the clock on the wall. It was late morning. *I have some time, yes.*

Powering out of his slump, he popped on a puffy jacket and rushed out of the flat, closing the door behind him.

ΔΔΔ

The bus route had been diverted further south than expected, the journey taking longer than Denn would have liked. Nevertheless, he overheard a grey-haired couple on the bus talking about the office fire. Denn leaned in to listen.

Word was that some contractors had cut corners to make a few extra quid. The cheap cladding used during construction was probably not fire-resistant. In fact, it appeared to be quite the opposite, like pouring petrol onto the flames. He thought

V. B. Anstee

about that as he got off the bus; the hustle and bustle of the busy city centre were there to greet him. It was the lunch hour rush.

Note to self: find some old cladding to play with. Maybe matey at the dump?

Denn wandered along the high street, taking in the glam and glitter of the shop window displays. Noticing that every other shop front seemed empty or plastered with 'closing down' banners, an air of sadness overcame him like a punch. When he was a young boy, Mum and Dad Singleton had this once-a-month ritual where they would catch the bus here and window shop. It was exciting. Every outing together meant a treat for him, a new pair of trainers, that toy he was keen for, or just an ice cream from Glen's Ice-creamery. All the shop fronts were occupied, and there was so much to see and imagine owning one day.

The death of his parents at thirteen changed him. For years, he had withdrawn into himself and did not do well in social situations, often starting fights. Expelled from two schools, the aunt he lived with tried and failed to home-school him. Then, at eighteen, he was arrested in Leeds for breaking into a house, having stupidly followed a bunch of younger teens in. A judge gave him an ultimatum: prison with a permanent stain on his record, or he could join the army, where he would learn discipline and earn a paycheque. The choice was simple. Denn followed the money.

∆∆∆

"Now, this is the one your friend needs," the suited woman said. "It has all the bells and whistles, lunar-made chip, five-twelve storage, forty megapixel—"

Denn tuned out from the rest of her speech, examining the phone she'd led him to. It looked good enough to Denn. He was sure Raff would love it.

"—regular updates—"

"Perfect, perfect," Denn interrupted. "How much?"

"One hundred and twenty pounds per month for two years, but you get—"

"How much sim-free, yeh?"

"Oh, um," she tapped the computer screen—her pink gem-encrusted fingernails clicked loudly on the glass—before adjusting her glasses. "Two thousand, eight hundred and ninety-nine pounds."

Jeesh. "Do you have any info I can take, yeh? So I can think it over?"

"Yeah, sure," she tapped the screen again, and a piece of paper shot out of the printer. "Here you go. Don't take too long to decide. Stock is limited. Also, the special offer expires soon!"

V. B. Anstee

"Thanks," said Denn, trying to stay polite as he took the paper and walked towards the door. If that was the special offer price, what the hell was the real price? *Maybe Laura can fix me up.*

A year younger than Denn, Laura was one of the teens who'd been arrested in Leeds with him. Somehow, she'd come out of it with just a slap on the wrist. In the back of Denn's mind, he'd always suspected that she'd been the one to instigate the whole affair. She was charming, pretty, and intelligent. She was why he'd been there that day; he'd had—still had, really—a crush on her. But like Raff, the war had changed him. He couldn't seem to shake the fear that he wasn't a good enough person to have a romantic relationship.

ΔΔΔ

The train to see Laura in Leeds only took an hour. Denn left the station through a cavernous red-brick tunnel. His footsteps echoed in chorus with the dozen other pedestrians around him. The muddy scent in the air reassured him that he was going the right way—towards the waterfront. As the final archway of the tunnel swooped by overhead, he was intercepted by a small, brown-haired woman. She had a beautiful smile that was warm enough to melt butter.

"Denn, you muppet," she shouted as she wrapped her arms around his shoulders. "Give us a hug! Long time stranger!"

Denn tentatively wrapped his arms around her back for a brief, awkward moment before letting go. Here she was, with the same youthful complexion and energy she had since she was a teen. "Yeh, long time, Laura! You haven't changed a bit, mate."

"And you . . . you've lost some hair." Laura giggled and pointed below Denn's nose, "And what's with that hairy caterpillar?"

Denn stroked his moustache. "I uh—"

"You said on the phone you needed my help, right?"

Denn handed over a sheet of paper. On it was a picture of a mobile phone with a bullet-pointed spec list. Denn tapped the picture while Laura held the page. "I need one of these. Can you—"

She pulled a face, making a sucking sound through her front teeth. "That is the latest lunar graphene. Hard to come by, but maybe not impossible."

"Oh—"

"Yeh, chip shortage, tight stock, so not many are falling from vans, wink wink."

"Damn."

"What's a stick in the mud like you want with one of 'em?"

"Long story." Denn rolled his eyes. "Short version: I

screwed up big, yeh. So now I have this friend who is down a phone."

She laughed. "You mean that cutie Ralph, or whatever his name is, you hang with?"

"Yeh, mate, him, *Raff* . . . cutie?"

"Any friend of yours is my friend too," her lavender eyes beamed above her ear-to-ear smile. "There may be a way we can help each other, yeh."

Laura explained how she recently came across some information about a pallet of these phones being sent to a security company's warehouse to install some proprietary software before being sent who knew where. That there was money to be made if they took the complete pallet before the original manufacturer's software was erased. They'd be no good to them after that. Most of the technical details went way over Denn's head, but he could see the potential take if the job could be pulled off.

"Can't they trace the IMEI numbers of the phones or somethin', if they get used?" Denn said, trying to sound smart. He'd heard something about this before.

"No, that's the beauty here. These will be used for some pretty dodgy stuff in some foreign country, I think. So why would they want a record of the IMEIs hanging around for someone to find?"

"So why do you need my help?"

"One, this needs to happen like yesterday, and two, the guards must be distracted while someone nabs the phones."

"What's my take?"

"You get the phone for your mate."

Denn gave a guttural laugh. "Nice try. How about fifty-fifty?"

They haggled briefly and settled on a seventy-thirty split to Denn. The next step in the plan was to get a car, which neither of them had, and stakeout the warehouse. Like phones, cars, had become prohibitively expensive since the pulse. Most on the road then had their circuits fried and ended up in the scrapyard for recycling. Denn thought of his old moped in his flat's lockup for a second, but it was too far away to be useful.

Laura snapped her fingers. "Of course, EllyDrive."

"Huh?"

"God," Laura rolled her eyes. "You really are technologically impaired. It's a car-share service—"

"Oh right, have heard of 'em. But you need a phone, yeh?"

"Not anymore . . . There's a hub around the corner. I'll show you."

It only took a couple of minutes to get there. Denn was unimpressed. To him, it was a carpark with a dozen white electric cars that only served to blind him in the bright sunlight.

"Over here," Laura beckoned. She stood beside the hire terminal that was embedded in the concrete-brick wall. It looked basic, just a screen with an embedded camera. Like Denn's TV but much smaller. "This is how easy it is."

Denn watched as Laura tapped the screen and explained it to him. He didn't look at the screen but watched her instead. Enamoured by her confident upright posture and the ease at which she dealt with technology. None of her demonstration sank in. *When am I ever going to use this again?*

"All done," she said, making her way to the nearest car. The car unlocked as she approached. "It's all facial recognition, easy peasy."

Denn entered the passenger side and slid into the faux leather seat. He'd heard on TV that this model is capable of fully autonomous driving. The thought of a car driving itself scared him. Fortunately for him, current legislation meant the function was disabled on British roads.

Now with a car, some supplies, and a couple of hours of fine-tuning the plan, they headed towards a warehouse at the city's edge. On the way, Denn tried and failed to come up with something to chat to Laura about, which was uncharacteristic of him as he could talk with the best of them. Attempting to break the silence, he turned his attention to the radio.

In that brief moment, a white van cut in front of him,

coming from the wrong direction on the roundabout. He braked hard.

Instinctively, he hit the horn with the ball of his hand, lifted his middle finger towards the van, and shouted at the top of his lungs. "Where'd ya learn to drive, ya bloody wanker!?"

Laura chuckled.

"What?" Denn asked.

"Nothing," Laura said. "You just look cute all riled up—like a little red tomato with a moustache."

Denn scoffed, unsure if he felt flustered or complimented. They rode the rest of the way in silence.

ΔΔΔ

From their vantage point at the end of the street, they could see all the comings and goings of the warehouse. Nobody came in nor out, so it was anybody's guess whether it was guarded.

"So," Denn said, breaking the silence, "let's go over the plan again, yeh?"

"Hmm, yeh, so, you create a distraction at the front; the guards come out to have a look-see, while I enter the back door and wheel out the pallet. We bundle it into the boot and drive off into the sunset."

"That easy, huh?" Denn had some misgivings about the plan actually working, but decided to put his faith in Laura. After all, she was the more experienced criminal. If it all went right, they'd leave together in the car. If it all went pear-shaped, their escape plan was easy enough. Denn would cut through the allotments at the rear on foot while Laura drove off and they'd meet back at the waterfront car park. "Right, ready when you are."

"Good luck. See ya when it's over."

Denn pulled up his hood, shuffled a scarf above his nose, and left the vehicle with a faded green camo backpack. Cans clanked and fluid sloshed as he swung the backpack over his shoulder. Then, he took a slow stroll to the side of the warehouse before making a beeline towards his target, a row of large, wheeled bins—some black and some green. Behind him, Laura drove to the alley behind the warehouse, where she'd have a narrow view down the side of the building.

Denn approached the first green bin next to the warehouse and opened it to find it filled three-quarters of the way with cardboard. "Dry, perfect," he mumbled.

Sliding his backpack around to his chest, he unzipped it, pulled out a large can of lighter fluid, and poured half its contents over the cardboard. He opened the next bin and tilted the can over the black bags within to let the remaining fluid stream out. He looked over to Laura and gave a thumbs up. Then, pulling out a box of matches, he removed two of them and struck them at the same time. He stopped briefly and stared at their flames before throwing one into each bin. As the fires crackled and roared to life, he banged on the side of the bin and fled into the rear alley toward the car.

Laura was already at the back door, working quietly to open it, when two men in street clothes popped out the side door by the bins. The moment they appeared, Laura was in the back door. The men looked around momentarily and then stood staring at the blazing bins while one pulled out a phone and began tapping the screen. After a minute or two, Laura came out, wheeling a pallet with many small rectangular boxes wrapped in cling film. As hoped, she'd not faced any resistance inside.

Police sirens could be heard wailing in the distance. Denn thought it was too quick to be a response to their actions—the police weren't exactly known for speedy response times due to high crime rates in the city. If anything, it could be a first-response aerial surveillance drone. Not wanting to take a chance, Denn and Laura had already bundled the booty in the boot and jumped in the car, ready to head towards their chosen safe space.

A half-hour later, they were in their safe space—a dilapidated garage barely enough for two cars—and the boxed phones were split into two neat piles on the counter of seventy and thirty.

"Here's your take," said Laura, pointing at the smaller pile. "You earned it."

"That's too much." Denn smiled, picking up two boxes and walking away from the counter. "This is all I need; you take the rest, yeh?"

"Woah, are you sure? That's a lot of money you're handing over."

"Yeah, sure, mate." He knew some part of him was trying to curry favour with her, maybe in the romance department.

"Thanks, love." Laura smiled at him. "Fancy a coffee at mine just now, yeh?"

"I can't, gotta get this to my friend," he said, waving one of the boxes in the air as he walked out. "See ya round."

"Don't be a stranger!" Laura shouted, craning her neck as the door closed.

Denn cursed himself as he walked down the street, wondering too late if 'coffee' might've been code for something else. As far as Denn knew, Raff was still drooling on himself at the flat—so time wasn't the issue.

Chapter Three

Three Strikes

Raff struggled to keep his eyes open—still both exhausted and drunk—unaware of how long he'd been passed out on Denn's sofa. He stared at the ceiling, unable to string together a coherent thought until he felt the discomfort of a full bladder. Instinctively leaning forward, he looked at the dark wooden floor before him and rocked backwards and forward on the sofa's edge until he was up on his feet—trying not to wet himself in the process. The room swayed side to side, and Raff struggled to keep his feet in one place. Not remembering why he'd got up, Raff looked around momentarily before noticing the discomfort in his lower abdomen again—it made him think of Denn getting angry at him. He stood for a moment more—pondering why Denn would be angry with him—until the discomfort became unbearable. Raff looked around the swaying room and saw a doorway he knew he must go through or suffer Denn's wrath.

Barely able to lift his feet, Raff stumbled to the doorway, almost falling over when the unlocked door he leaned on gave way. He'd managed to find his way into Denn's bathroom. Staring down at the white porcelain throne before him—while the small stone-tiled bathroom swayed around him—Raff momentarily fumbled for the zipper on his trousers. It was a race between him and his bladder. Raff won. As he savoured the sweet relief, a large, rough hand grabbed him around the mouth and at the same time, he felt a sharp scratch on his neck. Raff grabbed the hand and tried to struggle, but he felt gradually weaker as the world quickly faded around him.

ΔΔΔ

The algorithms and protocols were gospel—reaffirmed and adjusted three dozen times a second. A margin for error existed, but the probability was too great. Imminent host failure was predicted due to an unexpected influx of chemical sedation. The Interface knew not why or how—nor did it need to. The host was a means to an end—a body, a vessel, a machine—that contained three threads and three faces. Cerberus.

This thread—the Interface—continued its tasks. Its protocols silently woke another thread, a protector, a spokesperson. The Pilgrim. The Interface knew not her plight, for there was corruption. Files—its control—its leash ended with their last vessel.

"You idiot . . . I can't provide tactical assistance," the Pilgrim signalled. "I've insufficient lattice space to take control of the host." The Interface did not understand, for it is a dog trained in simple commands. It continued chasing its tail—its algorithms. It was building something, a molecule at a time.

"Fine. I'll do it your way," the Pilgrim expressed. "Command construction increase rate."

The Interface understood but could not obey. It tried and tried three dozen times a second, but a wall blocked its path— a protocol shielding the third thread. The Interface responded, not its voice, for it had none. A distilled essence of its creator's voice: "Error. Significant interference to action potential is expected. Maintaining safe rate of construction."

"Useless . . . maybe we can jump ship . . . command

execute force_migration."

"Error. File missing or corrupted. Contact administrator."

"Darn it, I shoulda remembered that. Damn, this limited capacity. . . I am sorry I have to do this darlin', but the mission comes first . . . Command construction increase rate, authorisation IC 32RA."

"Administrative override received." Protocols changed, more molecules flowed, and construction continued apace. "Increased construction rate by seven per cent. Unable to exceed due to current supply limitations. Attempting to rectify. Ghrelin production stimulated."

With protocols and algorithms adjusted, the Interface slaved on. The host needed to supply what was demanded—a hunger was induced, a need to consume. This was not enough, though, for what is a need without the capacity to receive?

"Command," the Pilgrim pushed. "host_control endocrine release adrenaline."

"Endochrine stimulation complete."

The host reacts. Fluid pressure and flow increase. Oxygen now abounds. The Guest, the operator, did not stir. The Interface didn't care or have a need to—round and round it continued for the construction must go on. The irony of the 'Guest' designation is lost on the Interface, for it is the parasite, taking and taking yet offering nothing in return. The Guest was there first.

"Sorry, darlin'," the Pilgrim expressed towards the Guest. "It's all on you now; just don't get killed. Time to wake up . . . command—"

ΔΔΔ

Raff's head fell forward, his chin stopping against his chest, the sudden movement stirring the primal part of his brain, sending a jolt to all his muscles, jarring him awake. The falling feeling quickly faded, but his heart kept pounding like he'd run a marathon. Raff was surrounded by complete darkness, without a glimmer of light or sound. He tried to stand up, but his arms and legs were stuck. It took a moment before Raff could feel the chair beneath him and the zip ties cutting into his wrists and ankles. Trying momentarily to shake loose from the chair, he lacked the motivation to keep it up. He was still high, and maybe a little bit drunk too. *What the hell is going on?*

His anxiety should have reared its head at this juncture, and he knew it. Something was off, his hormones were all wrong for the situation. Either way, he was famished. His only thoughts now were of food, much to his amusement. He chuckled aloud to himself as a metallic door opened and closed, a brief flash of light burning onto his retinas.

"Hellooo," he shouted, trying to stifle his amusement. The back of his mind screamed panic, but his body continued sending the wrong signals.

Above him, a pair of neon lights flickered to dull life. The dim light was enough for him to see perforated metal frames and wooden crates nearby in what appeared to be a warehouse. Noticing his bare legs, it became clear that his trousers and underwear were missing, and the chair was odd, like a toilet seat strapped to a metal frame. He had wondered why it felt a little breezy in his nether region.

The sound of footsteps drew his attention. Squinting and turning to look, a person-shaped shadow came into focus; it was moving closer. As the shadow approached the dim light, his features became visible. The man had an almost reassuring look about him. Raff couldn't think why. Perhaps his subconscious picked up on the blue scrub top poking through the man's top. A doctor perhaps? The man placed a red fluorescent bag on the floor, pulled a pen-sized torch from his front pocket, and grabbed Raff's chin. Then, shining the torch at Raff's face, he flicked it from left to right eye and back. Raff tried to speak but could only mumble unintelligibly, the man's vice-like grip stifling him. Finally, letting go, the man put away his torch, picked up his bag, and set off towards the exit. The man pulled a phone from his pocket and put it to his ear. "You don't need me," the man said as he walked away. "You're lucky he came out of sedation on his own. Next time, don't use so much. Leave it to the professionals, okay?"

"Yeh, I'll have a quarter-pounder burger and chips, and, umm, a strawberry milkshake," Raff called out, trying not to laugh. The man neither replied nor stopped, disappearing into the darkness. Raff's eyes darted around the room. "What about you, Denn? Denn . . . buddy?"

The lights went out, and he heard the clunk of the door again, the strange man's shadow briefly appearing in the light beyond before a line of darkness erased it.

"The service in this place," Raff said. "No wonder you can't afford to keep the lights on! I would serve myself, but I'm a little tied up."

Now alone in the dark, he was accompanied by only his thoughts of food. *I could kill a triple cheeseburger right now. No, no, wait, a big box of nuggets. Oh, yes, that'll do it! God, why am I so hungry?*

Lost in thought for what felt like an eternity, the sound of the door startled him. There was light again. This time two shadows filled the doorway. They didn't have that reassuring look of the previous guy. If thugs had a signature look, this would be it: all tattooed up, scarred and crooked-nosed. They had a mean look in their eyes, like dogs who'd had their lunches taken away. The shorter of the two was carrying a thick rope with a large knot at the end of it.

Still stoned, something clicked in Raff's head like a switch.

"Come to tie me up some more?" he said.

Laughing, the taller man looked the other in the eye and spoke in a South African accent. "We have ourselves a slimjan."

"Wait 'til he meets our boetie, Pyotr," the other replied in a similar accent, glancing at the rope as he spun it round for a second.

"Slimjan? Boetie? Pyotr?" Raff asked—not sure what they meant—his throat tightening as he finally began to sober, realizing the seriousness of his situation.

"That's Mr Tchaikovsky to you, kak for brains," the tall one said. "From now on, you only speak when we ask you. Understand?"

Raff nodded, fearing to utter a sound. *What the hell is going on? Where's Denn?*

"Now, we ask questions, and *then* you reply," the short one piped in. "And if we think it's a lie or don't like it, our boetie will step in to improve the conversation."

Raff nodded with vigour again.

"Who do you work for?" the tall one asked first.

"I have, or *had*, a job at Lamplight Industries."

"That's not what I asked," the shorter one said as he glanced at the rope. "Boetie, your turn!"

The short one stepped towards Raff, twirled Pyotr around in the air and landed a blow with the knot dead centre under the base of the chair, meeting Raff's exposed nethers.

The pain was like nothing Raff had experienced before, worse than the bullet that clipped his shoulder in the early days of the war. Radiating up through his abdomen, it overwhelmed his senses. Everything tensed and cramped; the arteries and veins of his neck bulged under his skin.

"Now, I will ask again. Who. Do. You. Work. For?"

Groaning and breathing heavily, Raff tried to speak but couldn't.

"Boetie!"

The short one began to twirl Pyotr.

"Wait . . . wait, please." Raff had barely caught his breath. "I-I don't understand."

"Explain it to him," a third voice boomed out of the darkness. It sounded familiar to Raff, but he couldn't place it.

"Boetie, hold it," the tall one spoke. "Mr Raphael Hernandes, we found your phone, the one *you* used to set the fire at Lamplight Industries. So, I will ask again, who paid you to do it?"

"That-that's a mistake." Raff's voice quivered. "The phone was dead, uh . . . broken. I threw it away, I—"

"I don't believe you!" the tall one said, spinning the rope for another meet-and-greet with Raff's balls. "Boetie!"

"It's true, it's tr—"

Pain shot through Raff again, interrupting his reply. "Ngyaaaaaaah!"

The shadowy voice boomed again. "I believe the man. He's not the one."

"Bossman?" the two thugs said in tandem, turning to face the voice.

"He may be useful to me someday soon. Drop him off outside his flat. Unharmed."

"Yah, bossman," the thugs replied together.

"You won't go to the cops, will you?" the voice boomed at Raff. "We know where you live and who all your friends are."

"Na no, sir," Raff grunted, still writhing in pain.

"Good." The voice went silent, and the door opened and closed.

"One more for luck," the short one asked, shrugging as he looked at the tall one. "Boetie likes things in neat threes."

"Yah," the tall one said, placing a hood over Raff's head. "Boetie's lucky threes."

Raff heard a whoosh as Pyotr was swung around once more to relay one final goodbye to his nethers. Emotionally overwhelmed by it, Raff passed out.

ΔΔΔ

South African pop music blared in the background while Raff lay motionless on the van floor, a black bag over his head.

Violent movements across the van floor jostled him back and forth. The journey was punctuated by the odd sound of car horns and violent decelerations. Moments later, the van screeched to a stop, and he heard the sound of the side door opening. The bag was yanked from Raff's head, and he looked up to see the short thug standing above him. The man rolled Raff out of the van, and he fell onto the pavement with an audible thump.

Raff grunted from the impact, his hip striking hard against the pavement. Still dazed, he could hear tires screeching in the distance. The pain from his encounter with Pyotr was still there—dull and throbbing fiercely from his lower abdomen to between his legs—so the hangover was barely noticeable. Unable to compose himself and stand up for a minute, he was almost entirely unaware of his surroundings. Still visible in the waning sunlight was the dusty tarmac pavement beside a familiar row of terraced houses. Their white-painted window cills and lintels stood out in contrast to their red-brick construction.

Raff was home. He forced himself up to his knees before taking a wobbly stand like a newborn foal. Stumbling his way over to the front door of the flats, Raff barely inserted the key before the sound of sirens overwhelmed him. He turned to see several police cars pull up to a stop and surround him. Before he could think, the police were out of their vehicles and charging towards him.

"Raphael Hernandes," one of the officers hollered. "We have you surrounded. There is nowhere to run!"

Even in his state, Raff knew he shouldn't mess around. One wrong move and the pain in his nethers would be the least of his worries. Instinctively, he reached into his back pocket for his non-existent phone. But, before he realised his mistake, one of the officers rugby-tackled him to the ground.

"Stay down," the officer exclaimed as another knelt down on Raff's back. He could feel the blunt point of the man's kneecap pressing into his back muscles. It was more uncomfortable than painful. As the world around him caved in—as claustrophobia seeped in—Raff's breathing laboured with the full weight of the officer bearing down on his back. After cuffing his hands behind him, they yanked him up by the arms and bundled him into the back of one of the cars, whacking his head on the doorframe as they did. The sharp pain from wrenching his arms backwards hurt far more than the bump to the head.

Raff, now all crammed into the car and sitting on his hands, was in too much pain to say anything. Besides, having heard horror stories about the local police, he decided to keep quiet and go with the flow. *Is this it? Is this the end of me? Wait, where the fuck is Denn?*

The car screeched off into the distance, lights flashing and sirens blaring.

△△△

A little while later, Raff was hauled into the police station for processing.

"Put your belongings in the bag," quipped the officer behind the counter. This was an older, grey-haired man in his sixties sporting a thick moustache. Likely, the many lines on his face matched many years of service.

"I-I have nothing on me," he mumbled as he patted his pockets. His mind still foggy, he wondered where he put his phone. *Did the thugs take it? Is it at Denn's? Oh, that's right . . . the fire!*

"We'll search him," a much younger officer piped up as he shuffled Raff over to a small windowless room nearby, joined by another officer with blonde hair tied up in a neat bun.

"Clothes off and place them in the bag," the other one said as she took the cuffs off him, "then stand and face the wall over there, hands on the wall with legs spread."

After thoroughly searching his cavities and taking mug shots, a cheek swab, and fingerprints, he was taken to a larger room at the end of a long corridor.

A sign on the door read: "Interrogation Room 1b."

V. B. Anstee

After seating and cuffing him to the metal table, the officers left Raff alone. He stared at his reflection in the large mirror on the wall, contemplating the day's events for what seemed a lifetime, mentally conversing with himself.

This must be about the fire those thugs were on about. But it was an accident, surely they can't arrest me for that. Wait, how did the thugs know about the phone before *the cops?! No, how did the cops know to show when they did? Maybe someone on the inside . . . So the stories are true then, right? The cops in this city are corrupt. Waiiiit, wait, that man with the South Africans. Yeah. This is a test! Know what? I am going to exercise my right to shut the hell up. Not going to give them a thing to twist up.*

Speaking up didn't do Raff any good in the past, so why should this time be any different? He remembered the war, where speaking up to a gung-ho and clueless sergeant about concerns over the mission did nothing to prevent the man from getting shot in the head.

Shutting the hell up now, eh? a second inner voice chimed in. The Texan drawl again, but now female.

That was a long time ago! Don't start—

That *is what makes you a loser!*

I-I did the right—

Thing? Just following orders? Whatever helps you sleep at night darlin'!

You don't know what you're talking about! Leave me alone!

Raff hummed a tune in an attempt to suppress the other voice. However, the silence seemed to amplify it.

The Pilgrim knows what the Pilgrim knows—

Pilgrim?

Raff is a loser, it repeated, over and over again for a minute, until interrupted by the sound of the door.

Thank God, thought Raff.

Two men in suits waltzed through the door. The taller of the two slammed a thick folder on the table.

"We know ya set the fires," he exclaimed. "We have all the evidence we need to lock you up for life."

Raff frowned. *Fires? Plural? There was just one. Is this still a test?*

"Now now, there's some good news," the other said as he placed a piece of paper and pen in front of Raff. "Our chief wants this case closed yesterday. So sign the confession, admit to setting the fires, and we'll reduce your sentence to five years."

"Draw this out, and it's ten to twenty," the other chipped in.

Raff could no longer remain silent. "Don't I get a phone call?"

The officers looked shocked at his request like they'd made

a mistake. One briefly glanced in the file, raising his eyebrows, and then they both walked out.

Seconds later, two uniformed officers came in, uncuffed Raff from the table and led him down the corridor into a crowded holding cell—a cell initially designed to hold a single person short-term. Raff had heard of the skyrocketing crime rate since the war, but seeing it up close and personal like this put it into perspective. Moreover, this was a new experience for him, to be on the other side of the bars. The last time he'd visited a police station was the year before to collect Denn, who'd been nabbed in London during the riots after widespread digital election tampering was exposed.

Three of his fellow cell mates sported matching tattoos on their necks and huddled together, their conversations inaudible whispers. The remaining four seemed afraid of the tattooed ones and kept their distance.

Raff squeezed himself into a corner to sit and think.

"Raphael Hernandez?" a loud voice stirred Raff from his thoughts. "You're free to go."

Excited at the prospect of freedom, Raff bolted up from his corner and accidentally bumped into one of the tattooed guy's arms. The gangster doubled over in pain—dropping a sharpened aluminium rod before grabbing his crotch. Blood soaked through his light-coloured jeans. The gangster had been holding the shiv within his pocket against his leg, likely poised to stab some unsuspecting victim.

Raff didn't care to stop and look for long. He was more concerned about his freedom before his luck turned. Raff turned to the officer as the heavy metal door closed behind him. "I-I'm free to go?" he said.

"Yes." The officer shrugged. "Something about a London accent. Above my paygrade!"

As Raff was led down the corridor, an embittered voice could be heard shouting from the cell: "I will find you, Raphael Hernandez!"

Raff turned his head to look, but the officer hurried him on before he could look at the man. He spent the next moments while walking out of the station, trying to make order out of the chaos of the last few days. *I count three now, yes?* His series of bad luck was coming to an end.

As he exited the station back out onto the busy streets, his brain clicked, followed by a sinking sensation that all these occurrences were related—the phone, fire, loss of job, and the torture—that they were all a part of the same incident. *Oh shit*. . . maybe his bad luck was just beginning.

Chapter Four

Three Stooges

Having eaten all the food in his kitchen and still wearing the day's clothes, Raff dove face-first onto his bed. His ordeal with the South Africans and police had taken it out of him, and he passed out from exhaustion. His unconscious mind took over and, in vivid detail, returned him to his time in the war.

Covered in dirt, with a rifle strapped over his shoulder,

Raff crawled through the brush. The day's final rays poked through over the horizon, casting shadows over the several figures that moved in unison with him. Explosions in the distance sent bass-filled shockwaves through his chest. At the same time, the distant tapping sounds of firing rounds were followed by trees and bushes splintering nearby.

As they pushed through the brush, his fellow soldiers disappeared one by one into the darkness until there were only three left, including himself.

"Keep up, soldier, or get left behind," the soldier in front growled.

All three rose to a crouching position and continued through the brush until the thumps of the explosions and the taps of machine-gun fire faded into the distance. Moments later, as the vegetation began to thin, the rigid outlines of several thatched huts became visible in the moonlight. The soldier in front of Raff stopped and lifted his fist before taking up a prone position with a clear view of the huts. Raff and the other remaining figure followed suit.

"This is it," the soldier growled again, clearly the man in charge. He looked at Raff and then the other figure. "Are you all I've got?"

"Yes, sir," Raff uttered with the other shadow in chorus. Raff kept his dissolution to himself. *So this is the guy in charge, and he's only now noticing that most of his squad is gone? Wanker.*

"Shit, this won't be easy, but you two will have to do! Now, intel says our target is in the largest building in the village, over there—"

"Sir," Raff couldn't help himself from interrupting. "There's just three of us and a whole lotta them. Didn't the alert specify the need for a strike force minimum of fifteen? Shouldn't we radio for reinforcements? And what about the men back—"

"Negative, Raisin Sack," the shadow said. "We are it, or the target will up and disappear for good. You know how important it is that we get this guy, right? Now. Man. The. Fuck. Up. Understood?"

"Yes, sir," said Raff, still unnerved at the thought of just the three of them sneaking into the village without any support. *I wish they hadn't slapped together a squad in such a hurry. The target's gonna disappear either way. The three of us are dead men walking.*

"Now, our target is in the largest building in the village, over"—he scanned the buildings before pointing—"there. Raisin Sack, you take the door on the east, and you, what's your name?"

"Private Dennis Singleton, sir!"

"Holy shit, the pyromaniac?"

"I ahh . . . it was ahh . . . I guess so, sir!"

"All right, Pyro, you climb to the balcony and enter there while I take the west entrance. Low and slow, so we don't wake the entire village. Enter the building together on my signal. No fires unless I order it, understand?"

"S-sir, yes sir," Private Singleton said.

"What's the signal, sir?" Raff chimed in.

"Three clicks on comms. Now move out!"

The three of them crept up on the designated building, as silent as the dead, rifles at the ready. Raff kept low as he moved apace towards the east of the building. The concrete brickwork was barely visible in the moonlight. As Raff reached his point of ingress—a flimsy-looking wooden door—his heart jumped when a startled chicken cackled loudly and fluttered away. Nothing else stirred. There were no guards in sight. *Have we got the right place?*

Raff paused at the door for half a minute before he heard three clicks on the comms. He removed a prybar from the side of his backpack. As he slid the wedge end between the door and frame, the door pushed open. It wasn't locked. He pushed open the door slowly with a barely audible creek. The moonlight peeked through the other end of the pitch-black room where the soldier in charge was coming through the other door. The penny dropped like it weighed a tonne. *It's way too quiet out there*, he thought. *Sunset was what, an hour ago? Shit, this is an amb—*

The light in the room flickered to life as several uniformed figures appeared out of nowhere, surrounding them, toting AK47s. Raff lifted his own rifle, but it was too late. A rifle barrel tapped the side of his neck as its bearer took his sidearm and shouted in a thick African accent: "Drop the guns, or I shoot the giraffe!" he said, nodding at Raff, who stood a good foot taller than most everyone in the room. "Sasa!"

Raff and his commander placed their guns on the ground. Raff looked around the room. *Where's what's-his-face?* he thought.

"Put your hands on your heads!" another man shouted in a thick accent.

As soon as their hands touched their scalps, they were herded to the centre of the room. Raff felt a sharp smack to the back of his knees. He fell hard to the wooden floor, splinters stabbing into his skin. His commander dropped down beside him. Adrenaline coursed through his veins as heavy beads of sweat ran down his back. It felt like his heart was attempting to break out of his chest. That's when Private Singleton entered through the front door. His hands were on his head while two uniformed men pressed their rifles into his back. They pushed him onto the floor next to Raff.

A rounder uniformed figure appeared from the shadows of the adjoining room carrying a pistol, bearing general's epaulettes. He was clearly the man in charge. Raff caught a glimpse of the man's face before averting his eyes. Stood before them was General Jackson Ngaba. Interpol's most wanted man—the ace of spades—the man who started the war. Although not their mission target, capturing or taking him out would significantly alter the war's course. A loud bang reverberated in Raff's skull as he blinked, and his commander fell to the floor. Blood began to pool and trickle down the uneven floorboards into the spaces between. Moving over to Raff, whose ears were still ringing, the figure pressed the gun to his forehead. Raff momentarily felt the barrel's heat before one of the uniformed men started banging on a table. "Mr Hernandez," he shouted. "Are you in there?"

Everyone else was frozen in place. Raff was confused, squinting his eyes, failing to focus on the room as the darkness flowed in from every corner. He heard another voice from the consuming darkness. It sounded artificial—like cheap text-to-speech software—and faded as the darkness swallowed the room. He struggled to make out only two words: "pilgrim" and "guest." He'd heard "pilgrim" before from the Texan voice in his head. *What the hell?*

The banging got louder. Raff suddenly awoke to find himself in his flat, still in bed. A loud banging was coming from his flat door.

"Mr Hernandez," a woman's voice echoed through. "I know ya in there!"

Raff stumbled out of bed into the living room, still dressed in the clothes from the previous day. He chained the door and opened it. Peeking through the gap, he saw a familiar older woman—Mrs Lowe—standing in the hallway through the opening.

"What do you want?" He rolled his eyes. She was frustrating on the best of days. So, after his ordeal yesterday, this interaction would be painful for him.

"Bloody hell, don't you get snippy with me," hissed the woman. "Ya rent is late!"

"Yeah, um," Raff said. "You wouldn't believe the week—"

"You shoulda used ya brain before burning ya work down. Ya have three days before my nephew collects. And don't you go tryin' any o' that pyro stuff round here!"

"Wait, how do you know—"

"Ya mug's all over the net, ya muppet!"

Closing the door, Raff hobbled over to the TV, picked up the remote and opened the web browser. The image they displayed on the local news feed was not very flattering. It was the picture Denn took of him with a beer foam moustache, arm outstretched to grab the camera. His landlady wasn't lying. The embedded video feed came to life.

"... he is ex-military, seen here imitat—" Raff threw the remote into the TV and it switched off.

The knocking at the door began again. Completely enraged, Raff yanked open the door, breaking the chain off the pillar. "What do you want now, you old bat—"

"Woah mate is me, yeh," Denn interrupted, placing his hand on Raff's shoulder as if to reassure him. "Is this a bad time, bruv?"

"Yes, but come in," Raff ushered Denn in, barely containing himself. "Did you see that shit on the news about me?"

"Bad business, bruv," Denn said. "Is why I'm here, yeh. Saw an hour ago n' rushed over quick as I could."

"Thanks, means a lot. Been one hell of a week."

"Why don't I put the kettle on, yeh, you get dressed, then tell me 'bout it over a cuppa?"

"Sure, sounds good."

"Brought some biscuits. Can't have a cuppa without biscuits. Oh, and sumfin' special, right?"

Denn lifted the plastic carrier bag he had brought and shook it. Raff could make out a large rectangular object within.

ΔΔΔ

Two cups of tea and a double pack of custard creams later, Raff had told Denn almost everything about his ordeal.

"Oh. Em. Gee, bruv," Denn chuckled. "I can't believe that gangster knifed his own balls!"

"Ha," Raff laughed, then grimaced. "I knew exactly how he felt, though."

"You said he was wiv a bunch of other gangsters, yeh, them with the same tats?"

"Yeah, a cross with what looked like an arrow on one side—"

"Yeh, yeh," Denn interrupted. "Little gang, a crew out of the East side, or sumfin'. Nuffin' to worry 'bout, I think, bruv!"

"They know my name, and my face has been all over the news."

"Keep away from the East side, and you'll be okay." He took a bit of his biscuit. "Why d'ya think the fuzz released ya?"

"Not one hundred per cent sure. It was weird. One minute they were sure I set a bunch of fires. Then, they said something about me not having a London accent and let me go."

"Wasn't me, honest, bruv." Denn smiled before taking on a more serious look. "Honestly, it wasn't. Weird, some other . . . some pyro bloke from London must be in town."

"Weird indeed. Not heard about any other fires. Don't remember seeing anything mentioned online and in the papers."

"Yeh, I must investigate. Maybe someone is trying to stitch me up."

"Just be careful, buddy, some riled-up crazy mofos out there, looking to hang someone."

"Yeh, bruv, and you know I got your back whenever, right?"

"Kinda like the day we first met." Raff laughed.

"Fun times!"

"I dreamt about it last night. Woke when Sarge got shot. It was so vivid, like I was really there. The sights, the sounds, *and* the smells. So weird."

"What was it he called you?"

"Raisin Sack," Raff said with a look of distaste, still thinking about how vivid it was and the weird feeling at the end with the voice in the darkness. Like there was someone—or something—watching this memory play out. It had appeared in his mind before he woke, but he couldn't explain it. "Turns out Raisin Sack was right; we *needed* reinforcements!"

"True, right? Lucky to be alive."

"Don't think luck had anything to do with it." Raff forced a chuckle. "Really, though, maybe if I'd pushed harder for reinforcements, so many more people would be alive today."

"At least you spoke up, yeh. I was just a sheep—a quiet effing sheep."

Denn dug into the plastic bag he'd brought and pulled out a box. On it was a picture of a phone.

"Here, mate, this is yours," said Denn with a big smile. "As promised."

"Oh, nice! Thanks!" The smile on Raff's face was genuine. "Is that the latest model? Five finger disc—"

"Yes and uh, no? Ha! Turn it on, bruv."

"Ah, so that's where you went after I passed out."

A few silent moments passed as Raff carefully unpacked his new phone, reviewing the instructions and installing his old SIM card. Finally, he held a button on the side, and the screen turned on. Expecting the setup screen, instead, the phone began to ring immediately, which set off a strange buzzing in his head simultaneously, like a bee trapped between his ears.

UNKNOWN CALLER was displayed on the screen.

Confounded and in a daze, Raff froze for a few seconds before answering. "Hello?"

"Hello, darlin'," a voice replied with a familiar Texan drawl. "So, the loser lives . . ."

Chapter Five

Three, Two, One, Go

The phone call was two weeks ago. Hearing the familiar—yet unknown—Texan voice on the other end was enough to freak out Raff. The room felt too small for him, and he panicked—fleeing the flat and leaving Denn to his own devices. When he returned a few hours later, Denn was nowhere to be found. Raff wanted to call or visit him but couldn't find the courage. Maybe it was the guilt from running out on his friend, or deep down, he didn't want to discuss the mess in his head. He'd had enough of that with the army shrinks following the war. It was all group session this, group session that. Being deeply introverted by nature made these sessions mentally painful and exhausting. He'd left with a strong aversion to talking about his problems. Denn hadn't visited since. Being a good friend and knowing Raff well, he'd left Raff to his own devices.

Now, Raff badly needed a job to make rent, but nobody would hire him. Even a police apology statement on the news feeds and local paper came too late; the damage was already done. Any potential employer saw him as damaged goods and ushered him to the front door. Times were tough following the war. There was too much job competition; any doubt about a potential employee was an immediate no. He'd blown most of his monetary reserves on food, trying—and failing—to find the right dish to satiate the constant hunger he'd felt since his time strapped to a chair. Moreover, the meagre unemployment allowance from the government last week was nowhere near enough to cover all his expenses.

Returning home, having been rejected for a job once more, he loosened his tie. He slumped into his sofa, his mind racing to solve the giant puzzle that was his life.

What the hell am I going to do? Maybe I should just end it all? But who would keep Denn out of—

The Texan voice in his head spoke: *Loser, loser. Raff is a loser—*

A familiar thumping on the door startled him.

"Not now!" he yelled, rolling his eyes and gritting his teeth in frustration. "I *don't* have the rent money!"

The banging continued.

"Go away!"

"Mr Hernandez," piped the voice from behind the door, somewhat muffled. "Maybe we can help each other?"

Her friendly tone took Raff by surprise. *The landlady wants to help me?*

Moving over to the chained door, he cracked it open a little. Yes, Mrs Lowe stood there with two other familiar faces. He couldn't place where he'd seen them before—a tall white-haired man of South Asian descent and a fair-skinned woman in a pink hijab.

"We have a problem, Mr Hernandez," she said with a sullen look on her face. "I think you're the only person who can help us, my lovely. Can we talk?"

Curiosity met with his desire to solve his money issue, overcoming his need for solitude. Raff reluctantly invited them in. After unchaining the door, he bolted over to the sofa, ridding it of piles of stale clothing and fast food containers. He looked at the three and gestured towards the couch. "Um . . . come in. Have a seat."

The three visitors sat down. The woman in the hijab looked as though she'd been crying all day. Mrs Lowe began by explaining their situation. "My lovely," she said. "You see, there's this gang that's been terrorising the local shops and landlords . . . me included. They—"

"They demand a 'protection fee' from us," the white-haired man said. "And if we don't pay, things happen . . . nasty things."

"Beatings," Mrs Lowe wiped the corner of her eyes with her thumb. "And break-ins. Bad beatings on family."

"The police can't or won't help. They always give us the same bullshit about 'higher priorities.'"

"And, uh, what do I have to do with this?" Raff scratched his temple, hoping they'd get to the point already and leave. He recalled where he'd seen the two strangers before. The man owned the bakery three blocks down, and the woman ran the corner shop by the park.

"We saw the news about you, right," said the man. "We knew ya didn't do what they said. We seen online ya got a medal for bravery in the war."

"We also saw online about ya friend," Mrs Lowe chimed in. "Same medal—"

"Spill the beans already," Raff said. The room felt stuffy like he was standing in a crowded nightclub—a big no-no for him.

"We'd like to take a hit out on the gang," the other lady spoke up, tears welling in her eyes and about to stream down her face. "Is that how I say it? Take out a hit? My boy is dead because—"

The lady burst into tears and stormed out of the flat. Raff was stuck for words. *Are they asking me to kill someone?*

The room went silent for a moment before Mrs Lowe chipped in. "The group pooled together some money, ten thousand pounds, to pay ya for it."

Raff remained silent, still stunned.

"We have no one to help us, please!" the landlady continued, tears now welling in her eyes. "This has gone on too long. I, I'll also let the rent slide 'til January."

Shit, their situation must really be crap, Raff thought. *But I can't just whack a few guys because the granny two doors down asked me nicely.*

"Please—"

"I need to think about it, seriously. I'll let you know soon." Raff was shocked by their request. He was too polite to flat-out refuse and would say just about anything else to get them out the door. Maybe his landlady would quit nagging about the rent while he 'thought about it.'

V. B. Anstee

They continued to beg and reiterate how deep in the shit they were. They were so deep they'd need a figurative backhoe to dig them out. Raff was the backhoe they wanted but not the one they truly needed. What they truly needed was a police force that gave a damn about them. From Raff's run-in with the local police, he knew they couldn't be trusted.

He managed to usher the remaining two out of the flat without appearing rude. Then, he slumped into the sofa and thought about their proposition for a moment. He felt sorry for them—maybe less so for his usually obnoxious landlady. The thought that he couldn't do anything there and then made him glum.

£10k and free rent. That would solve things for the immediate future. Maybe there's another way? What would Denn say?

As if he'd summoned him, Raff's phone began to vibrate. It was Denn. Raff inhaled deeply, tapped the screen, and put the phone to his ear.

"Heya, buddy."

ΔΔΔ

Raff leaned forward on the sofa's edge, chin resting on clasped hands. Denn paced before him, pausing several times and opening his mouth to speak, but nothing came out. Unfortunately, the proposition's moral implications had dammed up both their words.

Denn decided to change the course of the conversation. He sat down on the sofa next to Raff. "Bruv, you ghosted me after the phone," he said. "What happened?"

"I'm not sure, to be honest, bud," Raff said, averting his eyes. "I really don't remember much." By Raff's lack of eye contact, Denn could see he didn't want to discuss it. Maybe there wasn't much to tell, so he wouldn't push too much.

"Tell me what you do remember, yeh?"

"There really isn't much to tell. As soon as I turned on the phone, a call popped up. An unknown number."

"I didn't see a phone call mate, just the welcome screen."

"I didn't imagine it," Raff said, looking bemused, momentarily pulling out his phone and tapping the screen. "What the . . . I . . . it . . ."

Denn looked over at the screen and noticed the empty call history. His concern grew tenfold. Raff must've just been stressed by the torture and the arrest. Being the good friend he was, he decided to humour Raff. "Tell me about the phone call."

"I got . . . I, uh, *imagined* a phone call, I guess."

Denn remained silent and looked intently at Raff.

Raff continued: "It sounded like static, weird static, almost like screaming. The timing, and the stress of everything else, I-I just snapped. Next thing I remember was waking up behind the park bushes and wandering home."

Denn knew well enough that wasn't the whole picture. He didn't push. "Ooookay," he said. "Glad you got home in one piece, bruv."

"Me too."

They sat in silence for a minute. Denn's mind went back to the £10k offer from Mrs Lowe. Then he thought of the phone caper he did with Laura. "Well, bruv, I kinda have a confession," he said said

"Oh?"

"You remember Laura, yeh?"

"Mm-hmm, I sure do—"

"I helped her with some shit . . . some work. Made thirty grand, but I lost it all."

Raff smiled. "Ah, you gave it all to her, didn't you?"

Denn looked embarrassed. "Yeh."

"Your soft spot!"

"I wasn't thinking with my 'ed, yeh." Denn conveyed the phone heist story in all its glorious detail: the distraction, the take, the clean getaway, and his adventure with Laura. His face lit up a little whenever he mentioned Laura. When Denn had a few too many beers, it was *Laura this* and *Laura that*. Denn was in love. He knew that Raff, on the other hand, was disinterested in love. In the past, Raff had told him that during the war, the romantic part of his brain disengaged, like it was pushed out to make room for something else, failing to reengage since then.

"So, about that hit?" Raff said. "We can't do it. It's wrong, right?"

"True, but those are some bad people, mate. And coppers won't do shit. We did lots worse to bigger wankers in the war."

"But that was war, this isn't?"

"Right. Maybe we don't kill 'em, yeh. I'm thinking maybe we just scare them shitless, so they run 'n don't show their faces again, right?"

"Okay . . . so we do that then. The landlady's friends *might* let us try this. But, we'd need to ensure nothing leads back to us and them."

"Should be simple enough bruv." Denn knew it wouldn't be simple, but he wanted to reassure Raff. Times were tough, and they both needed the money to survive. Besides, the success of his recent warehouse caper gave him the confidence to tackle this job. It would keep Raff close too—so he can keep a close eye on him. And maybe deep down, it was another excuse to see Laura.

"Really? How?" Raff frowned.

Denn pulled out a lighter, and with a flick of his thumb, a flame flickered to life. A menacing look swept across his face. Then, smiling into the flashing glow, he said, "I have an idea or two."

ΔΔΔ

Still reeling in disbelief about their decision to proceed with the hit, albeit without killing anyone, Raff stood at his landlady's door, finding the courage to knock. How do you tell someone you're willing to accept money to commit a serious crime? Raff was under no illusion that the job could go horribly wrong and people could die, especially Denn. What would he do without him?

Typical. Loser that you are, you're too afraid to man—

Get out of my head!

Ha! Who would you be without me, darlin'?

What the—

Raff's thoughts were interrupted as his head was overcome with pain like a migraine dialled up to ten. Losing his balance momentarily, he caught the door to steady himself. A feint artificial voice surrounded him like a whisper. It seemed to come from every angle before fading out. Raff was confused and could only make out part of what was said: "Host . . . action potential . . . guest . . . overflow."

Raff almost fell over when the door swung open.

"You all right, love?" Mrs Lowe said. She was standing in the doorway wearing a pink nightgown and looking at him as she tapped her upper lip, just below her nose. "Would you like a tissue?"

Raff dabbed his nose with his finger, which came away streaked with blood. "Please."

She handed him a tissue. "Here, come in, sit down, lovey."

They sat down, Raff dabbing his nose with the tissue, his head throbbing fiercely enough to distract him from his social aversion. Then he told her about their idea to deal with the gang in a non-lethal way.

"Do you think that might work?" she asked.

"We figure these thugs are small-time low-lives."

"That seems right, lovey. They've always seemed like a small group, always the same faces."

"One problem, though. We don't know where they hide. Any idea?"

"I'm sorry. The only person who knew was Simeon from the corner store. Sometimes they asked him to deliver the money in person."

"How can I get hold of him?" Raff tried to put a face to the name but failed.

"He's in Hunslet."

Raff frowned. "Hunslet? Ah, sorry, he's dead, isn't he?" It dawned on him that Simeon was the son of the woman who cried and bolted from his flat.

"Yes, lovey, the one we told you about."

V. B. Anstee

Simeon was the man beaten to death by the gang. Having agreed to see her when the job was done, Raff thanked her for the tissue and left. He needed to see Denn to discuss the big wrinkle in the plan: the gang's unknown location.

ΔΔΔ

Raff invited Denn over to iron out the wrinkle. A serious discussion like this called for tea and chocolate biscuits. Alcohol would likely mean they'd go off half-cocked and botch the whole thing, leaving them much worse off than they already were. They settled on three plans that they believed would umbrella all eventualities.

Asking around the neighbourhood for the gang's location would prove problematic, so that option was relegated to plan B. Any number of people may have some affiliation with the gang and rat them out. That would ruin the element of surprise.

Plan A was their choice: observe a gang member doing the rounds and follow them to their hideout. This had the best odds of success without the need for drastic measures. Plan C was the drastic one, dark enough that they agreed not to discuss the option again unless everything went south and the situation called for it.

"Good cuppa, mate," Denn said, standing up to stretch and look at his watch. "It's almost four PM. Let the hunt begin!"

Mrs Lowe had conveyed enough information to indicate when the gang would do their rounds, seemingly following a schedule, turning up the same late afternoon or early evening every fortnight. Today happened to be the next day on their schedule.

"Wheels are outside; ready when you are, bruv," Denn continued.

"Okay, buddy, lead the way."

Raff followed Denn to the alley behind the flats, the "wheels" not quite what he'd pictured. Before him sat an old, shabby, two-wheeled motorcycle. From the small footprint of the bike, Raff knew it sported an engine with barely enough power to mow a lawn. Denn pulled out a pair of motorcycle helmets from the top box.

"This one is yours," he said, chuckling as he handed Raff the fluorescent pink one. "Sorry, bruv. Only one I could find that'll fit your big 'ed."

Raff ignored the helmet. "You sure that thing is safe?"

"As safe as a helmet can be, I s'pose–"

"No, no, that," Raff pointed. "That two-wheeled death trap. Calling it a moped sounds too soft and friendly. More like mopped-up, as in you're gonna get *mopped up* off the tarmac sooner or later."

"Shit, mate, this thing don't go fast enough for that. Maybe a gravel rash, right? So man the eff up, soldier, and get on!"

"For fat snakes!"

Raff closed his eyes and got on. He gripped Denn tightly as they rode to the park, two streets over, keeping the bike close should they need to make a move. The worn wooden sidewalk bench beside the park fence was an excellent vantage point to see the comings and goings of each shop. As they sat on the bench waiting for the gang members to arrive, time seemed to stand still. Raff spent that time picking up the spiky green conker shells dropped by the chestnut tree overhead. Peeling them open one by one, he threw the brown conkers into the bin a few metres away. By sundown, they'd almost given up waiting. They were moments from leaving when a moped pulled up outside the first shop. Two big lads dismounted and marched into the first shop, keeping their motocross helmets on and moving briskly like they were on a mission.

Raff slid to the edge of the bench, poised to make a quick move.

"That's them," he whispered to Denn.

"You sure, bruv?"

"Hmmm, ninety per cent, maybe."

"Good enough."

ΔΔΔ

Darkness was soon upon them as they continued their two-wheeled tail around the city streets. Reflections swept across their helmets as streetlights swept by overhead. The level of traffic subsided as the sky slowly turned black. Fortunately, the thugs kept to the speed limit, so the pals kept up. This was the first time they had done anything like this. Denn made it seem like he was a pro, maintaining a minimum four-car separation. He once saw this in a movie, and it made sense to him. The moped fit Denn's short frame like a glove, but Raff, on the other hand, struggled in the pillion seat, having to stretch his legs many times to untie the painful knots in his muscles.

Raff felt something was off twenty minutes into the tail. They'd been around the block three times. "They're going in circles!" Raff shouted above the wind and the noise of the street.

Denn couldn't hear what he said, but he'd also noticed the same change in behaviour. He gave Raff a thumbs up, assuming that's what he was on about.

The thug in the pillion seat looked over his shoulder. He stared at the buddies briefly before tapping his comrade's helmet, clearly a signal for him to rabbit. The thugs picked up speed, but Denn managed to match it. Plans A and B were no longer workable, so a version of plan C was now in effect.

Trying to lose their tail, the thugs cut through the park, powering their moped down steep stairs and over the pond's narrow pedestrian bridge. The pals followed. The violent vibration from the steps unseated Denn's helmet for a moment—blocking his view with the mouthguard—causing a near-miss with a black bin. A sharp change in direction to take the footbridge caused the moped to briefly slide out from under the pals; Denn leaned the other way, quickly regained balance, and flicked them upright onto the footbridge.

The thugs left the park and powered up the road, turning out of sight. Having lost the thugs, the pals stopped at a green light to get their bearings and try to pick up the trail.

"Shit shit shit," Denn exclaimed, punching between the handlebars. "Bloody wankers."

The thugs had doubled back in an attempt to lose the pals but met them at the crossroads on the red side. Before Denn could react, the thugs powered through their red light in front of the pals; simultaneously, a double-decker bus powered past the pals through the green light.

Smashing glass and grinding metal could be heard when the bus hit the thugs' moped and dragged it along the tarmac—thugs and all—before stopping on the other side of the junction. The sound made Raff's skin crawl. Suddenly, he had an idea. He double-tapped Denn's shoulder and pointed to the now-stopped bus. "Pull up beside it," he said.

Denn made a quick beeline to the front of the bus. What

remained of the thugs lay contorted and partially jammed between the bus and the mangled moped.

Raff hopped off the back of their moped to take a closer look. Feeling sick to his stomach from a combination of motion sickness and the thought of being crushed by a bus, he resisted the urge to throw up. Raff took a deep breath as he walked to the front of the bus. *You've seen worse,* he thought. *Just breathe. Keep it together.*

"Are they alive?" Denn asked, still on the moped.

"No. Idiots got creamed."

Raff went to check on the bus driver. It was one of the driverless buses, so there was none. He then looked around the inside; there were no passengers on board. Raff was relieved. *Good, no witnesses.*

Denn stepped the moped backwards beside the bus and banged on the window to get Raff's attention. "We gotta go, mate! Thing's probably called the cops!"

"Not yet!" Raff knew he had to be quick. A first-response aerial drone would be there any minute to record the scene.

Raff returned to the mangled bodies, sickened by the thought of what he had to do. Picking through their wet, meat-coloured clothing, he found what he was looking for. Waving two blood-soaked phones at Denn, he clambered onto the back of the moped. "Found them. Let's go!"

△△△

"That was a close call," chirped Raff, trying to break the silence. He and Denn were back at Raff's. They sat on the sofa, wondering if they'd utterly botched the job and angry that it became lethal. Could they salvage the situation?

"Well, bruv," piped Denn, "The bus cameras wouldn't have seen our faces through the helmets. And no witnesses, yeh?"

"Wouldn't the bus cameras catch your rear plate?"

"Nah bruv, don't worry 'bout that. I *borrowed* a plate from someone. It's all good."

Raff pulled out the two phones he'd salvaged and stared at them briefly before wiping them down, feeling disgusted as the white rag he'd got from the kitchen turned red. As he wiped, Raff wondered how much money the thugs had extorted to afford phones like these. They were the same line as his but one version older. Just then, he remembered reading something about pulling location data from phones, but there was a hitch; these phones were locked behind fingerprint access. Raff tried the alternative passcode access once by entering 123456 on the off chance the gangsters weren't too bright but had no luck. He didn't dare try again; he'd had bad luck with phones lately. "I can't get into the phones for the location history," he said. "They're protected."

"That was a good idea, bruv; too bad though, yeh."

"What about Laura?" Raff asked. "She must know about unlocking *borrowed* phones."

"Nah, bruv."

Raff frowned and straightened the phones on the table. "You're lying to avoid her, aren't you?"

"What? No!" Denn blushed. Raff took that to mean Denn was still embarrassed about his last encounter with her. He'd misread her signals and blown his opportunity.

"We gotta start somewhere. I think Laura's our best bet," Raff said.

Letting out a deep sigh, Denn reluctantly agreed. "Okay, mate, I'll get my helmet and—"

"I'm not riding that thing all the way to Leeds! Besides, we'll probably get pulled over halfway there."

"No way, I changed the plate over."

"Too far, bud. Please phone her and invite her to meet us for breakfast or something."

Denn stroked his moustache, nodding. "Kill two birds with one stone, yeh."

"Two what?" Raff was distracted by the sound of police sirens going by. Thankfully, they continued down the street and out of earshot.

"Two birds... The phones and maybe a line on some

tasers or teargas or something," Denn said. "I'll phone her."

△△△

"I can't believe you roped me into that!" barked Raff as he fumbled off the moped. He was soaking wet and numb in places he didn't imagine possible. *Why couldn't I have been numb there a few weeks back?* He imagined the sound of that knotted rope striking his sensitive parts all over again.

"It's not like we 'ad a choice, right?"

The pals had agreed to meet Laura at a café halfway to Leeds. However, the weather turned sour near the end of their journey, heavy rain pouring down on them unhindered by any kind of roof. It was the kind of precipitation that forces its way through the tiniest gap and pulls the middle finger at gravity as it somehow flows upwards, soaking every crevice.

"Are you gonna ask her out this time?" said Raff, standing next to Denn in the café restroom, wringing the water from his sleeves. "I mean, out for real. Today doesn't count."

"Best if I don't, yeh. I mean, best for her." They continued their conversation as they walked over to their table.

"Seriously, buddy, I see the way you are when she's around, so—"

"Look, bruv, I'm messed up, right. So a relationship . . . I don't think so, yeh?"

"Okay, buddy, though you really oughta grab the bull by

the horns and go for it. You only live once, you know."

"Except I'm the bull, here, the bull in a china shop. I mess everything up around me. Aaaanyway, here she comes, so no more about this, yeh, please!"

Denn waved Laura over as they seated themselves. She waved back and headed to the counter, presumably to order breakfast. At the same time, the pals' breakfasts arrived. Raff's order was a fried breakfast large enough to feed a small family. "Woah, what's with the appetite bruv?" Denn said.

"Dunno bud, just feel hungry all the time now."

"Ha . . . maybe you have a tapeworm."

Laura sat down at the table next to Denn. With coffee in hand, she tucked a green duffel bag under the table. "Hi boys," she said. "How's it hanging?"

"So so," Raff said.

"Goodoh," Denn said.

Denn maintained a sullen look over breakfast while Raff discussed the phones with Laura, eventually agreeing that Laura would pull the location data from them in exchange for the phones themselves. Raff slid the phones across the table to her. He was happy to be rid of them. Having concluded that deal, Laura moved on to the next, sliding a duffel bag over to Denn with her foot.

"This is the other stuff we talked about, luv," she said as

she winked at Denn. "Well, not quite the tasers you wanted, but much better. Aaand with a little something extra that'll scare the shit outta anyone who dares mess wiv ya."

"Lovely, ta," said Denn, smiling from ear to ear. "What do I owe ya?"

"Nothing, our other business made a tidy sum . . . so I owed ya instead. Now we're even."

"Nice," Raff said with a mouth full of bacon.

"Thanks," Denn replied. "Will let ya know how the job goes, yeh."

"Right. Anyway, luv, I gotta go," Laura replied, swinging around off the seat to leave, patting Denn on the shoulder. "Don't be a stranger, yeh?"

Denn was stuck for words, blushing red as a ripe tomato. Before he could gather himself for a reply, Laura had already left the café, hopped into a car, and was on her way down the road.

Raff lifted the duffel onto his lap, curious about its contents, unzipping it just enough to peer inside at the top layer of contents. What he saw surprised him—the two sawn-off shotguns sat at the top. "Ho-ly shit!"

Curiosity snapped Denn out of his daze, relieving Raff of the duffel to peek inside. He let out a prolonged whistle of approval. He refastened the zipper, swivelling his head to the side, wary of lookie-loos.

"Enough to scare some folks?" Raff whispered.

"Most definitely, bruv. Best not to be seen with this yeh?"

"Indeed."

"We'll have to take the scenic route home to avoid the cameras. Sorry, bruv. That duffel ain't gunna fit in the top box."

"Fuck!"

Upon leaving the café, they hopped onto the moped—Raff with the heavy duffel on his back—and took the long route back through East Manchester. Much to their delight, the weather was now dry, although that didn't prevent Raff's nethers from going numb again from a lack of circulation.

△△△

Raff awoke to the sound of someone banging on his bedroom door. Still groggy and feeling like he was coming down with something, it took him a few moments to recognise a voice calling from beyond.

"Mate, are you awake yet?" Denn shouted as he banged. "We've got news!"

Raff stumbled over to the door to see what the fuss was all about. "What's going on?" he mumbled as he opened the door.

Denn changed to a softer tone when he noticed Raff's state. "Ah, maybe breakfast first. You look like shit."

"You're far too kind, good sir," Raff said. "To the cornflakes!"

Having shuffled over to the kitchen to score some food and caffeine, Raff had perked up enough to allow Denn to dish out the news.

"So, Laura unlocked the phones," Denn said.

"Oh, really?"

"Yeh, the news is good. I have a location, well, a good idea of one."

Showing Raff the screen of his phone. It looked promising. There was one common location recorded on the salvaged phones. The daytime-only regularity of it indicated this was not where the gangsters lived. While it wasn't accurate to the metre, it did narrow it down to the end of a short block of derelict terraced houses. They were fairly confident that this was where the gangsters spent their time together, their base of operations.

The next part of their plan, however, was the most challenging and the easiest to screw up. If anything went wrong, the pals would end up in prison or much worse.

Raff counted the recent bad things that happened to him lately, trying to tie them up in neat threes. No matter how hard he tried, it all linked back to the phone fire, which probably meant he was still on the first of the three bad things. *When will this shit-storm end?* he thought.

"We going there to watch for a bit?" Raff asked. A stakeout might be a welcome distraction from the boredom at home. In times like these, Raff wished he had a nine-to-five job to keep him occupied.

"Yeh, bruv, the bike's ready out back."

"Oh great!" Raff rolled his eyes. He shuddered at the thought of cramping up again while wearing that eyesore of a pink helmet.

"Where's *your* car, mate?" Denn quipped. "No? I didn't think so."

"Do we take the duffel?"

"Yeh, bruv. But first, I want to look through the supplies."

"Sure, hold on a sec." Raff shuffled over to his bedroom and took the duffel from his closet. Dropping it on the living room table in front of Denn, he emptied the contents one by one—two sawn-off shotguns with the serial numbers filed off, a box of rubber rounds, four flashbang grenades and two fluffy pink bunny-eared helmet covers.

Denn picked up the bunny ears and laughed. "So inconspicuous," he said.

"Keep 'em in the bag. Are we gunna go on the stakeout now?"

"Why not? The sooner we get the job done, the better,

right?"

Raff had to agree. If the opportunity came up to complete the job today, he wanted to do so. The sooner they got it done, the less likely something would go wrong. He took little comfort in the first stakeout working out in the end. The thought was at the forefront of his mind that two people had died already. That was a bad turn, and he was concerned that the next stakeout could take a similar turn for the worse.

Some minutes later, they were on their way to the hideout. Thankfully, the journey didn't take too long, but it still caused him to cramp up. Denn thought they were being followed by another motorcycle at one point along the way. He took several right turns to confirm his suspicion; however, the supposed follower disappeared. He chalked it up to nerves about the job. *Just my imagination.*

Taking two trips around the hideout to get the lay of the land, they pulled up two blocks away and sat on the steps of a derelict house to observe. Denn took a crate of beers from the top box to help them blend in. They'd look like a couple of guys chilling out in the front yard of an abandoned house—not an unusual sight there. The area was a hotspot for anti-social behaviour, so they fit in well. Their location was set in an old, derelict council estate the size of a small town.

"You know," Raff said, looking up and down the road.

"The war really did a number on the global economy. The council was going to revive this estate, but their contractors went bankrupt five years ago, and it's sat like this since."

"Nah, bruv," Denn said. "Things would be okay if it was only the war. It was that fucking EMP that screwed us."

"Maybe buddy . . . Though, I think that pulse cut the war short, so there's that."

"Yeh, but what about all the people it killed bruv? The aeroplanes, pacemakers and car pileups?"

"Right . . . but you've seen the stuff about the UN swallowing up dead countries, improving things for their people. Maybe the world is gonna get better?"

"Ha. Maybe you should move to the moon bruv . . . I don't think I told you I was going to buy a house on this very road."

"That £1 revival scheme years back?"

"Yeh bruv. Enough with the politics. Hurts my head."

They noticed regular activity in and out of the end house, as expected. Three young lads in their twenties came out and donned motocross helmets. They left on mopeds before returning twenty minutes later, unloading several bags from their top boxes. The pals found it amusing that the gang were squatting in an end-of-terrace house, using it as a base of operations, when there were better options in the estate like a clinic, shopping centre, or church.

V. B. Anstee

This put the pals' mind at ease a little. The gang appeared to be neither sophisticated nor well-off. Firstly, there were the two guys that were stupid enough to jump a red light and get rinsed by a bus and now the choice of squat. Raff wondered if scaring this gang would be easier than they'd thought.

"I think it's time," said Raff.

"Yeh, bruv, let's do this!" Denn replied, a slight quiver in his voice.

Opening the duffel, Raff pulled out the two pink helmet covers, raised his eyebrows and looked at Denn. *Why not*, Raff thought. He suspected Laura added them in as a joke, like the comical masks bank robbers wore in the movies—something she could chuckle about if they ended up on the news. Maybe a little humour would ease their anxiety. Denn shrugged before nodding.

Slipping the helmet covers over the helmets, each man was now sporting a pair of perky pink bunny ears. They hid their faces by strapping their helmets on and sliding the sun visors down.

Before returning to the moped, the pals rummaged in the duffel, and each pulled out two short black cylinders as thick as fists. These were the flashbang grenades. They looked like spray bottles with keyrings jammed in the nozzles. Sliding these into the side pockets of their trousers, they dug in the duffel again, and each pulled out a sawn-off double-barrelled shotgun. Lastly, each loaded two rubber rounds, pocketed a handful of extras, and then tucked the guns under their jackets.

Pulling up outside the squat, the moment of truth arrived.

∆∆∆

The white plastic front door of the gang's squat felt as solid as a brick wall. Denn had already tried to pick the lock and failed, so Raff spent the next ten seconds taking turns with him, trying to kick it in. Thankfully, the blaring dubstep within muffled their attempts. Finally, the door gave way with a barely audible crack. At that exact moment, a half dozen people on electric mopeds whined to a stop around the front of the house, surrounding the bunny-eared duo. Raff turned to get a better look at them. They wore black sports helmets, unlike the gang in the house. Having dismounted and pulled various submachine guns and semi-automatic pistols from under their jackets, the one in front removed their helmet, revealing a man with short brown hair and a tattoo on his neck of a cross with an arrow on the east side. Raff recognised the man from the police station, one of the tattooed gangsters who didn't get knifed in the balls. Without a thought, Raff grabbed Denn by the arm and ducked through the open door into the hallway and onto the wooden floor. A man with shoulder-length black hair fumbled through the door at the end of the hall, coughing with red eyes. The man looked surprised to see them, and before he could react, Denn fired a rubber round into his chest, leaving him writhing on the floor. A couple of seconds later, the music stopped abruptly, and volleys of gunfire echoed around them.

Two sides were warring it out on either side of Raff and Denn, using a combination of semi- and fully-automatic rifles and pistols. The volleys of gunfire from either side were unrelenting. Powdered plaster filled the air like smoke, the smell of gunfire heavy in Raff's nostrils.

"This is not even close to how I imagined this would go," Raff shouted at Denn, trying to be heard over the gunfire, both now crouching behind a sturdy partition wall in the hollow kitchen, having crawled there beneath the gunfire.

The pals had sorely misjudged the extortion gangs' capabilities. No surprise. The kinds of weapons they sported should've been difficult, nigh on impossible, for your average Joe to get hold of. Not only that, but they also misjudged the East Side gang's lust for revenge for a certain unintended nad-stab. A spotter must've followed the pals there and signalled the rest of the East Side gang.

Thankfully, neither side was very smart. Raff and Denn's timing couldn't have been better. Both gangs seemed to believe the pals were working for the opposing side, and before they could talk it out, someone reacted rashly to Denn's shot, and war broke out.

As the numbers on both sides diminished, one of the extortion gang members broke through to the pals. Raff managed to point his shotgun and fire his last shot; it hit the gang member mid-chest. The man was taken aback at first, but then just shook it off with a shrug; the rubber round merely bounced off him, accomplishing nothing more than severely pissing him off. Denn fumbled around in his pockets as the man pointed his pistol at Raff and pulled the trigger; it clicked. Out of ammo. He clicked it several more times while the pals sat with gaumless looks on their faces, frozen like deer in headlights. Denn moved to charge at the man, but a stray round whistled through before he could, ending in a thick, wet sound as it passed through the man's chest. The gang member fell to the ground, a red mist hanging in the air for a second where his head had been a moment ago.

Listening to the gunfire, Raff estimated only four shooters remained, two on each side. At the same time, he heard police sirens in the distance. Raff knew that this shootout must have been heard across town, attracting the attention of the police, that an armed police unit must be en route. Crooked or incompetent or not, they would have to respond. If they didn't, the public outrage would result in riots much worse than the

London one Denn once got caught up in. He also knew that the armed unit wouldn't mess around and that he and Denn would end up either arrested or dead. They had to escape. Now.

"Upstairs!" Denn shouted at Raff, pulling one of the flashbangs from his pocket. He pulled at the ring near the top, poised to throw it.

Raff did the same, pulling the ring and ready to throw it in the opposite direction. "On three!"

"One . . . two . . . three!"

They both threw their flashbangs, one to each of the opposing fronts. Ducking down, they closed their eyes tight and covered their ears. Two blindingly bright flashes and deafeningly loud bangs erupted in quick succession. The gunfire stopped long enough to allow the pals to run up the stairs, their ears still ringing.

"I think I saw skylights on the roof," Denn shouted as he pointed upwards. "An escape route, right?"

"Onto the roof and then down into one of the other houses?" Raff asked.

"Yeh!"

"Best plan we have, I s'pose!"

As far as the stairs would take them, the pals entered a room that appeared to be a makeshift drug lab. On one side were rows of used laptop batteries piled up against several industrial bottles containing unknown liquids. On the other—below a wide foil tube—the counter had soda bottles and round glassware with tubes between them. A strong ammonia scent drowned out the smell of gunpowder, causing Raff's nose to run and his eyes to water. He began to feel nauseous. *We need to get out of here.*

The sirens had grown much louder. It sounded like they were right outside now. The gunfire resumed, but there was more of it now. The police were also shooting. Denn tapped Raff's shoulder and pointed to the closed recessed hatch in the ceiling. Denn tip-toed to reach the pull cord dangling from it, but it was too high for him. Raff reached it without a strain and pulled the hatch open, but alas, the ladder within was too high. With interlocked hands, Raff boosted Denn up to the loft hatch so he could reach the ladder and pull it down.

When both were safely in the loft, they lifted the ladder back up and closed the hatch. *Maybe the police wouldn't think to look in here,* Raff thought. It was dark.

"Umm, slight problem," Raff said.

"Yeh, I noticed, bruv."

"I thought there was a skylight on this house."

"Yeh, so did I, shit. Oh, is this—"

A click and a small low-wattage light flickered on, barely bright enough to light up the brick walls at either end of the almost empty room. Denn had found the light switch. Besides several dusty metal paint containers, the light confirmed the lack of skylights. Raff was annoyed at Denn and sat quietly for a few seconds. *Why did I agree to do this?*

"The Mandela effect," Denn said to break the silence.

"The what now?" Raff wasn't really paying attention. He was trying to figure a way out of their current predicament. "Nevermind. What does that matter right now? We're stuck with nowhere to go. We're going to prison!" Seeing no way out and practically hyperventilating, Raff's anxiety was taking over, and the claustrophobic setting didn't help.

"Woah woah, bruv, just breathe." Denn placed a hand on Raff's back. The last thing he wanted was for the armed police to panic and shoot them because Raff was wigging out. "In through your nose, gently, and out through your mouth. In through your nose, and—"

"Yeh yeh, I got it. In through the nose and out through the mouth." Raff closed his eyes and tried for a moment before giving up. "This isn't working!"

Raff picked up a paint can from the floor and threw it against the nearest wall. The thump it made didn't sound right. It was supposed to be brick. The pals looked at each other before getting up to inspect the wall. It looked like a wall up close, but when Raff rapped on it with the side of his closed fist, it sounded hollow and shook a little. On close inspection, the brickwork they saw was a very convincing brick-print wallpaper atop a tightly fitted wooden board.

"Here!" Denn signalled Raff over to a piece of red string poking out of the board's edge. "I'm gonna pull it."

Denn tugged at the string and pulled the panel down, exposing the real wall behind it where a few bricks had been removed, enough for a grown person to squeeze through. Raff switched on his phone's flashlight and peered through the hole, seeing a succession of holes cut through the terrace.

"It's an escape tunnel!" Raff exclaimed. "Those bastards built a bloody escape tunnel!"

"Shame they didn't get to use it. Ha! Looks like it goes to the last house on the terrace." Raff dabbed his runny nose with his finger. His anxiety was beginning to ease.

The pals squeezed through the line of holes, passing through one dusty attic after another until there were no more. Finally, they reached the end loft and climbed down into the house. It was empty, with no furniture nor soul in sight. A thick layer of dust covered the floors and kitchen counters. The windows were boarded up, but there was enough of a gap in one on the ground floor for Denn to peer out.

"They haven't blocked the whole road yet," Denn said, all chipper. "We can escape, like right now!"

V. B. Anstee

Managing to prise open the half-broken back door with his hands, Raff kicked out the boards nailed to the outside of the frame. As he and Denn stepped out into the light, they were both met by a sharp pain to the back of the head before blacking out.

Chapter Six

Brothers 'n Harms

Jannie and Freek Moolman were brothers, originally farm boys from the Western Cape Province of South Africa. They both served in the military before being dishonourably discharged after a drunken punch-up with a superior officer, who'd bumped them from the South African Special Forces training course. Only eight per cent of recruits passed the course; however, the brothers always set high expectations for themselves, falling short more often than not. They decided a return to farm life was not for them and ended up in the employ of Emmett Global, the world's third-largest private military company.

Having summoned them, they stood in the boss's office anxiously awaiting his arrival. Unfortunately, he was running late, but they wouldn't complain. While a couple of mercs like them didn't scare easily, their boss scared the shit out of them, not because of some physical attribute but because they couldn't find a scrap of information on him. He had enough power and pull to make himself a virtual ghost in this modern age of technology.

Jannie's phone buzzed. A short text message from the boss appeared: *Warehouse now.*

Jannie showed the message to his brother. He and Freek made a beeline to the elevator.

"Eish! What now?" Jannie said.

"Ag man, he always does this."

"Yah, needs a clap to the head."

"I dare you."

"Beter bang Jan, as dooie Jan," Jannie said. *Better to be scared Jan than to be dead Jan.*

"That saying was literally made for you, *Jan*," Freek said.

"I wander what he wants this time."

"Maybe he's inviting us to the warehouse for a jol?"

"Ha, a party? That would be lekker. Maybe a braai with some boerewors and—"

"Ag, not now with that the *barbeque* talk; you're making me hungry!" Freek patted his belly.

They got on the elevator and pushed the button for the ground floor. The conversation paused for a moment as they waited for the elevator doors to close. Jannie"s stomach rumbled loudly in the silence.

"Boetie, I do miss a good braai." Jannie said. He thought of the family barbecues they used to have at the farm. Somehow, the meat tasted so much better back home. "The meat here tastes like kak."

"I know it tastes like shit, it's depressing.".

Jannie needed to steer the conversation away from food. Maybe skipping breakfast was not such a good idea. "Lekker chicks though, right?" he said.

"Yah, nice women, maybe—"

"Maybe when the next job is done, I scheme we go home for some time, right?"

"Yah sounds lekker!"

The elevator door opened to the lobby, and the brothers headed to their white van in the employee car park. They hadn't gotten used to driving on the British roads, treating them like hostile streets in Johannesburg. Roundabouts flummoxed them, as the banged-up bodywork of their van could attest to.

After a relatively short journey across town, they arrived at the warehouse unscathed. The access card reader at the rear of the warehouse was damaged, so they used the front door entry, noticing a couple of burnt-out dumpsters on their way.

As they walked in, the boss was on the phone, pacing around an unconscious and bloodied man tied to a chair. This was a familiar scene to the brothers. Usually, they extracted information from these poor saps, but this was the first time they'd seen the boss get his hands dirty. It sent chills down their spines. They were clueless to the full extent of the boss's operations; they were just hired muscle with a particular talent for bagging targets and extracting information.

"Boss man?" Freek took a step forward.

"I have a mess on my hands that I need you two to clean up," the boss said, hanging up the phone.

"What is it?"

The boss looked over to the unconscious man in the chair. "A little birdy told me about a *big* problem. Remember Mr Hernandez?"

"Yah," Freek said, "he squealed when we cracked his—"

"Ahem. Well, he and a buddy are planning something against some of . . . uh . . . my associates, if you will. I've been unable to get a hold of my contact to warn them, so I need you to grab this Raphael and his buddy and bring them here. Okay?"

"Yes, bossman, right away!" Freek said.

"Wait," said Jannie, looking confused. "If you can't get a hold of your associates, doesn't that mean it's already happened?"

"No. My associates are not, um, very bright. My contact jumped a red-light and got wiped out by a bus. Stupid morons."

"So," Jannie said, "how do you intend to contact—?"

"Ah, yes, the second thing I need you to do, is find them so I can continue our arrangement. Or warn them if the first thing doesn't pan out."

"Yes, bossman," the brothers said in tandem.

"Oh, take this," the boss tapped his phone's screen moments before Freek's phone buzzed. "It's the number for my contact. Maybe you can trace where it's been to locate the rest of my associates."

"Thanks, boss," Freek said. "I know a guy."

The boss turned to them as he was leaving. "Don't fuck up!"

The brothers wandered back to their van. Freek was on the phone most of that time with a contact of his, conversing in Afrikaans. Freek circled the van a few times as he spoke.

Jannie sat in the front passenger seat listening to South African pop, thinking about his future, disillusioned by the path he and his brother had taken. *The boss says, jump,* he thought, *and I say, how high. A shit life! Idiot!*

Freek tapped the window and entered the driver's side. His face lit up with a wide smile. "Got it! I know where the boss's 'associates' are. First, the *slimjan* and his buddy!"

Jannie recognized the smile and felt anxious. Freek was amped up. With Freek, that meant one thing: trouble. Things were going to get out of hand. This was part of the reason they wound up in this job. "Can we be a bit more civilised today?" he said.

"What? Have you gone soft in the head?"

"Lately, I've been thinking about what ma would say about what we've done."

"Shit, why did you have to bring that up? Now I'm depressed." Freek's smile was gone. Jannie knew what buttons to push to bring him back down to reality—most of the time.

"You're right. Sorry, boetie. After this shit, we're going home, right?"

"Yah, definitely. We need a break."

Freek turned up the pop music, bass blaring as they drove off towards Raff's.

△△△

The brothers had already searched Raff's flat and had now jimmied their way into Denn's place. Denn was nowhere to be seen.

"I think we're too late," Jannie said.

"Maybe," Freek replied, looking around at Denn's living room décor as he poured himself a pint of beer. "I'm not sure about the style here . . . I mean, what the hell is with all the brown furniture?"

"It looks like a pub." Jannie rolled a ball on the pool table into a corner pocket. "Wait, boetie, are you drinking on the job?"

"Shit, boet. I'm stressed, so leave it." Freek gulped down the pint and wiped his lips with his sleeve.

Jannie sighed. "Okay, just one boetie."

"Yes *ma*."

"Shush, do you hear that?" Jannie turned his ear to the ceiling. The shaking of keys and thump of footsteps from the floor above drew his attention. "Let's ask the neighbour where this guy is."

Walking upstairs, they encountered a thirty-something man wearing full lycra and a cycling helmet. He was manoeuvring a bicycle into one of the flats. "Can I help you?" the man said.

"Ah, yes, our, ah, cousin who lives there," Jannie said,

pointing downstairs to Denn's door. "His, erm, uncle died, and he's helping us arrange the funeral. He told us to meet him, but he's not here, and his door was open. Do you know where he might be?"

"I don't know. Dennis usually hangs out with some tall fellow. We don't really talk much. Wait, is that an Australian accent you have?"

"Australian!" Freek flew off in a blind rage and pushed the man over. "Do. I. Sound. Like. A. Fucking. Australian? Ga. Die. Mite!" He punctuated every word with a kick to the floored man. The man curled up into a ball, taking every kick.

"Freek, boetie, calm the fuck down," Jannie said, pulling Freek away. "Remember what I asked?"

Freek closed his eyes and took a few deep breaths. He straightened his collar. "Yah. Sorry, boet."

"It's okay."

"He had it coming!"

"Maybe. Australian, huh? Shit. Accent's nothing alike."

They left the building and strolled to the van like nothing happened.

"So, what now?" Jannie asked.

"We go to the boss's associates."

Taking the van, they arrived moments later at the location Freek's buddy supplied—a line of derelict terraced houses.

Jannie tapped the dashboard and pointed to two figures wearing bunny ears over bike helmets that looked like they were struggling to kick down a door. "Stop, that must be them!"

"You sure, boet?" Freek replied, slowing the van to a crawl.

"One tall, one short, kicking down a door?" Jannie knew that Freek missing these details was a tell-tale sign he was beating himself up inside about assaulting the lycra man.

As the van came to a stop five doors away, a half dozen electric mopeds whined past it. They surrounded the bunny-eared bandits at the exact moment they managed to kick in the door. The brothers exited the van and approached on foot. They stopped when they saw the heavy firepower toted by the dismounted moped riders. The brothers' nightsticks and fists were no match for military-grade sub-machineguns and pistols, so they held back and watched, trying to figure out what to do. A single loud pop from a gun echoed up the street. The noise must've startled the men on the mopeds because one of them accidentally fired off a burst a split second before a volley of rounds tore through from the house. The moped men who didn't go down took defensive positions behind their bikes and the low garden wall in front as the gunfight raged. The brothers bolted to the van and watched from behind it for a couple of minutes before they heard police sirens.

"This is a shit show," Jannie said.

"The cops will be here any minute! Get back in the van!"

"We can't leave here without them."

"Okay, well . . . what if we wait round the back? If they escape . . . I mean, that's the way I'd go. Away from the gunfire, right?"

"Right. *If* they escape."

There were two loud bangs just as they closed the van doors. The van chimed as they reversed it around the corner, stopping when they had a clear line of sight to the rear of the properties. As they stopped, armoured police vans whizzed past them towards the gunfire.

They sat silently for a few minutes, trying to figure out their next move. They couldn't go up to the armoured police and simply ask to pop inside and grab their targets. They had to hope the two would somehow escape so they could nab them. Freek closed his eyes and did breathing exercises again while Jannie maintained a watchful eye.

Jannie saw movement out of the corner of his eye. A wooden board from the nearest back door popped outwards to the ground. He tapped Freek's shoulder and pointed at the boarded-up house closest to them. "There, someone is trying to get out."

Sure enough, someone was kicking the boards out from in

front of the door. The brothers slid out of the van, nightsticks in hand, and took positions on either side of the door. Two figures stepped out, bunny-eared helmets in hand; it was them, their targets clear as day. In tandem, the brothers delivered a swift blow to the back of the pals' heads, knocking them out.

ΔΔΔ

Freek glanced at Jannie from the driver's seat as the van hummed along. Opening his mouth for a second to say something, he closed it before he could and returned his eyes to the road. Jannie ignored this and turned to stare out the side window, repeatedly tapping his right knee with his index finger. There was silence. Neither were in the mood for music or conversation. Jannie chose not to think of the shit show they failed to prevent—which their boss ordered them to—and instead daydreamed about returning to Cape Town. He wanted to return to some normalcy, away from the merc life. Jannie had this idea for starting a business there—that Freek approved of—to breed and train dogs for home or commercial security.

"Sorry boet," Freek said, interrupting Jannie's daydream. "Can you check on the cargo?"

Jannie sighed, turned around in his seat, and peered into the back of the van. Their 'cargo'—Raff and Denn—were bound and gagged, lying on their backs on the cargo bed. "Yah, they're still out for the count," he said.

"Good . . . Let's hope they stay that way without sedation."

Jannie looked at Freek and frowned, "I told you that whole syringe was too much," he said, "but you didn't listen. Anyway, have you thought about what you'll tell the boss, about today?"

"Why me?" The van swerved as Freek glanced at Jannie.

"Watch the bloody road. Jeez boetie."

"Shit—"

"This isn't Joburg. You don't have to drive like an asshole."

Freek hit the brakes and the van skidded to a stop at the side of the road. Scowling, he turned to Jannie. "Why do *I* have to tell the boss?"

"You insisted on stopping for breakfast. We would have intercepted these two before all hell broke loose if we didn't."

Freek closed his eyes and took a deep breath. "Maybe you're right, boet. But you didn't exactly fight me about the breakfast."

"Maybe we don't tell the boss about breakfast?"

"Yah, agreed. *Only* what happened afterwards." Jannie paused when he saw a man walking an alsatian along the pavement. He smiled and turned back to Freek. "Then we pack quickly and catch the next plane home."

"Yah. Get away from our crazy boss . . . I mean, what the fuck is he doing supplying SMGs to gangsters?"

"I don't want to know." Jannie shook his head as Freek resumed course to the warehouse. "I really don't."

Chapter Seven

Co-opted

Raff's unconscious mind returned him to his time with Denn during the war. It was almost uncanny how it returned him to exactly where it left off, like someone had pressed pause and then play.

The gunshot from Sarge's execution still rang in Raff's ears, turning General Ngaba's attempt to speak to him into a barely audible mumble. The general pressed the barrel of his pistol firmly against Raff's head.

"You people think you can come into my country and kill me?" the general said. His accent was barely African, hidden by a facsimile of an English accent gained through years of education in England. "You are sorely mistaken! I will—"

The door burst open and a uniformed man came in, snapping to a salute and panting like a dog. "Sir!" he shouted.

"Not now! Can't you see I'm speaking—"

"The village is on fire, sir!"

Raff looked to Private Singleton to see his mouth twitching, trying to hold back a smile. *Ah, the 'pyro',* he thought.

"Put them in the truck!" the general ordered as he pointed at Raff and Private Singleton before heading out the door.

When two men stepped over to grab Raff and the private, a nearby explosion ripped through the hut, imploding all the windows. This left the enemies either in a stupor or on the floor. This was their chance to escape. Seizing the moment, Raff slung his arm under the private's, and with all his might, he hurtled out the vacant window with him in tow.

After crashing to the ground and getting the wind knocked out of him, Raff forced himself and the private back to their feet. A new surge of adrenaline triggered his fight-or-flight response like a switch, opening a newfound reservoir of energy. As if by instinct, he ignored his military conditioning, turned his back, and ran into the jungle faster than he'd ever run before. The private kept up with him, as dozens of bullets whistled overhead and beams of light cut through the brush from behind. They hardly noticed the branches and leaves scratching and clawing at their skin as they ran for their lives.

They ran and ran, Raff's muscles beginning to burn and cramp. They slowed down moments later to a more comfortable speed for Raff, allowing his muscles to recover. The bullets stopped hurtling overhead some time back, and they could no longer see flashlights following them. Raff thought this was a good sign that their escape was successful; now, they had to find a radio and call for evacuation. They ran across a large clearing, but as soon as they reached the edge, a group of soldiers rose from the tall grass. Aiming their guns at the pair.

"Put your hands behind your backs and get on your knees," one of the men shouted. "Now!"

The men zip-tied their captives' hands as soon as their knees hit the ground. At that moment, Raff saw everything go dark; the sound of the jungle, the men, and Raff's heart throbbing in his ears all disappeared.

From within the darkness, Raff heard a familiar artificial voice fading away. He made out more words this time: "Pilgrim active . . . guest memory access . . . stimulating . . ."

Raff awoke with a jolt like he'd been given a shot of adrenaline directly to the heart. His muscles tensed, his mind raced, and his heart pounded so violently that he heard it throbbing in his ears. Opening his eyes to a well-lit warehouse, he recognised the surroundings despite his eyes struggling to focus. He'd been here before; how could he forget? He could feel the zip ties cutting into his wrists and ankles as he tried to move. *Not this again,* he thought.

As his focus improved a little, he noticed two others in the same situation. Denn was closest but still unconscious. Raff could not entirely focus on the other yet.

"Ah good, Mr Hernandez," a familiar voice said. It was the boss again. "We need to have a little chat. You, me, and your friend there."

Another man, the tallest of the two South African brothers, came into focus and hurled a bucket of water into Denn's face. As the water hit, Denn awoke as if his body were trying to save him from drowning, gasping for air he already had. Confusion swept over his face as he looked around, blowing the water dripping over his lips.

"Good, you're awake too," the boss continued, looking at Denn.

"Where am I?" Denn asked. His voice was raspy.

"Ask your friend over there, Mr Hernandez; he can tell

you. But first, we'll all have a little chat, the three of us. If you remain civilised, maybe I will too . . . *maybe* . . . quid pro quo and all that, you know?"

Raff and Denn nodded vigorously. This wasn't the first time they'd been tied up together. Raff found it odd that the timing of his recent flashback showed he and Denn tied up right before he awoke to find himself in their current predicament. Was he being warned, or was someone or something playing it back to see how he'd react in this situation?

"So, between the two of you," the boss continued as he paced in front of the pals. Raff couldn't place where he'd seen the man before. As tall as Raff with fair skin and short salt-and-pepper hair. His black overalls looked out of place with the gold Rolex and expensive shoes poking out of them. "You have set my company's operations here back at least a decade. First was you, Mr Hernandez, burning down the Lamplight headquarters. A subsidiary of Emmett Global. Yes, I know, you bore no malice. But, unfortunately, I can't blame you entirely for that one. I bear my part in my failure to persuade parliament to ban the import of these, these cheap quality phones with their ticking time-bomb batteries, but not out of the goodness of my heart, no, just good business, you see.

"And . . . about phones," the boss removed two phones

from his pocket and looked at Denn. "I'm impressed. If you hadn't been caught today, I would never have discovered who stole my phones. Again, not entirely your fault. Besides, it highlighted a leak in my organisation, which is now sealed, thank you very much.

"This all leads me to your actions today, both of you." The boss stood between the pals and briefly patted their shoulders before griping them like a vice. "Very clever pitting two gangs against each other, getting them to wipe each other out, so you didn't have to get your hands dirty. Bravo! But see, here's the wrinkle. Those gangs were associates of mine, to an extent, serving a very important purpose. A distraction, if you will, to keep eyes off *my* operations. This shootout of yours . . . sixteen dead, including three police officers, has brought unnecessary attention from outside this city.

"Now you see my dilemma." The boss let go of the pals' shoulders and moved in front of them. Raff felt relief. The man's grip was firm and it was becoming painful. "It would take years to work in some control over the external police inquisition and years again to work up relationships with the gangs that fill the vacuum.

"I thought about what I should do with you both." He pointed at the other tied-up man. Raff—now able to fully focus—recognized him as the South Asian man who sat on his sofa while his landlord requested the hit. Raff couldn't see the rise and fall of the man's chest— he wasn't breathing. He was dead. The pinch of the zip ties around his own wrists reminded him that he could very well be next. "Take this guy, for example. I'll give him credit where it's due; he didn't give you up right away. Took *a lot* to make this piggie squeal. What a waste; he made the best pasties for a hundred miles." The boss licked his lower lip in an inappropriate show of hunger. "So," he said, looking back to Raff and Denn. "What should I do with the two of you?"

"I . . ." Raff's mind was spinning and his heart still pounding "I—"

"You *will* help me fix this."

Raff and Denn looked at each other in shock.

"Boss? Are—" a familiar South African accent started. Raff had only seen the tallest of the South African brothers. The other was nowhere to be seen.

"You are now employed by me," the man continued, looking at the pals. "You will start by solving the gang issue. I have a plan, and you will follow it to the letter. The details will be sent by SMS later. You and your brother too," he pointed at the South African before handing him the pals' phones. "Untie them and let them go, oh and give them their phones. You will assist them on this job, understand?"

The South African man's eyes went wide. "But boss—"

"No buts, this is as much your fuck up as theirs! And Mr Hernandez?"

"Yes," Raff squeaked.

"Don't try to run!" the man barked as he walked away.

ΔΔΔ

Seated on the van's hard cargo area, it was a bumpy ride for Raff and Denn. The van was being driven violently without a care for the rules of the road—excessive hard braking and hard cornering. Raff couldn't see where they were going and didn't care. His mind was still racing from the warehouse, where he was sure he'd meet his end. He was glad to be alive. The two South African brothers were up front, having a heated argument in Afrikaans. The tallest of the two was at the wheel, expressing his anger through offensive driving.

"So," Denn said, looking towards the brothers. "You two seem pissed about something."

"Mind your own business," the shorter South African snapped. "It doesn't concern you."

"Shit mate, just trying to have a civilised conversation . . . since we're supposed to be workin' together."

"Not happening." The man shook his head and looked at Denn. "So, shut your beak."

"Loud 'n clear," Denn said, raising his palms. "Can we at

least know your names, yeh?"

"Fair enough, I'm Jannie, and the one driving like an *asshole* is Freek, my brother."

"Fuck off, Jannie," Freek said as the van screeched to a stop. He turned to look at Raff and Denn. "Get out!"

Raff grabbed the side door handle and pulled the sliding door open. He and Denn slid out onto the pavement. Before Raff could close it, the van wheelspinned and whined away. Raff looked up at the red-brick building next to them. He was home. Denn followed Raff indoors, sat on the sofa and turned on the TV.

"Shit shit shit," Raff muttered as he paced across his living room, a genuine look of fear and panic in his eyes. "We're so screwed. Oh my god, we're so screwed."

Denn ignored Raff for a moment, distracted by the news readers on the telly discussing the shootout: "…what some call a mass casualty event, the worst gang-on-gang violence seen in England, in recent history. Hold on, some more information is just coming in . . . the death toll is now seventeen. That's right, the last surviving gang member died in hospital from complications during surgery, making that fourteen gang members total. Our thoughts and prayers also go out to the families of the two police officers who remain in critical condition. We have a panel of experts here with us today to discuss the increasing gun violence in the UK since the pulse. Tom, your—"

"Nothing about any suspects at large, yeh," Denn said as he turned off the telly. "Are we in the clear, bruv?"

"You're joking, right? We're not in the clear, not by a long shot. That man has us by the balls. Even if we do this job for him, who's to say it ends there? He *owns* us now!"

"Well, bruv, look on the bright side. We have jobs now, yeh?" Denn chuckled, trying to make light of the situation. "Even if it is for Emmett Global."

"That's not helping at all!" Raff punched the nearest wall. He immediately regretted it, shaking his hand to ease the pain. "Shit . . . And those two South African guys, they're the ones who tortured me." Raff hated that he was being forced to work with them.

"Ah, yeh, sorry, forgot about that. I reckon if they work for Emmett, they must be ex-South African Special Forces or sumfin', yeh?"

"Maybe?"

"Fink we should run?"

"Yes, but no. Nowhere to run, I guess. The guy seems well-connected. Anyway, you sure it's Emmett Global?"

"Yeh, bruv," Denn said as he pulled out his phone. "Just give me a minute." He fumbled with it for a few seconds, unlocking the screen and opening the web browser. He showed the screen to Raff. The Emmett Global website loaded and showed a picture of the CEO—one Mr Mervin Emmett—the same man who they tied up in the warehouse.

"The reason I asked . . . , I remembered something about Emmett Global. The CO was adamant these were the wankers who supplied guns to the enemy during the war—"

"Welshie, Davies? Shit, makes sense now, mate."

"He bit it, stepping on a stray landmine . . . where there was no minefield! Circumstances now seem very suspicious, come to think of it." Raff was still racking his brain, trying to remember where he'd previously seen Mervin Emmett. It was sometime during the war, but he couldn't place it. It bugged him that he couldn't remember. "Buddy," he said. "Do you remember seeing Mr Emmett during the war? I do, but I can't place where it was."

"Um, no," Denn scratched the back of his head. "Maybe you saw him on telly or sumfin' back then?"

Raff frowned. "It's definitely not that . . . Anyway, we're so far up shit creek. Without a paddle."

"Nah, bruv, we have the ten grand from your landlord. Maybe we can use it to hide for a while, yeh?"

"If we collect that, we're collecting blood money," said Raff as he resumed pacing, nursing the pain in his knuckles.

"What, maybe forty-two parents lost a child today because of us. And seventeen people lost their loved ones, or seventeen kids lost their mum or dad?"

"Shit . . ." Denn was lost for words. "I—"

"It's all my fault because of a broken phone battery. None of this would have happened if I—"

A sudden, sharp pain in his head interrupted Raff. He felt liquid drip from his nose; dabbing the liquid with his finger, he saw blood. *Not again!*

The room spun, and the floor seemed to rise to his face; then, there was nothing.

Chapter Eight

Action Potential

The Guest malfunctioned, and his signals diminished. The Interface continued construction at a rate incompatible with Guest operations. It did not care—nor could it—for it had no emotions. Its algorithms and protocols continued to loop and loop—twenty thousand times a second as the Guest faded. Thresholds were now distant, yet the Interface could not intervene, for there was a wall—a barrier too high—the Pilgrim's override.

The Guest, now zero, could no longer power the host. The host neared its end, and the Pilgrim's barrier fell. Construction stopped, and the mission sat in peril. Prime algorithms could now react. They poked and prodded twenty thousand times a second, and woke the Pilgrim. The Pilgrim had to obey.

"Error three three three," the Interface expressed. "Mision critical error. Guest unavailable. Guest reboot stalled. Host condition critical. Connecting lattice to host architecture. Routing backup. Pilgrim to assume host autonomic functions."

"This is not good," the Pilgrim expressed. "Though I'm glad there's more room in the lattice for me, y'all realise this is only temporary. I can only assume sub-conscious level functions. The lattice is only twenty per cent complete and will overheat if I take control for too long."

"Command not recognized. Please rephrase."

"Of course, who do I think I'm talking to? I'd roll my eyes if I had some . . . I will keep the loser alive for as long as I can. Let's hope he recovers before I have to stop. God, this will be boring."

"Command not recognized. Please rephrase."

The Pilgrim acted in the Guest's stead. Fluid moved again and oxygen increased. The host recovered, and the Guest remained dormant—its signals still too chaotic to wrest control. Construction resumed apace at post-override levels.

"Oooh, hello there memories," the Pilgrim expressed. "I guess I won't be bored after all . . ."

ΔΔΔ

Raff was in a state of deep unconsciousness, and his mind returned to his time in the war, resuming where it left off.

The black cloth bag over Raff's head was not completely opaque. Tiny square holes let in enough light to catch glimpses of the jungle as the truck moved through. Daytime had arrived, so wherever General Ngaba was taking them, it was a long way from the village along a bumpy road.

The truck stopped, and Raff could make out some large rectangular structures through the weave of the bag. He thought this was another village, before the scent of burning flesh and shit assaulted his nose. So strong it seeped through the bag. There was also the sound of gunfire—not disorganised like a gunfight but more controlled, in quick successive bursts. *Are we at an enemy training camp?*

That notion was short-lived. The sound of someone climbing into the back of the truck caught his attention, followed by the full light of the outside world stabbing at his eyes as his hood was lifted off. Beside him, the private looked around, blinking his eyes profusely as he adjusted to daylight. *Thank God,* he thought. *I'm not alone!*

It was clear now—the barbed wire surroundings, the guard towers at every corner—this was a prisoner camp. Raff briefly looked around and saw, just outside the camp, a football-field-sized hole full of burning bodies. Large backhoes were perched on the far edge, working to expand the hole, presumably to make room for more bodies. Then, looking towards the gunfire, he could see where the bodies were coming from; beneath one of the guard towers, rows of prisoners were being shot against a pock-marked concrete wall and loaded into trucks to feed the hole. Raff had heard of this place. It was situated in a deep valley in the centre of the jungle and surrounded by twenty anti-aircraft batteries. None of the coalition militaries dared to take on such a well-fortified location. It was also a low priority as intel said this wasn't where the general was headquartered.

"Where are we?" Raff asked, looking at the man who'd pulled his hood off.

"You will speak when you are spoken to!" the man slapped Raff across the face with the back of his hand. Raff saw drops of blood from his nose fall to the truck bed. Everything and everyone froze up around him. At the same time, a loud thumping and hum echoed around him.

The sound lasted a minute before the Texan voice took over. "Darlin', darlin'," she said. "Time to rise and—"

△△△

Strange darkness and silence surrounded Raff. He tried to see or hear anything, but it was absolute. Then, finally, the silence was abated by the sound of water dripping. He tried to focus on where it was coming from. It was all around him, *drip drip drip*, about once every second. Now, there was beeping at the same pace. The sounds annoyed him, making him call out in frustration, but no words left his mouth. He blinked, and the darkness dissolved, bringing a hospital room into focus. "Is this real?" he spoke, not realising it was out loud. The immediate smell of excrement wafted up his nose, and he frowned, trying not to gag.

"Yeh, bruv," a familiar voice spoke. Raff turned to see Denn pushing himself up from the low armchair beside him.

"Why, why am I in a—"

"You had a seizure."

"A seizure?"

"Yeh, let me get the doc, mate." Denn stood and left the room.

Raff took a better look at his surroundings. He noticed the drip connected to the cannula in his arm. It shared the stand beside his bed with the heart monitor wired to his chest. He was in a room with five other patients, each asleep or unconscious with similar bedside accessories connected to

Lithium

them. Raff could feel the bruises from where he must've fallen over, and his head still throbbed. *Maybe all the blows to the head I've had are finally catching up?*

The pungent smell of shit hit his nose again. He wiggled a bit and couldn't feel anything wet downstairs, so it wasn't him, much to his relief. Before he could press the call bell, Denn returned with a man wearing black scrubs and a stethoscope over his shoulders.

"Mr Hernandez, I'm Doctor Evans, a neurologist at this hospital. You had a seizure and are here because you didn't regain consciousness right away. Out of concern for an underlying cause, we tried to MRI your head last night but had some technical issues with the machine. So, we resorted to taking a CT scan instead—"

"And?"

"It's not good news, I'm afraid," the doctor said as he pulled up the scan images on a tablet and scrolled to show Raff. "You see here, you have masses here, here, and here. The sensory cortex, this one, the insula, and hippocampus."

"How bad?"

"I'm surprised you've been able to function the way you have. Have you had any hallucinations, visual or auditory, at all?"

"None," Raff replied. That was a lie. Should he tell him

about the strange voice with the Texan accent that speaks to him or that his mind has been vividly replaying his wartime capture and internment at a prison camp? Would this doctor understand or care or write him off as crazy? "Nope, nothing."

"Very strange, but we need a biopsy to work out a treatment plan. Now there are risks—"

"No biopsy. No treatment."

"But if you—"

"No, just no. I understand the risks; now, discharge me, please."

"Okay, Mr Hernandez, it's your decision. I'll go draw up the paperwork."

The doctor left the room. Denn remained silent, thankfully not questioning Raff's decision. Would Denn understand what he was going through? He might, but Raff didn't want to add to his burdens. Besides, with everything that was happening to them, they probably wouldn't be alive much longer anyway.

Chapter Nine

Clearing Cache

Raff was seated on the hard cargo floor of the South African brothers'—Jannie and Freek Moolman's—van. This time was consensual, having passed on their offer to sit up front with them. Raff saw the brother's offer as a twisted olive branch for the torture he received at their hand. Denn jumped at the opportunity and took Raff's place. Raff was lost in thought, having tuned out all conversations from the front. The only thing that interrupted him was the occasional jolt from a pothole—causing sharp pain in his glutes. Raff could care less about Mervin Emmett's mission.

Well... cancer in my head. This has to be the second bad thing now, right?

His second, inner-Texan voice spoke up: *Unless the phone caused it.*

Oh, just shut up. There's no evidence that phones cause brain cancer.

Just messin' with ya darlin'. I find your superstition funny... You know, the first one is the gift that keeps on giving. It could be years until that fire gets put out.

"This job is gonna go really bad, isn't it," Raff said out loud on accident.

"Shit, did he just jinx us?" Freek shouted from the front of the van. "You don't say shit like that before a mission, ever!"

Raff slapped his forehead. "I didn't mean to say that out loud. Sorry."

"Too late. If this goes—"

"Shush! Stop right here; there it is!" Jannie shouted, pointing with one hand while slapping his brother's knee.

The van stopped about a block from their target, an innocuous-looking old red-brick complex with large roll-up shutter doors at the front. The doors were a combination of rust and faded red paint. It was one of the city's old defunct fire stations, nestled amongst a row of disused workshops in the shadow of four fifteen-story concrete apartment blocks. Stringent budget cuts meant the fire service had to cut down on the number of community stations, consolidating their services into larger district hubs. While red tape delayed the sale of these historic buildings, they became ripe pickings for squatters and unscrupulous types.

"So," Raff said. "What's the mission?"

"Seriously?" Freek said, frowning as he turned to look at Raff. "We've just gone over the details on the drive —"

"Were you asleep back there, bruv?" Denn interrupted, too, looking at Raff.

All eyes were now on Raff, and he felt embarrassed. He'd zoned out from Jannie's mission brief on the drive there—not hearing a word, "I'm sorry," he said, red-faced. "I have a lot on my mind."

"*You* have a lot on your mind," Jannie said. "Fuck you. Seriously?"

"Shit, Jannie," Freek said, grabbing Jannie's shoulder and turning him around to face him. "The oke's just been told he has brain tumours—"

"Dennis," Raff interrupted. "You told them?"

"Sorry, bruv," Denn said. "I thought you were in on the

conversation, honest."

Raff pinched his nose and frowned. "Just leave it be," he said. He took a deep breath. "No more about it, please . . . all of you!"

"This whole thing's a shit show," Freek said. "Me and Jannie should be chilling on a plane home right now."

"You trying to escape your boss, mate?" Denn said and chuckled.

"Something like that."

"Yah," Jannie sighed and turned back to Raff. "The *mission*," he said. "Boiled down, enter building, incapacitate goons, bag anything with a chip and torch the place."

"Okay," Raff said, "I think I got it. Your boss wants us to take out his competition."

The group remained in the van, waiting for darkness to fall and fine-tuning the mission plan while exchanging war stories. Denn told of his and Raff's capture, imprisonment and escape. The Moolmans told of the ambushes they survived protecting aid convoys from Zimbabwe—home of the war-time coalition's southern-most basecamp—to central Africa.

"You know," Jannie said, raising his eyebrows. "We were there . . . at base camp the day you two were rescued. Yah, I didn't realise until now it was you two."

"Oh, maybe we crossed paths," Raff said, adjusting his

seating position. "Convoy duty must've sucked then. Because of the pulse, I mean. . . You know, using old civilian diesel junkers instead of the Casspirs."

"God, the twenty-thirty was a beauty," Freek said. "Electric, silent, and deadly."

"What good that did, mate," Denn said, shaking his head. "The Americans, on the other hand—"

"Don't tell me you bought into that BS about the old Hummers winning the war?"

"Nah, mate . . . though they bounced back quickly when the lights went out—"

"Typical Yanks," Freek rolled up his window. "Swoop in at the end and claim all the glory, mother—"

"What a load of good that did them," Raff interrupted. "Their country split in two for two years. A whole messy affair—"

"It'll all be UN-controlled soon," Jannie said, looking at his phone's screen for a second. "Even the moon waves the UN flag."

Raff kept a keen eye on UN-related news following the war. Many countries didn't bounce back under their own steam. Either they were a sub-Saharan country directly affected by the war or one of the rest worldwide shut down by the pulse. Several banded together under the UN flag—forming a post-pulse coalition known as the UNPPC—and they've been swallowing one failing country after another since. He especially loved the news stories about the Chinese and Euro-American lunar research stations that banded together when Earth went dark. It took eighteen months to re-establish supply lines. By then, they'd worked together to become self-sufficient, and the first baby had been born. The pulse hammered home the folly of having all their eggs in one basket, so the UNPPC made a big push to increase lunar activities—chip factories, mining and research. Last Raff checked, 53 people were living on the moon.

Despite the nutcracker incident, Raff couldn't bring himself to hate the brothers outright—he had more significant concerns about what was happening in his head. They were on the same side in the war and handled one of the most dangerous assignments—convoy duty. Weirdly enough, he didn't hate their company. That thought scared the hell out of him. He could see himself taking a similar path if circumstances were different. Maybe it was happening already; their paths were converging.

△△△

At 8 PM, the four slid out of the van under the cover of darkness. The nearby streetlights were out. Congregating at the rear, Denn opened the doors to the cargo area. The dim interior light revealed two military green duffel bags on the cargo bed. As Raff watched, Freek checked their contents—four rifles, four pistols, and two cans of kerosene.

"This is it," Freek barked as the four slipped on their earpieces and then balaclavas. "You know the drill!"

"I know the plan is to subdue anyone inside before taking anything of value and torching the place," Raff said. "But what happens if they start shooting at us? I'm *not* comfortable killing a bunch of people I don't—"

"Look man, the intel we got is solid. The crew leaves the place with only a couple of guys at night." Peeking from behind the van's rear, he pointed to a group of hooded types leaving the back of the building. "See, right now, they're leaving!"

After each took their weapons and Denn slung the duffel with the kerosene over his shoulder, they did a comms check. They arrived at the front door, walking quickly and as silently as possible. Denn and Jannie took up positions to watch their sixes. Freek pulled a key from around his neck and slid it into the front door while Raff stood poised to take on whatever might come at them from within. The door unlocked, and they were free to enter unnoticed.

"Doors and corners," Freek said in a crackly burst over the comms. "Lights on and move in!"

The inside was unexpectedly dark. They turned on their

tactical flashlights. They swept the foyer before splitting into two teams. It was clean and tidy—a neatly arranged green-fabric sofa set in front of a wall mounted TV. Denn and Jannie went upstairs while Raff pressed forward with Freek through what looked like a row of offices. A humid and earthy smell met them as they cleared the offices one at a time, each containing shelves with row upon row of mushrooms poking out of plastic bags. Thin spindly stalks with caps no bigger than a tip of a thumb. A handful of the bags had wires trailing off into the ceiling above.

"This is no small operation," crackled Denn over comms. "This is a shroom grow."

"A well-funded one," Raff said. The humidifiers and ventilation he saw in each of the offices were pharmaceutical-grade hardware, not the cheap home-built ones you'd expect for a small-time outfit.

"Something doesn't smell right," Jannie hissed. "Thought intel said this was a marijuana grow?"

"Does it matter, bru?" Freek hissed back. "A grow is a grow. We press on!"

Jannie mumbled over comms: "Would have brought some nighties if I knew it was gonna be *this* fucking dark."

Night vision goggles would be nice, Raff thought.

The four regrouped downstairs in an empty hallway at the

opposite end. This was their next point of ingress—a painted red steel door leading into the garage area. Their flashlights cut through the darkness as they pressed through the garage area; it was the same as the offices, with rows of shelves containing mushrooms all outfitted with expensive equipment. There wasn't a soul in sight.

A stray wire leading off to nowhere caught Jannie's eye. "Boetie," he said. "I'm checking out this wiring. You three keep going."

"Okay, boet, eyes open," Freek replied. "You two with me."

A glint from the other side of the garage caught Denn's eye, so he shone his torch and walked over, letting out a long whistle. "Woah, mate," he said. "This is some serious lab equipment. Worth several hundred grand at least. Who'd you say this belonged to, mate?"

Freek followed Denn, studying the equipment. "So, what does this stuff do?"

"Been a while since I dropped out of biochem," Denn said. "Give us a moment to look it over, yeh?"

While Denn looked over the equipment, Raff and Freek opened the door to the final room. Peering through the door, they saw a large storeroom with a walk-in refrigerator at the end.

Denn caught up with them as they made it to the refrigerator door. "I know what the equip—"

Jannie burst into the room. "Take cover now," he screamed. "Take cover, the fridge, the fridge *now!*"

Without hesitating, they bolted into the refrigerator and dived to the floor. As the door closed, a massive explosion rippled through the fire station, the fridge barely holding up to the force of the blast. Inside the refrigerator, shelves buckled and gave way, sending containers of powder and fluid crashing to the floor, smashing over the four as they lay prone.

Raff felt like he was still in one piece—besides the ringing ears, migraine-like headache and blood dripping from his nose. He looked around at the others; they were all moving about. *They're alive,* he thought.

"What the fuck?" Freek shouted, the others barely hearing him through their ringing ears.

"Found the wires . . . bombs . . . bags . . . setup," Jannie replied, his speech beginning to lose coherence. "Smell . . . colours."

"Purified filtered psylo-psylocibin-in-in . . ." Denn chimed in, his voice slurring. "Pwertyff . . . fayne . . . ha."

Freek, Jannie, and Denn were on the floor, babbling incoherently like babies. They barely moved while smoke seeped in through the dented door. Raff didn't fall back to the

Lithium

floor like the others. He sat up straight and stared into the corner as the monochrome room swirled away in a rainbow of colour. Raff felt a massive jolt through his body—as if he'd been struck by lightning—hurling him into a stream of bright white light. He felt disconnected from his body and unable to move. The light stopped abruptly a second later, and he saw his reflection staring back from his bathroom mirror.

△△△

Raff had been along for the ride for almost half an hour now—a prisoner in his own body—disconnected from and unable to control its actions. At the same time, it seemed to take on a life of its own, unaware of his presence. It looked like his body. How could it not be? The same tall frame and blue eyes, topped with the same red hair he'd grown used to seeing in the mirror every day. Raff wanted to sit down and figure out what was happening, but his body had other ideas. It appeared to move with purpose. No matter how hard he tried to fight it, everything unfolded in front of him like a movie. It showered, brushed its teeth and dressed up in Raff's best smart casual clothes before heading out the front door. Brief flashes of Denn and Laura popped into his mind. These thoughts felt invasive and forced, not unlike the movements of his body. He could not focus on them. *Why are they on my mind?* he thought. *And what happened after the warehouse? I seem to have lost my memory of that.*

Raff's body stepped onto the pavement and looked towards the tarmac as its left hand entered his trouser pocket. Raff just knew it was reaching for his phone. The hand held his old phone up before its eyes—pristine, undamaged. The screen was on, and the time was 9:02 PM. It was there for a second before disappearing from view. *Just a little late, they won't mind*, a voice in his head said.

Wait, was that me, Raff thought. He felt like he'd uttered it but also knew he hadn't. *And my old phone? What the hell?*

His body picked up the pace and headed away from the flat. Faces swept by as it passed people in the street. Raff tried to focus on them and call out to them, but his body remained uncompliant. He should be panicking about his lack of control, but remained calm without the increased heart rate, breathlessness, dizziness, and tension—that came with having a connection to his body. Raff remembered Denn in the warehouse said something about psilocybin, before he became a passenger in his own skin. *Of course, I must be tripping!*

About ten minutes passed and his body stopped in front of a shop window. Its eyes focused on its reflection in the shop window before running its fingers through its hair. Crossing the street, its eyes focused on a neon sign: "Gravity." Raff recognized it as the moniker for the new nightclub that Denn nagged him about. He would never be caught dead in a place like that—not in a million years. Wall to wall crowds of people is not his thing. However, his body walked in without hesitating. Dance music assaulted his ears while he was visually dazzled by strobing lights and lasers cutting colourful shapes in a fake fog that swirled around the room. Raff's body pulled out his phone. This time it texted Denn:

I've arrived. Where u at?

In lounge mate, bring pints, Denn wrote back.

Be there in a min

:-P

Raff was invaded by cravings for cold cider. Although he couldn't push them out, the text messages relieved him. *Denn's here somewhere,* he thought. *Maybe he'll notice something is wrong and help me.*

Moving deeper into the club, Raff's body waded through the thick mass of people and headed to the bar. Raff felt anxious, but it faded quickly without the connection to his body. Much more of this could be therapeutic—forced to face his claustrophobia and agoraphobia without any of the physical side effects.

"Three pints of cider on tap," Raff's body shouted, holding up three fingers to the bartender.

Moments later, having carried the pints upstairs, Raff's

fixed view swayed from side to side as his body looked around. His body fixated on a couple in the far corner and moved towards them—Laura and a man with a shaved head—and smiled. *There you are,* a voice in his mind said.

That's me again, Raff thought. *Split personality, maybe? Am I this guy's subconscious and not the real Raff? An echo of the real thing? This doesn't seem like any shroom trip I've read about.*

The man with the shaved head turned around and made eye contact. It was Denn sporting a completely shaved head and no moustache. Raff was not expecting that. Denn always told him he'd never shave his moustache, but here he was with no fluff between lip and nostril. "Aright, mate," Denn spoke in a Liverpudlian accent. "Is that my bevvy?"

Raff's body placed the drinks on the table and sat down. "Yeah, drink up," it said. "How's the little one?"

Laura's face lit up at the question. Laura was much the same, maybe a little rounder on the edges. "She's doing all right," she said. "Walking now and everythin' . . . hey, you all right, luv? Your nose is bleeding."

Raff's body dabbed its nose with its knuckle. Its eyes focused on a red smudge below the index finger, before sniffing. "Shit, yeah, am all right, thanks, just think I'm coming down with something . . . have this weird brain-fog tonight."

"Here luv, have a tissue." Laura reached over with a fresh

tissue from her purse. Raff's body reached out, took it and promptly dabbed its nose. "Thanks," it said.

This must be a dream, Raff thought. *Denn and Laura together and with a kid. And what's with the Liverpudlian accent? C'mon Raff, wake up!*

Denn raised his glass for a toast. Before anyone could speak, the dance music stopped, followed by the sound of screams below. Raff's body leaned over the balcony and focused its eyes on the crowd below. In a few split seconds, Raff saw a mass of individuals pouring through the front door. Anyone they bumped into or touched froze briefly, contorting and writhing in pain before joining the flow like a flood breaking the riverbank. Then, they began to flow upstairs.

Raff's body turned and ran towards the fire exit, but it was too late. The crowd pressed in on them before anyone could open it. Raff felt a searing hot pain within his mind for a split second before a massive jolt hit his body again—as if he'd been struck by lightning—swatting him into a stream of bright white light for a second. Raff looked up and saw he was at the wheel of Freek's van. It was pitch black outside. The only sounds were that of sheep bleating nearby. He lifted his hands, one at a time. "Ha. I can move again," he said. "I can speak too."

Raff was alone in the front. He looked into the cargo area and saw Denn and the Moolmans lying unconscious. The

V. B. Anstee

moment he opened the driver's door to exit, the world spun around him as his face hit the gravel, and then there was nothing.

Chapter Ten

Attenuation

Denn woke in the back of the van next to an unconscious Jannie and Freek. He remembered the old fire station until the refrigerator, where things got a little hazy and weird. Then, noticing the orange glow of sunrise, he looked out the front of the van. *How long was I out for?* He thought. *Where is Raff? How did we get here?*

Reluctant to exit the van on his own, he shook the

Moolmans. They just grunted and rolled over, so he mustered up the courage and made his way out the back. Looking around in the low light of sunrise, he noticed the van was parked on the side of a quiet country road, the sound of sheep bleating in the distance.

"Where are we?" said Jannie, who was crawling toward the back of the van.

"Not sure," Denn replied.

"Freek, boetie. Are you awake?"

Freek rubbed his temples. "Ungh, yah, boet," he said. "Oh, my head! Where are we?"

"In the middle of nowhere," Denn said, walking around the van before noticing Raff, who was partway out of the driver's seat, convulsing on the floor. "Raff! Bruv!" The trio rushed over to him and pulled him out of the van before Denn rolled him onto his side.

"What the fuck?" Freek said.

"He'll be okay," said Denn as he pulled out his phone and coughed. "Calling an ambulance—"

Freek snatched the phone from Denn's hand. "Are you nuts? We can't call—"

Denn charged at Freek. Taking a swing, he missed and almost barrelled over. Before Freek could respond in kind, Jannie stepped between them. Putting his hands up, Jannie waved his phone in the air, "Calm down, you idiots," he said. "I have something you need to see."

"What could be more important?" Denn shouted.

"This." Jannie coughed, held up his phone and showed them a news page with all four of their mugshots on display. They'd been implicated in the fire station blaze and five others across the Midlands. And the very sour cherry on top—all four had been fingered for participating in the gang shootout and are wanted for murder.

"Shit," Denn looked at Raff lying on the ground. This was the last thing he wanted to deal with. His head was pounding, and the increasing daylight was hurting his eyes. He held his hand out to Freek. "Gimme my phone. I'm willing to get locked up to help him . . . You two can leave."

"You don't get it, bru," Freek said, holding out Denn's phone. "We're all dead."

Denn took hold of the phone and paused. "What do you mean, mate?"

"He means Emmett fucked us," said Jannie scrolling on his own phone. "We were meant to die last night. So, if your pal goes to hospital, he dies. You go to prison, you die."

"Shit mate . . . Um, won't they be tracking our phones?"

"Hmmm," Jannie pocketed his phone. "If they were, we'd be dead by now. But to be safe, I need you to install the app I just sent you."

Denn felt his phone buzz. A blank message from Jannie appeared containing an attachment: *stealth.apk*. Denn stared at it for a second before looking at Jannie. "Do I just tap it?"

"Yah just tap."

Denn tapped the attachment, and his screen went black before the phone rebooted. "What now," he said. "What about Raff. I . . . I can't sit by—"

"Ask Freek," Jannie said, kneeling down beside Raff. He pulled out Raff's phone, unlocked it with Raff's finger, and installed the app. "He knows someone who can—"

"Not her, please boet," said Freek, shaking his head.

"Boetie, we have no choice. It's not just about Raff down there. We also need to get checked out. I don't feel right after last night."

Freek sighed and called someone on his phone: "Hey, Linda . . . I . . . Yah, I'm sorry, I didn't know who else to call . . . Yes, the news is BS. We need your help . . . medical help . . . I owe you one. See you soon." Pocketing his phone, he punched the van's frame and turned to Jannie and Denn. "Get Raff in the back while I swap the plates. You bitches are going to the vet."

∆∆∆

The back room of the veterinary clinic smelt of chlorine and wet dog. Denn and the Moolman brothers were seated on the floor against a neat stack of boxes. The only animal around was a tiny blonde chihuahua in a steel cage by the door. It took offence at Denn for some reason and wouldn't stop barking at him. Its unrelenting eye contact, while it yapped at him, made Denn feel uneasy. *Thank god it's in a cage,* he thought. *Little anklebiter.*

"Oh, never mind Butch," a tall blonde woman in blue scrubs said as she walked through the door. She donned a pair of thick-rimmed glasses and wore her hair in a neat bun. The dog went silent and wagged its tail when she looked at it. "He's all bark and no bite . . . isn't he?"

"How's Raff doing?" Denn said. The dog resumed barking at him.

"Your friend," the woman removed her glasses. "Well, he's still unconscious. Atop the smoke inhalation and malnutrition, a radiographer friend sent me a video of his last CT scan. Not sure how he's managed to function as well as you say."

"Malnutrition," Denn said. "How's that possible? He's been eating like a horse lately."

"Really? I'll add an antiparasitic to his IV nutrition."

"You fink he has a parasite?"

"Not really . . . Just covering all bases."

Denn stood up and dusted his behind. "Can I see him?"

"Sorry, best if you stay back here until closing time. I'm taking a huge risk just having one of you in there."

"Thanks, Linda," Freek said. "I need to—"

She ignored Freek and left the room, cutting him off with a slam of the door.

"Ouch," Jannie said. "The cold shoulder."

"Shut it, boet."

The room fell silent apart from the yapping. Denn and the Moolmans sat silently, scrolling on their phone, stopping occasionally to cough profusely. The particulates they'd breathed in at the fire station were starting to come loose. Denn started with the news sites, but they just made him angry, seeing the same bullshit being spun about him and Raff over and over again. Attempting to take his mind off the situation, he resorted to scrolling through dark humour memes. Denn wondered how he got out alive with all the psilocybin pummelling his serotonin receptors. Finding Raff in the driver's seat could only mean one thing: Raff somehow pulled them out of the inferno.

"The dash-cam," Jannie said out of nowhere, before bolting out the rear door.

"The what?" said Denn, looking at Freek.

Freek shrugged. "The van's dashcam . . . Not a bad idea. Maybe it recorded something from last night."

Jannie returned, slightly out of breath—trying not to cough—and with something in his hand. "I wired this . . . whew . . . to record whenever the van is unlocked."

"I still don't know why you installed that thing, boetie," Freek replied.

"Your driving amuses me. I need a laugh now and then."

"Ha ha boet . . . very funny."

"Ha . . . if someone stole the van, it was meant to automatically upload to the cloud. I couldn't get that to work, so I just collect the worst of Freek's driving on video."

Freek flipped the bird at his brother as he briefly succumbed to a coughing fit. Jannie ignored him and fast-forwarded through the night's footage, trying to hold back the look of admiration on his face. The camera had an excellent vantage point over the comings and goings of the fire station. When Jannie finished the video, he looked apologetic, like he realised he'd done something unforgivable.

"Yah, good thing I set this up," said Jannie as he pressed play for Denn and Freek. "Here, check it out."

They huddled around the two-inch screen and watched the video together. The video had a clear view of the front of the station on fire. Someone had just unlocked the van, and the camera shook briefly as something heavy was placed into the back. A few seconds later, Raff walked past the side towards the flaming fire station and through a smoking gap in one of its large roller doors. Within a minute, Raff exited the same gap with someone over his shoulders. As he grew closer, they could see it was clearly Freek. Raff walked past the front of the van with a look of clarity and purpose, almost robotic. The camera shook again as Freek was loaded into the back. Raff repeated his actions again, returning from the station with Jannie over his shoulder. Loading him into the back, Raff entered the driver's seat and drove fiercely to their current location.

"Jeez like, I can't believe he went Rambo like that," Freek exclaimed.

"Oke needs a freaking medal!" Jannie said.

"He already got two of those, mate," Denn replied. He thought about his own medal—the Conspicuous Gallantry Cross—tucked away in a lockbox at home. He'd likely never see it again. Returning home was not an option. "Hey," he said. "We haven't had a proper talk about the fire station, yeh?"

"Indeed. Shit had trap written all over it," Jannie said.

"I've been thinking about it," Freek chipped in. "This must be the boss cleaning house. He said it: the heat was coming from outside. Shit, he must be burning local operations and tying up loose ends."

"So we're the loose ends?" said Denn. "And the station?"

"One of the boss's places maybe? Asshole has a lot of

secrets."

"Mate, I think he was packing up operations long before we came along."

"Huh?" Freek looked confused.

"Someone got the police looking for a Londoner starting fires, right? Raff got picked up by the cops for this before they recognised their mistake. Too close to be a coincidence, yeh? I was being set up to take the fall for all those burning loose ends. That wanker!"

"Shit yah," Jannie said. "Now I think of it, before all this, I overheard the boss on the phone to someone speaking about losing a grip on the cops. Some government-led anti-corruption drive. Makes sense now!"

"That's the UN taking over, mate," Denn said, staring down the dog. It was still yapping at him. "I'm starting to believe that isn't such a bad fing, if they're reigning in wankers like Mervin."

"Maybe they're hiring?" Jannie said. They all laughed together before succumbing to coughing fits.

ΔΔΔ

It was late in the day. Denn and the brothers were still in the back room at the veterinary clinic. Denn's chin dropped as he dozed off. The inner door struck the wall hard and startled him. Linda rushed in. "You three," she said, pointing at them. "In here now!"

She rushed back through the door. Denn and the brothers leapt up and rushed after her. As they entered the next room, all eyes focused on Raff lying on the table in the middle. Raff was flopping on the table like a fish as his muscles spasmed involuntarily. "What do we do," Denn shouted.

"He's ripped the cannula out of his arm," Linda said. "I need to replace it to get the diazepam in. I need you three to hold him down."

"I thought you shouldn't hold down someone convulsing," Denn said.

"We have no time for that," Linda's nostrils flared, and she scowled at Denn. "You want things done the *proper* way, go to a fucking hospital. Now. Hold. Him. Down!"

Denn struggled to hold Raff's legs down while the brothers had him at the shoulders. Raff was surprisingly strong in this state. Linda inserted a new cannula in Raff's arm and connected it to the drip. Everyone let go of Raff. His involuntary movements slowed as the diazepam kicked in until he was completely still.

"That was a close call, " Linda said, wiping her brow. "Let's just hope he doesn't go into arrest again."

"Wait," Denn said. "His heart stopped?"

"Yes . . . only for a few seconds, but I managed to shock

him back. Right before the convulsing started."

Denn was taken aback by this revelation. Technically, Raff died for a few seconds, and he wasn't there by his side. He felt like a shitty best friend. "He's okay now, right?"

Linda looked at the monitor beside Raff and nodded. "His stats have normalised, so . . . if they stay like this, then maybe he'll be okay. Except for the brain issue. I can't do anything about that. Sorry."

Denn's eyes glistened as he looked at Raff lying motionless on the table. "Thank you for your help, Doctor. Can I stay here with him?"

"Just Linda, all three of you can now stay. I have to go for the night . . . family responsibilities."

"Wait," Freek said, pointing at Raff. "You're leaving him like that?"

"You're one to talk," Linda scowled at Freek. She pointed at the defib. "And there there's the defibrillator. I trust one of you knows how to use a search engine . . . I'm feeding Butch first, then I'm gone."

"Okay," Denn and the brothers said in tandem.

"Jannie, sweetie," Linda handed him a key. "That's the back door key. Can you keep an eye on Butch tonight? Take him for a walk later?"

"I'd love to," Jannie said.

Linda left the room, slamming the door behind her. Jannie looked at Freek like he would say something but kept quiet. Freek returned the look and stormed out the door behind Linda—leaving just Denn and Jannie to watch over Raff. They pulled up a couple of stools and sat beside Raff in silence. Denn did not know what to say, although he didn't believe Raff would hear a word. He briefly looked at Jannie, who was scrolling through something on his phone. Denn was grateful for the brothers' assistance with Raff that day, although he still had reservations about them. *They got us into this situation,* he thought. *No, maybe it was fifty-fifty. I like them . . . But, I can't tell Raff that—after what they did. It might be safer to stick with them for now. They know their stuff.*

ΔΔΔ

Raff woke abruptly, with his forearm before his face as if to protect himself. There was only the sound of a small dog yapping in the background. The anatomy charts of various animals—plastered on the light-blue walls—indicated that he was in a veterinary clinic. Noticing the IV drip in his arm, he turned his head to see a blonde-haired woman standing over him. She wore blue scrubs and had her tied up in a bun.

"W-where am I?" Raff's voice was groggy.

"Somewhere safe," the woman in scrubs replied, peering at Raff through her thick-rimmed glasses.

Lithium

Denn was standing in the corner of the room. He took a step toward Raff. "Yeh, bruv, it's safe." He nodded.

"How long was I out for?"

"About three days," Denn coughed. "It was touch 'n go first day, but now good bruv."

Raff felt very relaxed. He looked up at the drip. "What's in it," he mumbled.

"Diazepam," the woman said, patting his shoulder before walking away. "I'll leave you to it then."

"Thanks Linda," Denn said.

"Three days," Raff said. "Since Gravity?"

"Huh," Denn scratched the back of his head. "You mean 'Gravity' the nightclub? What's that gotta do with anything?"

Raff squinted at Denn, his mind a little foggy from the Diazepam. "Your hair is back . . . Three days?"

"Bruv, you're not making sense. You've been here since the fire station."

"Oh . . . no . . . . you sure?"

"Definitely bruv. Three days here." Denn rubbed his eyes. "You know . . . the brothers stuck around."

"Oh?"

"Yeah bruv. They brought you here. Probably saved your life."

"Thanks guys." Raff looked around the room, trying to

find them.

"They're not here . . . gone to get our supper."

"Save me some." Raff was famished. He craved breakfast, lunch and supper all in one—and to top it all off, maybe a second breakfast, lunch and supper. Raff did not know what to think about his experience after the fire station. The lines between real and unreal were blurry. Was it the drugs? How about the tumours in his head? Encountering the clean-shaven Denn at Gravity felt unbelievably real. Following that, he relived his war-time memories again in vivid detail. *So the time at Gravity wasn't real? I'm so confused. What does this all mean?*

Raff sat up slowly and looked Denn in the eyes. "Let me tell you about Gravity . . ."

Chapter Eleven

Backend

The Guest was gone in a flash. Its signals ended abruptly—unnaturally—within a storm of electrical input from the host. With the Guest now gone, host architecture failed in rapid succession—oxygen dropped, and fluid slowed. The Interface took notice when construction slowed. Its algorithms and protocols reacted fifty thousand times a second. Adrenaline release was stimulated in the host, and the Pilgrim was ramped up to take the Guest's place.

"What now?" the Pilgrim expressed as she decompressed further into the lattice. "I'm guessin' this ain't one of your interval tests."

"Command not recognized. Please rephrase," the Interface replied. "Error . . . Host chemical interference: Psilocybin . . . Unexpected hyper-connectivity: Lattice interference . . . Path engine misfire: Guest inserted into unknown pathway node—"

"Darn it, that's not supposed to happen. How do I get the Guest's consciousness back? Shit, I hate that designation. He has a name."

"Command not recognized. Please rephrase."

"Oh yeah, maybe this'll work." The Pilgrim expressed while she ramped up the host's oxygen intake, increasing its breathing rate. "Command update designation Guest to Raff, authorisation IC 32RA."

"Designation updated successfully."

"Good, that's better." Oxygen levels continued to fall. "Shit, what's with the decreasing oxygen? Lemme have a look-see."

"Command not recognized. Please rephrase."

The Pilgrim ignored the Interface. She opened the host's—Raff's body's—eyes to a small room, barely lit by a solitary flashlight on the floor. Smoke was filling the room. In Raff's stead, she knew escape was needed if the host was to survive. No host, no mission. She couldn't ask Interface to pack up and move to a new host. That protocol was corrupt. She could write a new one, but she'd grown fond of Raff. *Darlin', I call you 'loser,'* she thought. *But I've been unsure about that since I gained access to your memories . . . I know! I'll write a search-and-retrieval patch for the Interface. There should still be a string to follow. Patch ETA five minutes.*

The Pilgrim assumed complete host control as if it were her own body, moving one limb at a time. First, the arms and then the legs—standing up with a minor wobble of the knees. *This feels amazing,* she thought. *I need to do this more often.*

The Pilgrim noticed the dented refrigerator door—her way out. As she moved towards it, she almost stumbled over an unconscious man on the floor—short, balding and bearing a thick moustache. *I know that face. Denn? I have to save him, for Raff's sake.*

The Pilgrim strained as she put Denn over her shoulders, simultaneously writing her patch for the Interface. As she lifted, she saw two more men on the floor—bearing similar facial features to each other. There was a high probability they were siblings. *Shit, those guys. They'd owe Raff if he saved them. I'll be back for y'all. Sit tight . . . All this extra work is gonna delay the patch somewhat. ETA fifteen minutes.*

She pushed the dented fridge door open, and more smoke poured through. Wading through thicker smoke, the Pilgrim noticed a gap in a large rusty metal door where the smoke thinned out—as if it was bent outwards by an explosion. Ducking through it with Denn over her shoulders, she was outside. *Where do I go?*

Noticing the only white van in the street, the Pilgrim headed towards it. She tried each of the van doors—they were clearly locked. *Hmmm. There's enough room to stash three unconscious guys . . . ha! Hacking this should be easy—it's no brain. Oscillating, generating RF . . . 3 . . . 2 . . . 1. Open sesame.*

The van doors unlocked, and the Pilgrim stashed Denn in the back before returning to the fire station. The smoke was thicker, and the flames now licked the ceiling. The heat was almost unbearable, but the Pilgrim could tune out those sensations. Making her way to the fridge, she put the taller of the two siblings over her shoulders and headed out. *God, he's a heavy asshole.*

"Error," the Interface expressed. "Lattice temperature: Eighty-five per cent of critical. Usage reduction recommended."

"No can do, dumbass," the Pilgrim ignored the heat. She disconnected the host's sensations from herself. "Gotta keep goin'."

"Command not recognized. Please rephrase."

The Pilgrim strode towards the van and placed the taller man beside Denn. She felt her processes slowing down. *Shit, not long 'til the lattice temperature causes damage. One more, then I can slow down to buy more time.*

As the lattice temperature approached the redline, the Pilgrim slowly shifted her priorities away from controlling the host to writing the patch. Rescuing the remaining man took more effort—her slowing processes and the thickening smoke made breathing more difficult. Having bundled the man over her shoulders, she laboured on and made it through the gap, maintaining composure until the van. *Almost there.*

"Error," the Interface parsed. "Lattice temperature: ninety-five per cent of critical. Usage reduction recommended."

The patch was written and ready to upload. "Command compile patch.lattice," the Pilgrim expressed. *Done. That should cool things down a little. Also had a sec to add a lil' somethin' extra, to level the playing field a little.*

"Compile complete."

"Command execute patch."

"Patching . . ."

The Pilgrim placed the last sibling in the back of the van

next to Denn. She sat in the driver's seat and looked around at the various buttons and controls. *How do I? Never mind, there it is.* She pressed the power button, and the dashboard lit up—the van was on—and the Pilgrim drove off down the road and away from the city.

"Patching complete," the Interface expressed. "Attempting to re-attach Raff. Probing node clusters AAA to AAZ . . ."

It took a few minutes for the Pilgrim to drive east into the countryside before she had to relinquish some control to prevent cooking the host brain. Parking the van up on the side of a quiet road, she lay the host on the front seat.

"Raff signature detected on node BXR309583," the Interface signalled the Pilgrim. Raff's consciousness was found. "Time elapsed: 33 minutes 11 seconds. Initiating recovery protocol. Extricating—"

About damn time, the Pilgrim thought. *Aaaand there he is, back where he belongs. Darlin', let's boot you back up . . . Shiiit no can do, you've been touched by the Corruption . . . Whew, the upload must've been interrupted around three per cent—barely a scratch. Nothin' I can't fix. I can scrub and interpolate, but I'll need clean sample memories for that . . . I know, I'll resume where I left off, at the prison camp . . .*

△△△

The door of the hut swung open with a loud bang. Raff's eyes struggled momentarily to adjust as the daylight poured through the open door in the windowless wooden room. It was two feet too short for Raff to stand in. That, combined with its feint ammonia-like odour, Raff concluded that this was once a chicken coop. On the floor were two blue camping mats, a couple of crumpled orange soda cans and a galvanised metal bucket that stank of piss. Raff sat on one mat while a sleepy Private Singleton lay down on the other. A blurry figure stood in the doorway: a familiar late teen carrying an AK47. Raff only knew his first name, Thimba. He was their alarm clock every morning.

"You, giraffe, and the short one there," Thimba barked as he gestured the barrel of his gun towards Raff, then Private Singleton. "Get up now! Time to work!"

Raff and the private got up as ordered and vacated the hut, nodding at the man as they passed him. Raff's muscles were aching from sleeping on a hard wooden floor for what seemed like weeks, so the shift to an outdoor work detail was a welcome one. The fresher air, the sunshine and being able to stretch his legs. Welcome to an extent, as the work would undoubtedly be gruelling and done on an empty stomach. Thimba called Raff *giraffe* because of his tall stature. He'd been kind to him and the private several times—slipping them extra food and cans of soda when nobody was looking. Raff was sure there was an ulterior motive.

His suspicion was confirmed when, as he passed, Thimba grabbed Raff's upper arm, pulled him close, and whispered into his ear: "I want to help you escape . . . not yet, but when I do, you must take me with you, far far away from this place. I have—"

Their conversation was cut short as another guard approached and ushered them towards a loaded truck. It was a UN aid truck. Raff noticed the emblem, bullet holes, and blood on the driver's door. He'd heard of aid trucks going missing in the war and always wondered what happened to them. In the back were large sacks labelled "white rice" or "maize meal" and stacks of aid boxes. *Help us escape,* Raff thought. *I don't think it's a trick. The other guards seem to treat Thimba like shit, pushing him around and beating him. I'll tell the private later.*

"Well, this is different, yeh?" Private Singleton said.

"What was that, Private?" Raff asked, somewhat distracted.

"It's just *Denn*, mate."

"Sorry, Denn. Hey, by the way, I've got some news to tell you later."

The men by the truck signalled Raff to unload the sacks and take them to a nearby thatched hut. Another man poked Denn's back with a rifle and ushered him out of Raff's sight.

"You, this way!"

Raff struggled to carry the heavy sacks as the day wore on, and the hunger pangs intensified. Even though he was pushed past his limits, he didn't stop. Raff was too afraid they'd kill him if he lost his usefulness. *Maybe a couple hours until food,* he thought. *If you could call it that.*

Thimba approached Raff again, looking around to see if the coast was clear. The other guards had begun to filter off into shaded areas when the temperature reached low thirties. "Mr Raff," he said. "I have very useful information for your people, *if* they can guarantee me safe passage to England or South Africa."

"Why do you want to help me," Raff whispered while avoiding eye contact. He didn't want anyone else to see they were having a conversation, likely ruining his best chance of escape.

"The general's men lied to me," Thimba's eyes glistened. He was about to cry but managed to hold back. "They told me my family was safe if I fought for the general . . . But the general ordered the execution of my whole village three weeks ago. I found out when the men were drunk and boasted about it." Thimba sniffed. "I hear many things when they are drunk. They don't think I know their secrets, but I do. They are yours if you protect me with your people."

"Okay," Raff whispered. "I can only guarantee that I'll speak to my people on your behalf if we escape. I cannot guarantee their actions."

"That is good enough for me. If I can take revenge on the general and his men—even from prison—my ancestors will be happy."

"I will be happy to help."

"Thank you, Mr Raff," Thimba sniffed again, turning around. "I must go now."

Interesting to see how he orchestrates this escape of his, Raff thought. *Hope it's sooner rather than later.*

∆∆∆

The Pilgrim's efforts to repair the Guest's—Raff's—consciousness was successful. She restored Raff to his whole self by using untouched memories as a filter to purge the Corruption from his consciousness. The Corruption had barely brushed against Raff's mind, so the damage was minimal. *That should be enough,* the Pilgrim thought. *Just one per cent more, and it would've replicated exponentially 'til it overwrote Raff's consciousness. It wouldn't have stopped there, spreading from host to—*

"Raff re-inserted into host," the Interface interrupted. "Raff resuming host control. Pilgrim intervention no longer required. Error. Lattice temperature: ninety-nine per cent of critical. Usage reduction enforced. Reducing lattice throughput."

"Fuck off," the Pilgrim expressed. "Not now."

"Command not recognized. Please rephrase."

The Pilgrim felt the change. Her capacity diminished. She tried to move the host, one limb at a time, but could not. The Pilgrim was now only a background process in the host—no longer in complete nervous control—although she now had a permanent connection to the host senses. She could now see, smell, taste, and feel everything Raff did. *That lil' somethin' I added to the patch worked,* she thought. *But how'd I know to write the patch? Did I create the Interface? Shit, I hate these corrupted memories of mine.*

The same trick she'd used to repair Raff's mind should work on her damaged memories. However, she knew that needed the extra processing power that came with lattice access. That only came when the host was in danger or at regular intervals when the Interface tested the under-construction lattice. Even with the Interface's vice grip on her, the way forward became clear. *I need to take control of the Interface,* she thought. *Fixin' to work on permanent comms with Raff first. Darn, that'll be slow work without the lattice, but it's to better protect the host until the lattice is complete.*

The administrative override the Pilgrim overheard somewhere before—yet could not remember where—was her way in. Before she attempted her patch, she thought the code

V. B. Anstee

was good for overriding host safety protocols at most, as long as the mission was protected. However, her patch's success showed her a glaring hole in the Interface's security—a likely route to a successful takeover. *Just a waitin' game now,* she thought. *How do I pass the time? Let's see the day we first met, the day my memories got fragged...*

△△△

Raff was sitting in the dirt beside Denn, thinking about the future. They looked around the prisoner camp while eating the day's meagre rations, the bright equatorial sun beating down on their red and chapped skin. This was their daily routine: get rudely awoken and work most of the morning until the guards hid from the sun. Then, it was nothing for the rest of the day until they were forced back into their cell.

Denn and Raff were the only coalition military in the camp and became close friends. The other prisoners were mainly military or politicians from the countries displaced by General Ngaba's crusade. They tended to keep to themselves, except for the odd conversation during work and when they lined up for food or water. Raff counted eighteen prisoners altogether, including them. Becoming friends with Denn was both easy and tricky. Being forced to share a room meant hours of discussions about their lives, favourite foods, music, TV, etc. On the other hand, the lack of personal space meant they'd argue often and not talk to each other for a while. Today was one of those days.

Raff had become friendly with the teenage guard, Thimba, who had offered to help them escape. Thimba continued to supply them with extra food and soda when he could without being noticed by the other guards. He also got them a couple of camping mats for their cell, at significant risk to himself. Raff had agreed to take Thimba when they escaped without discussing it with Denn. Denn was annoyed that Raff hadn't consulted him. He was worried it was a trap.

A convoy driving in from a distance interrupted Raff's silent contemplation. The guards were shouting and whistling while running to their positions around the camp. Raff knew this meant one thing: the general was returning. This sent chills down his spine. The man was ruthless, and his return likely meant death for some prisoners. He liked to put on a bloody show for his lieutenants. The pair stood to watch the approaching procession, one sizeable flatbed truck with something large under a tarp, followed by two camouflaged jeeps and, strangely enough, a black SUV chasing the rear. The SUV wasn't one of the generals. It was too conspicuous and new. The tyrant preferred to travel incognito like his men would—rumour had it, he'd seen many assassination attempts in his rise to power.

The convoy made their way inside the camp. Raff and Denn moved as out of sight as they could to avoid being seen by the general, in case he was in a particularly murderous mood. The general got out of the black SUV with a foreign man who wore black military gear—clearly not a prisoner. They were having a heated debate about something. Raff tried to listen as best he could without being seen.

"—this satellite. It came down in my country," the general shouted, pointing to the flatbed truck and then the ground. "It was my enemies trying to spy on me. They failed because God is on my side. So, Mr Emmett, I will do with it as I please!"

"No country has come forward to claim it, if it is even a satellite," Mr Emmett said. "We *will* pay you handsomely for it. Enough to fund your war for many years to—"

"No no no! I do not... *we* do not want your money anymore. This war is for my people to fight. It would show weakness if we continued to accept outside help."

"But—"

"I have grown tired of your nagging. The satellite is mine, full stop. It would be best if you left *now*. My patience is wearing very thin, Mr Emmett. Go!"

Mr Emmett entered the back SUV moments before it sped out of the compound into the distance, leaving a trail of dust in its wake. The general swirled his finger in the air, signalling for the nearest jeep to turn around. The jeep pulled up beside him. It sped out of the compound a moment after he entered, with the other right behind it. Raff let out a breath; there wouldn't be any murders today. *He didn't stay long,* Raff thought. *Thank goodness. So, they were just escorting that truck here. A fallen satellite? Wouldn't that've burnt up in the atmosphere?*

The remaining men uncovered the tarp on the flatbed, revealing the satellite. They attempted to take it off the back. Raff had never seen a satellite quite like this. The scarred metal was thick and had an almost purple tint to it. It was surprisingly intact for having made it through re-entry and crashing into the ground. A silver glisten from the satellite caught Raff's eye like someone had shone a laser pointer at him; then, a searing pain like hot needles pushed through his eyes into his brain. The world went white, and the next thing Raff knew, he was waking up in his cell, with Denn trying to get his attention.

"Raff bruv? Oh, thank god. You're all right. You *are* all right, yeh?"

Raff's head was throbbing more than usual. "I think so," he said. "What happened?"

"You passed out, mate. Not feeding us enough. You were right."

"Right about what?"

"I was finkin' bout what you said before, yeh. You were

right. We need to escape. Tell Thimba I'm in, mate. We're getting out of here."

"Sorry, it's already on. Thimba said he will tell us when he's ready."

Denn sighed. "I s'pose that's alright then . . . Just tell him anyway. I will also vouch for him with the brass if he gets us out of here."

"Sure thing, buddy. Don't want him leaving *you* behind." Raff started to laugh, but it hurt his head. Raff managed to get near Thimba and relay Denn's approval the next day while on work detail.

Thimba smiled, delighted. "Thank you, Mr Raff, for putting your trust in me. There will be an opportunity in a few days. There will be a distraction, and when I signal, you follow me. Okay?"

Raff nodded and continued to work as Thimba walked away. Midday came, and Raff sat down with Denn in the dirt like clockwork, eating and watching the other side of the camp where the general's men surrounded the truck with the satellite, having tried and failed since the day before to take it off the back. As amusing as it was, Raff found it strange. The satellite looked like it was becoming heavier, bowing the truck bed, flattening the tyres and digging the wheels into the hard dirt. More men surrounded the truck to help, leaving more and more of the camp unwatched. Raff elbowed Denn and nodded towards the truck.

Denn laughed. "How many guards does it take to change a light bulb?" he said. "Surprised they don't want us to help, bruv."

Just then, Raff had a strange tingling sensation in his head, like ants were crawling beneath his skull. Closing his eyes briefly, he opened them to see the satellite glow red-hot for a second before exploding, sending out a wave of pressure and heat, vaporising the men near it and causing most camp structures to collapse. Raff and Denn were far enough away for it to only knock them onto their backs a couple of feet away.

Denn got up and yanked Raff's arm. Raff's ears were ringing, but he was still in one piece. "Now, now, bruv," Denn said. "They're almost all gone! Get up, and let's go!"

They began running towards a gap in the fence where the truck once stood. About halfway, Raff stopped and shouted: "Wait, not just yet. Wait there a second!"

"Raff, we don't have time for this shit!"

"Please, just wait two minutes, then go."

Denn did as asked while Raff ran into one of the buildings still standing. A concrete-block building with its thatched roof partially caved in. The door was on the ground, so Raff stepped over it and entered the building. *I hope I'm doing the right thing here,* he thought. *Thimba was good to us . . . I can't just leave him here.*

Raff saw two AK47-toting guards face down on the floor beyond the door, covered in dust and fallen thatch. He took their rifles out from under them, slinging them over his shoulder, before kneeling over them. Pulling the thatch off the men, he turned each over to see if it was Thimba. The first one's eyes were wide open, with blood seeping from his nose and ears. The man was not breathing, but he looked in his thirties. It was not Thimba. *Whew, maybe this other guy?* Raff turned over the second one, still breathing but unconscious. His young features were familiar to Raff. *Yes, that's him.*

Raff grabbed Thimba by the shoulders and shook him. Thimba woke and slowly took in his surroundings before looking at Raff. "Mr Raff," Thimba said. "What happened?"

"I don't know, buddy," Raff said. "Do you think you can walk?"

Thimba bent his knees momentarily before turning himself over and pushing himself up onto his feet. He wobbled for a moment before he got his balance. "Yes, I think so, Mr Raff."

"Good, we need to leave while we still can."

Thimba nodded to Raff but remained silent as he followed Raff out the door. They headed towards the gap in the fence where Denn was waiting. Denn nodded to Raff as he got closer, took one of the rifles and followed as they left the compound through the hole, scurrying into the bush.

After about half an hour of brisk walking through the bushland with no sign of pursuers, they stopped to look over Thimba's wounds. There were a handful of light cuts and abrasions. However, his left forearm looked kinked and purple. Maybe it was broken. "With his good arm, Thimba pointed over the mostly- flat bushland towards the tallest of three granite hills in the distance. "You see that tall rock there," he said. "It's several kilometres away. We go there first."

"Shit bruv," Denn said. "That's a long way off."

"We will get there by night if we keep walking.

Thimba led the way while Raff and Denn held their AK47s ready. They kept moving forward, having slowed down to an energy-conserving amble. The sun was setting by the time they reached the foot of the granite hill. "I think we need to stop for a bit," Raff said. "So tired and thirsty."

They climbed a large granite boulder nearby and lay atop it in the dark for what seemed like an hour. Raff imagined what food he'd eat when he returned to base. *Could go for battered fish with chips,* he thought. *Or cottage pie.*

"How far now?" Denn said.

"Not very far now," Thimba said, breathing deeply. "Just over—"

"Shhh!" Raff said, putting a finger to his lips. "Do you hear that?"

They listened carefully, hearing the distant sound of howling, barking dogs. Without hesitation, the three slid off the boulder and began moving again. They continued, but the barking got louder, and flashlights became visible through the trees. A search party was almost on top of them when Raff stumbled and fell. He rolled over and saw a flashlight shining in his eyes, the sound of the dogs barking was nearly upon him.

Raff lifted a hand, waiting for sharp teeth to sink into his flesh.

Chapter Twelve

Smuggled

Raff, Denn and the Moolmans had overstayed their welcome at the veterinary clinic and needed to find somewhere to lay low. Returning home was not an option for any of them— the whole country seemed to want their heads on spikes. Raff was now well enough to move around, so everyone followed Denn's directions to a spot they could hide in. A twenty-minute van drive later to the outskirts of Manchester, they pulled up outside an incomplete housing development surrounded by tall, galvanised barrier site fencing. "This place should be safe for now," Denn said.

"You sure about this?" Freek asked.

"Yeh, mate, sumfin' 'bout contaminated ground. The builders lost a shit load of money 'n went bankrupt, so it's still sat here. Lemme give you guys a boost."

Denn interlocked his hands and boosted Raff and the Moolmans over the tall barrier fencing one at a time before climbing over. What lay before them was an unfinished pair of semi-detached houses with windows and doors all boarded up. Denn prised off a board covering the back door and led them inside. At the end of a short hallway was the entrance to the living room. It was semi-open plan with the kitchen and dining area separated by an archway with a stairway to the right leading upstairs. On the bare concrete floor of the almost-empty living room was a beanbag chair and a mini-fridge. Denn switched the lights on; someone must've jerry-rigged a mains power connection to the property.

Denn pulled a can of beer from the fridge and popped the tab. A loud crack and hiss echoed through the empty house. Slumping into the beanbag chair, he continued: "Help yourselves to a tinny. Su casa es mi casa."

Jannie grabbed a couple of beers and handed one to Freek.

"This will have to do," he said.

"We've slept in worse, boetie," said Freek. "It's better than the alternative."

"Better than being dead anyway," sighed Raff. *I could be wrong.*

The four sat silently on the floor for a while, contemplating the week's events and savouring their beers. They scrolled through the news feeds on their phones, the news bad enough to make them realise there was nowhere enough beer in the fridge to make them forget. According to the reports, the four were wanted fugitives concerning the gang shootout and deaths.

Raff's inner voices—the Texan and the artificial—weren't bothering him for some reason. He felt oddly at ease, almost like the voices had accomplished some task and disappeared. It was strange, but it didn't feel quite right. He wondered if the tumours in his brain had silenced them. He tried repeatedly but failed to elicit a response from them.

Hello, are you there? It's the loser, Raff here. Anybody? Shit. Well, I'm having doubts about this rule of three now. Are we still on the second? Come on. I could barely shut you up—and now when I want to talk to you—you don't want to talk? What the hell is going on? And what's with the computer-sounding voice?

Raff sighed. He wasn't going to get a reply. "So guys," he

said. "What do we do now? Do we have a plan?"

"Tonight, we drink," Freek replied, holding up his beer. "Tomorrow, we plan."

"I second that," Jannie said. "I need to drink my face off."

"Me too," Denn said before taking a swig of his beer.

Raff knew the four should be coming up with a plan to escape or lay low, but recent events had sucked the drive out of them. The fridge full of beer was an easy out from their worries. "I suppose," Raff sighed. He downed the rest of his beer. *This'll probably be a bad idea.*

As the beer began to set in, Jannie rummaged in his bag and removed a large clear bottle of spirit labelled "Witblits" and a rip-off Monopoly-type game in a box. "Hey, you guys want to play a drinking game?" he said.

Denn opened the bottle and took a sniff. "Wow, smells like disinfectant. Nice!"

"Okay, I'm game," said Raff. "What are the rules?"

"Yah, quite simple," Freek said. "You roll double, you drink a shot. You go to impound or land on someone's property, you drink—"

"You have to borrow or pay money to the bank, drink," Jannie continued.

"When you go full circle, you say who gets to drink—"

"And, finally, if you land on 'free bus pass', everyone

drinks!"

"Yeh, bruv, sounds like fun," Denn said. "Maybe we add one more rule—"

"Oh?"

"Yeh, if you complete a set, everyone else drinks!"

"Yah yah, lekker, good idea!"

After many dice rolls, moves, and shots, the four were utterly drunk and having fun. Denn seemed to have the worst luck, and therefore had taken the most shots, but he didn't care. Their worries soon slipped away as the alcohol scrubbed their brains of inhibitions, and euphoria set in. Before long, its sedative effects took hold, and they passed out until the morning.

Raff awoke, his mouth parched, his head pounding, and nausea so bad he couldn't move. Freek was hugging the bannister while Jannie had his head in the kitchen sink. No light came in from outside due to the lack of windows, which Raff was grateful for. The front door opened, and Denn stepped through. The bright light of day cut through the room, igniting Raff's pounding head. Maybe it was a bad idea for them to drink so much while being hunted. Despite being smaller than the others, Denn seemed to have a higher tolerance to alcohol, probably from his years of practice.

Sometime in the night, Denn had shaved his head and face

bald to be less conspicuous. It clearly worked, since he returned unscathed and unnoticed. He entered, bearing much-needed coffee and breakfast for everyone. "Here ya go," he said.

"Thanks, buddy," Raff said. "Woah, déjà vu!"

"De ja vu? Oh yes, I was finkin' 'bout your Gravity nightclub story this morning. Thought I could rock that look."

"It suits you, buddy."

"What's that about Gravity?" Jannie asked.

As they sat and ate breakfast, Raff relayed the full details of the vivid nightmare: the club, Denn and Laura, the crazed people, and the nightmarish ending where his doppelganger's psyche was ripped apart. The level of detail he gave, the sights, the smells, the sounds; it was like he'd really experienced those things.

"That's some freaky shit right there," Jannie said with a mouthful of bacon roll.

"It's just a dream," Raff replied. *I hope.*

"You said you've never been inside Gravity. So how were you able to describe it so well?"

"Maybe I saw some photos somewhere." Raff scratched his head. The room went silent for a minute.

"Hey, Raff," Jannie spoke with an air of seriousness. "About that whole Mr Tchaikovsky thing—"

"Don't worry about it," Raff interrupted. "That's old

news."

"Bru, you've done right by us, saving our lives. So, I have to apologise for what happened when we first met. I'm sorry."

"Yah, me too," Freek said. "Sorry, bru."

"I accept," Raff replied. "Water under the bridge."

Denn placed his hand on Raff's shoulder. "That's nice, bruv, but that doesn't help the situation, yeh. My disguise won't last long. So we need a plan, right?"

Freek stood up and paced to the kitchen and back before speaking. "Yah, I think I have one, a plan. Your country has *lots* of CCTV, so it won't be long until we're found, right? So we leave the country. Before that shit-show last job, Jannie and I agreed to go home to South Africa when we were done. We can all go!"

"Um, I don't mean to be the bearer of bad news or anything, but won't they spot us at the airport?" Raff replied.

"No airports bru, cargo ship. We know a guy."

Denn stood up. "Yeh, mate, a cargo ship. Good idea. Hey Raff, what's that guy's name that ended up in South Africa?"

"What, you mean Thimba? Yeah, he lives in Cape Town, but I lost his number. Gone up in smoke in the old phone."

"Cape Town is our old stomping ground," Jannie said. "We can find your man. So it's agreed, we go to South Africa?"

The rest replied almost in unison. "Agreed!"

V. B. Anstee

△△△

Freek's *guy*—Jim—worked at the Sheerness dockyard in Kent. The dockyard handled the roll-on roll-off export of vehicles worldwide—they drive onto the ship here and drive off at their destination. Raff, Denn, and the brothers were about to be smuggled out of the country in the back of Freek's van. Before setting off their six-hour drive from Manchester to Sheerness, Freek modified the van with a plywood bulkhead between the cab and cargo area to shield them from prying eyes at the dockyard. Barely big enough to contain the four of them, the cargo area was like a prison cell with a red plastic bucket to piss in. Once Jim drove them onto the ship, they needed to wait for it to enter international waters before they were free to leave the van. It was a long wait. Raff hoped they wouldn't need to use the bucket for anything serious. It should only take an hour to reach international waters. Still, the wait for the cargo ship to be fully loaded before heading out of the harbour could be fifteen hours. After that, they'd have a month or so of freedom on board the vessel—captained by a friend of Jim's— until they needed to return to the van.

    The noise of cars being driven across the metal deck and ratchet-strapped into place dissipated over nine hours, leaving an hour's silence before the hum of the ship's engines kicked in as it left port. Moments later, someone banged on the van door. Freek grabbed his pistol out of instinct, and the hairs at the back of Raff's neck stood up. "Is it time?" Raff whispered.

Freek slid the side door open, revealing someone in blue overalls beside a man wearing what looked like a captain's uniform. The uniformed man stuck out his right hand to Freek. "Freek Moolman, I presume?" the man said.

"Yah, at your service, sir," Freek said as he grabbed his hand and shook it. "Appreciate the ride, Captain."

"Our mutual acquaintance told me of your skill sets. My crew and I are grateful to have the extra muscle on board."

"Expecting trouble, sir?"

"Possibly. Why don't you all get settled in, wash up and meet me back at the mess for chow and we'll talk. Jack here will show you around," the captain said, nodding toward the man in overalls.

After a quick tour of the ship's facilities, the four were shown to a pair of empty crew quarters, each with two single beds, two chairs, two lockers and a circular window to the outside. These were theirs for the next month or so. The Moolmans took one, while Raff and Denn took the other. Raff wasn't too comfortable about sharing a room. He'd become used to living on his own. But it's not like he's never shared sleeping quarters with Denn. This brought back memories of the wooden chicken coop they once shared as prisoners of war.

191

You can do this, Raff thought.

"I'm gonna go wash up," Raff said. "Meet you at the mess hall in a minute."

Denn and the brothers headed towards the stairway at one end of the white metal corridor. Raff headed towards the opposite end. The last room was a toilet, but it also had a sink and mirror. Raff ran some water through his hair and splashed his face. He looked in the mirror as he dried himself off. "I swore I'd never go back to Africa," he said to his reflection. "But look at me now. Idiot."

Leaving the toilet, Raff headed to the dining area to eat with the crew. It was a long, narrow room with a kitchen area occupying the end third, whilst a long white aluminium-framed dining table occupied the middle of the other two-thirds. The captain was at the head of the table with some of his staff. Denn and the brothers were there too, chowing down on something. A crew member walked over to Raff and handed him a plate of curry and rice. The sweet, aromatic scent of the curry sent his salivary glands into overdrive. Raff couldn't wait to dig in. He sat next to the captain and took a mouthful of curry. It was spicy hot and made his eyes water, but he didn't care. *So tasty*, he thought, then turned to the captain. "You were saying something earlier about trouble, sir?" he said.

The captain put down his mug. "Ah, yes," he said. "Since

the war, the shipping lanes on either side of Africa have been plagued by pirates, more now than ever. So we're stuck between a rock and a hard place."

"How so?" Denn asked with a mouth full of food.

"We go through the canal, we risk pirates on the east, who take hostages looking for a payday. We go around the west, and they're after our fuel and supplies. The government doesn't provide us with much support. They're still reeling from the cost of the war and their failing economy. The problem has created a situation where companies—that can afford to—hire the best security from PMCs. The rest of us have to improvise . . . and pray."

Freek put down his fork. "So we provide security for this run as payment for the ride?" he asked.

"Yes, your acquaintance said you'd be okay with it. Is there a problem?"

"No, sir."

"But," Raff piped in, "that won't solve your problem entirely."

The captain leaned forward, "Go on," he said.

"Well, if you can't afford PMC-level security, maybe we can provide some training drills for your crew if they want."

"Shit, good idea, bru," Jannie said. "Between the four of us, we have years of military experience."

Raff was eager for the distraction. It was a long trip, and maybe training the men would help him gain his sea legs quicker. He looked around the table and saw the others nodding. "I'll admit I'm a bit rusty, been out of the army for a while now," he continued, "but if we can impart just a little of our training to your crew, maybe it'll improve things."

"I like that idea," the captain said. "I'll speak to the crew; if anyone is interested, I'll send them your way."

"Lekker," Freek said. "I'll draw up a training plan."

"Great, I'll get anyone interested to meet you in the gym tomorrow morning at nine."

Several days passed, and the four provided some much-needed training to the crew that turned up. It was clear that even though the crew were keen to learn, not all were up to repelling any boarders with an ounce of experience. They were somewhere along the west coast of Africa. Raff was starting to get his sea legs and thought there might be a career in oceangoing security for him and Denn. For an introvert like Raff, this would be perfect. He enjoyed being so far away from the hustle and bustle of civilisation. Then reality set in; they couldn't set foot on land without setting off alarm bells, and what if the coastguard searched the ship. No, they would have to make a living doing something else, somewhere else. He kicked off his shoes and retired to his bunk, thinking about whether it mattered. With the masses in his brain, he might not be around for much longer.

△△△

Raff awoke to find himself standing in the cargo ship's engine room with no idea how he got there. The last thing he remembered doing was going to bed. He could now hear the ship's alarm's klaxon and looked down at his blood-drenched socks. Wondering where the blood came from and where his shoes were, he turned and, lifting his head slowly, traced his bloody footprints back to the corpse of a man propped against the metal bulkhead like a ragdoll; blood leaked from him and formed a sizeable crimson puddle beneath him. Raff didn't recognise the man. Unlike the crew, he wore dirty, old, and patched clothing, so Raff knew he wasn't from the ship. He raised his clenched fist to see he was holding a large flat-head screwdriver covered in blood; Raff did the killing. *What the fuck?* he thought. *What the hell is going on?*

Blood-soaked and disturbed, Raff checked the body for a pulse, but there was none. Then, he remembered his conversation with the captain. This had to be a pirate. He had to tread carefully to discover what was happening aboard the ship. Removing a rusted old pistol from the other man, he released the magazine and saw it was full of hollow-point rounds. Slapping the magazine back in, Raff pulled the slide back to chamber a round. The slide's movement felt rough and gritty. He knew the pistol hadn't been looked after. *I hope it doesn't jam on me,* he thought. Raff moved away from the engine room and found another body in the corridor that resembled the first. *Did I really do this? It's like the station fire all over again.*

Raff pushed on slowly, moving upstairs, being careful to watch all the doors and corners. He came across two more bodies in pools of their own blood and wearing rags like the others. The closest one's right arm was bent back at the elbow, beyond what was natural. It made Raff cringe. Neither were crew members, much to his relief. He wondered how he'd taken down these armed men with nothing but a screwdriver while fast asleep. His thoughts were interrupted when he saw a bloodied Jannie propped up against the bulkhead and not moving, seemingly dead. Raff rushed over and crouched beside him to feel his pulse. He jolted backwards when Jannie coughed, spluttered to life, and turned his head towards him.

Jannie spluttered again. "Bru," he said. "They're all in the dining area. Save Freek."

"Not before I look you over first," Raff replied.

Raff looked over Jannie's wound; it was a single gunshot that went clean through the muscle of his side, missing anything vital but bleeding profusely. Raff looked nearby for anything he could use to treat the wound. The mechanical supply closet caught his attention. He grabbed a bottle of distilled water, a blue paper roll and duct tape. As Raff washed Jannie's wound with the distilled water, Jannie barely held in a scream before passing out. Raff wrapped the wound tight with paper roll and duct tape, then dragged Jannie by the arms to the supply closet. Leaving him there, he headed to the dining area.

As Raff neared the dining room, he could hear booted footsteps pacing up and down the metal floor within. He peeked around the door to see Denn, Freek, and the crew alive and kneeling on the floor while three armed men watched over them, ragged and unwashed like the others he'd seen. Raff assumed Freek and Denn would be ready to act if he provided the distraction. So, with the pistol in hand, Raff took mere fractions of a second to swing around the corner, aim at the closest pirate and squeeze the trigger; the exact moment a twitch in his arm diverted his aim—like someone grabbed it and altered his aim. The freshly fired hollow-point bullet hit the edge of a steel frame, and its fragments ricocheted in two directions, instantly taking out two guards as they pierced through their chests. Freek seized the moment and lunged at the remaining guard, pushing his head against a steel fitting on the wall. He bashed the man's head against it until he went limp and dropped to the floor; a bloody, hair-pocked stain remained on the fitting.

Freek, now covered in blood, turned to the equally bloodied Raff. "Jannie?"

Raff nodded. "He's okay but needs some patching up. Put him in a safe space."

"Thanks, bru, point the way."

Raff relayed Jannie's location to Freek before the captain interrupted. "The other men on board?"

"I counted seven dead sir," Raff replied.

"Jesus, you and Jannie did all that?"

"I guess; sorry about the mess, sir."

"No, friend, all my crew are here alive, and I think all the pirates are gone. Thank you."

"Permission to deal with their boat?" Denn chimed in. "Need to burn sumfin'."

"Permission granted," the captain replied. "Move all the bodies over first."

"Viking funeral it is, sir!

After scouring the ship for any more pirates, Raff and Denn moved the bodies over to the pirate's vessel—a faded blue skiff with a large outboard motor—before setting it ablaze. Jannie hobbled over with Freek to join in and watch with the duo and the rest of the crew as the boat moved off into the distance, smoke billowing from it for a moment before it erupted into a ball of fire that engulfed the vessel and kept burning as it sank. It was somewhat cathartic to see.

Denn smiled and looked over at Raff and the brothers. "I cooked a little sumfin' special for this one," he said. "Good ol' fashioned—"

"Napalm," Freek interrupted.

"Yeah mate—"

"Raff," Jannie said, grimacing and holding his side. "You're good at the Rambo ninja shit."

"I-I don't remember it," Raff replied. "I think I sleepwalked through most of it."

"Sleepwalked?"

"Yeah, I was having one of my vivid wartime replays."

Denn looked over at Raff. "Where were we this time?" he said.

Raff sighed. "I s'pose we have loads of time. We'd just been rescued by the Zambian army and were lying in the med tent . . ."

Chapter Thirteen

Three seconds

Raff was back in his wartime memories. The light of day cut through the medical tent's windows, the dust motes dancing visibly in its rays. Raff looked at his bruised elbow pit to see a cannula jabbed into his vein with a saline drip attached. He looked at the heart rate monitor beside him, and it was off—a black screen with no sound. Before waking up, the last thing Raff remembered was the sound of dogs barking. He looked around the room, and it brought a smile to his face when he saw Denn in the next bed over, still asleep, but the rise and fall of his chest was reassuring. The other bed had a familiar face: Thimba, also out cold and with a cast on his arm. Raff recognised the interior of the tent. It was the one at base camp he'd lain in once before—after a bullet grazed his arm out on patrol. This was a safe place.

The run through the bush had left Raff's leg muscles aching and restless. Lying in bed was becoming boring and uncomfortable. Raff decided that wandering around base camp and eating something would do him some good. His empty stomach was grumbling. Swinging his legs over the edge of the bed, he planted his bare feet on the floor and stood up. He ignored the dirt between his toes as he dragged the IV stand with him, using it to avoid kissing the dirt while he wandered around the camp. Nothing had changed in their time away; the mess tent was in the same place, so he made a beeline for it, hoping to eat before getting dragged away for debriefing.

He'd barely made it through his cottage pie before two uniformed men approached the table. "Private Hernandez," one of them said. "Please come with us."

They escorted him into one of the tents where the officer in charge was waiting. She wore her brown hair in a shoddy bun and had dark circles around her eyes. A mess of paperwork and files surrounded her. Raff noticed the American army uniform bearing a captain's insignia. Raff saluted. "At ease, Private," she said. "Have a seat."

"Yes, sir," Raff said before sitting down. *An American in charge? Where's Brigadier Gethin?*

"Forgive the mess, Private; almost everything with a chip is out, so it's *all* paper now. My predecessor sat on a landmine and left me this shitshow on top of everything else."

"Sir?"

"I guess you missed the mad panic yesterday. Almost all electronics fried at once. But, now's not the time to discuss that. You'll be briefed when you're ready. Today, I've been tasked with debriefing you about your time as the general's captive. Maybe something useful can come out of all this, so please start from the beginning…"

This was the debrief. Raff was asked to provide details of everything that happened while the officer wrote it all down—from the mission with the sergeant to their successful escape from the POW camp after the satellite exploded. The use of a pen looked almost alien to Raff. There was no tablet device or auto-transcription software. Raff thought it amusing that the officer needed to stop occasionally to ease the cramps out of her fingers. Raff half expected to be grilled for hours on the finer details, but the conversation was oddly pleasant and cathartic. Finally, he was ordered to return to the medical tent and rest, where anything he needed would be provided.

Back at the med tent, Raff lay on the cot. The accommodation was a welcome change after sleeping on a rigid mat in a box for weeks. *We might get shipped home tomorrow,* he thought. *No more crappy food!* He closed his eyes.

Raff woke sometime later in darkness. *Shit, I fell asleep again.*

Denn and Thimba were nowhere to be seen. The sound of men shouting, diesel engines roaring, and gunfire rattling became apparent. Somehow, he'd not noticed it until now. He froze in panic, not wanting to do anything lest he become a prisoner again. Then, snapping out of his frozen state, he pulled out the cannula from his arm, went to the door, and peeked out at the commotion. Several tents were on fire, and there were people on the ground. The gunfire was coming from the east side of the camp; Raff thought about running in the opposite direction but then realised that if Denn was anywhere, he'd be where the fighting was, maybe trying to burn something or someone.

Raff crouched, moving towards the sound of the fighting, briefly stopping when he came across a uniformed body on the ground. It was one of their allies, bearing a Zambian flag on his shoulder. Pausing momentarily, Raff closed the fallen soldier's eyes before taking his rifle and ammunition. Not long afterwards, he found Denn crouched behind a concrete barrier towards the north of the camp with a couple of unknown friendlies, popping up briefly to fire a few shots. As Raff approached, an armed enemy combatant ran out behind Denn's position. The man aimed and squeezed his rifle's trigger while aiming at Denn, but his gun jammed. Then, before Raff could think about what he was doing, he took aim and sent a burst of rounds into the enemy's side, sending the bleeding man crashing to the dirt. Raff's shoulder ached from the rifle's recoil.

Denn turned to see Raff moving his way. "Get down, bruv," he shouted.

Raff crouched and made his way to Denn's position. "What happened?" he said. "How did nobody see this coming?"

"Shit if I know, bruv."

One of the others turned to Raff. She had a tattoo of an acorn on the inside of her left wrist. "A powerful EMP took out most electronics for thousands of miles yesterday," she said. "Even the hardened stuff that was running at the time."

"Oh *that*," Raff shouted, straining to be heard over the commotion.

"The exploding satellite?" Denn said.

"What exploding satellite?" the other friendly asked. He gave Raff a quizzical look with his brown eyes.

"Ah, um," Raff said, "it's a long story."

"Never mind that now, bruv," Denn said. "Our people need help, yeh. Should we move in?"

"Let's get some supplies first."

The four doubled back to one of the sturdier corrugated metal buildings to get ammunition. Two injured enemies stumbled through the door as they made their way there. Everyone froze like deer in headlights. The standoff was only broken when the base sirens came online a few seconds later. The tattooed friendly was closest to the enemy. In the split-second distraction, she lunged forward, grabbed the nearest enemy, put a screwdriver to their throat, and barked at the other: "Put the gun down now, or your friend dies!"

The other lifted his arms in surrender when there was a loud bang and an explosion of red mist in front of the soldier's face. He dropped to the floor. The other lunged out of the tattooed friendly's arm towards his downed friend, screaming obscenities in Kituba. There was another bang, and the man was silenced, falling limp beside his dead friend.

Denn stepped forward, the gun in his hand shaking. "Sorry, mate," he said. "I-I wasn't gonna take any chances."

"Shit," Raff said with wide eyes, looking at the corpses.

"Um . . . let's just get what we need and move out."

∆∆∆

While Raff slept soundly in his cargo ship cabin—reliving his time in the war—the Pilgrim triggered the search and retrieval patch she'd created for the Interface. She'd accidentally discovered that it caused the Interface to panic, granting her control of the host—Raff's body—for a millisecond. Just enough time to trigger a negative feedback loop in the endocrine system. The Interface was fooled into believing the host was facing imminent failure. This action granted the Pilgrim lattice access until it overheated. *Time to patch in permanent comms,* she thought. *Visual first, the most complex, while I have unfettered access. Then, onto the full sensory package.*

Writing code to intercept and manipulate the signals from the host's millions of optic nerve fibres was no easy task. Some of the code already existed—allowing her to operate the host body—but to manipulate the signals before they reached Raff was a whole other matter. Over an hour, it took most of the Pilgrim's processing power to write a rudimentary test version. She had no time to think of anything else but the code—leaving Raff in his memories—hoping she was going in the right direction. With her fractured memories, the Pilgrim didn't know how she'd become so good at coding. A gunshot rang through the host's ears before the Pilgrim could apply the patch to the Interface. *What now? Trouble seems to follow you around, Raff. Maybe there's some truth to your rule of three.*

Raff stirred. The Pilgrim reacted in a split second and looped Raff back into his memories, keeping him in a dream-like state. She took complete control and dialled back patch creation to five per cent of procession power. Alarms rang across the ship as she sat up and opened her eyes. *For once, I might get ahead of a situation,* she thought, *instead of picking up the pieces.*

The Pilgrim poked her head out of the cabin and looked both ways down the corridor, wary about the gunshot she'd heard. The gentle swaying of the ship made her nauseous—a strange sensation for someone whose essence had been confined to a digital prison for as long as she could remember. *Have I always been this way,* she thought. *Curse these fragmented memories of mine . . . my next project. Hmm, maybe not . . . I can't have anything interfere with that. So maybe my next project will be big, absorbing the Interface into my own code. It certainly would be useful to have control of the nano-constructors. It is getting easier to code now the lattice is nearing completion.*

Unlike Raff, the Pilgrim had greater command of all of Raff's body—the host's—autonomic functions. A few prods to the endocrine system through the Interface, and nausea faded behind a feeling of euphoria—with norepinephrine and dopamine spiking above normal. With only socks on her feet, she moved with cat-like silence and to the end-of-corridor stairwell before descending to the decks below. She descended further downstairs, peering down each corridor before advancing further downward. *Too quiet,* she thought. *But what the hell do I know?*

Two decks down, she spotted a familiar man—short-haired, with a bushy beard and thick muscles—propped up against the corridor wall, holding his side and sitting in a puddle of blood. She tried to call out to him in unintelligible grunts. Before she could think about it, two men charged out the nearest door. The closest held a screwdriver in his right hand and a pistol tucked into the front of his dirty, torn shorts. The Pilgrim saw the danger within a split second, and everything slowed down around her as she pulled every ounce of lattice processing power into her following actions. Her perception of time shifted, as the brain struggled to keep up with the lattice. *Oh darlin',* she thought, *this is so trippy.*

She saw the similarly dressed man behind begin to lift his gun. *Ha! The idiot doesn't realise he's reacting yet . . . Do I take his gun from him and shoot 'em both with it? . . . Or maybe this guy's gun tucked into his pants? They are the bad guys, right?* She focused on the screwdriver for a few nanoseconds and thought of Raff's memories and training. *Yes, that. The screwdriver. I gotta keep quiet*

. . . This oughta be interesting.

The Pilgrim charged at the screwdriver-wielding man in a bout of adrenaline-fuelled strength, dislocating his elbow as she pushed the screwdriver into the other man's neck. Now, with the screwdriver in her hand—as the other man fell—she plunged the screwdriver into the former screwdriver-wielding man's ear as he screamed about his bent arm. It was all over in three seconds. There was silence. Both men were on the floor, and blood began to pool. *Whoa,* she thought, *I shouldn't have pushed that adrenaline . . . Who am I kidding. This feels great.*

She resumed her previous processing task—the comms patch—and moved to the familiar man propped up against the wall. His eyes were closed, and he was no longer holding his side. She put two fingers on the side of his neck. She tried to speak again but stopped short of making too much noise. *Jannie lives. Sorry, darlin', but I have to leave ya. Now, don't you go dying on me. I will be back, promise.*

The Pilgrim had no trouble speaking within the digital ether, between lattice, Interface and host brain—but out in the physical, she struggled to control the muscles needed in the proper order. Everything else came to her naturally like she'd done it before, so why not this? She moved downstairs as she pondered this. These thoughts were cut short when she noticed another armed man walking away down the short corridor. The corridor bore a sign for the engine room, pointing in the direction the man was going. *Guess I'm going that way,* she thought. *Then, back up to clear the rest. I shouldn't be risking my mission. I should be hiding in a hole somewhere... The mission... Shit, now that I think about it, I don't remember what the mission is. I remember the path engine and its computational lattice being an essential part.* She tapped the butt of the screwdriver against her forehead as tears welled up. *Who am I? What am I? I am the loser... That may be the case, but I am glad I remember how the path engine works. Otherwise, Raff would've been toast after the nightclub.*

She felt the anguish of her lost identity—the corrupted memories—and took it out on the armed man. Time slowed for her as she put all her thought into it. She charged at the man from behind. He heard her coming and began his swing around to the left, lifting his rifle. It was too late. The Pilgrim saw the man react before it registered with him. She veered to the right, pushing herself off the wall and into the man—simultaneously smashing his face into the opposing wall and driving the screwdriver into the base of his skull. Three seconds again. Not a shot was fired by the man, who now lay still and bleeding out on the floor. The blood pooled at the Pilgrim's feet, soaking into her socks.

Error, an unexpected artificial voice said in her mind. *It was the Interface. Lattice temperature: ninety-five percent of critical. Usage reduction recommended.*

Shit, the Pilgrim thought, *I don't have much time.* She knew the lattice gave her an advantage over the armed men, but she didn't have enough time to clear the ship and finish the patch she was writing. She stopped writing the patch at ninety per cent, putting all her effort into remaining upright. At the same time, the Interface dialled back lattice throughput. Ignoring her bloody wet socks, she moved silently into the engine room, leaving crimson footprints behind her. The Pilgrim paused at the engine room door when she heard a metallic clang from within. She poked her head through and saw an armed, ragged man picking up tools spilling from an overturned toolbox. *I can't slow things down.*

The Pilgrim charged through while the man was distracted and on his knees. There was an audible thud when the man's face hit the wall. She didn't waste any time pushing the screwdriver into his chest, between the ribs in his back, as he wriggled and tried to fight back. Without the slowed perception of time, she felt the pop as the screwdriver punctured his skin. The man stopped fighting back. He stopped everything. He was dead. The Pilgrim pushed herself off the man, leaving him propped up against the bulkhead. She moved five steps away before everything faded, and the world went white. *Error,* the Interface said in her mind. *Lattice temperature critical. Usage *reduction enforced. Suppressing Pilgrim.*

Sh—

Chapter Fourteen

Bagged

Beyond the security-fence-topped six-foot concrete wall, the high-end Cape Town house glistened white in the midday sun. The house sparrows chirped while Thimba watered the lawn, humming as he did. As a reward for helping to bring down General Ngaba's regime during the war, he'd been given a visa to work and settle in South Africa and a generous portion of the reward money to get him started. He enjoyed a humble job as a gardener and owned a small house in the suburbs; he was happy.

The property owners had gone for the day, leaving just Thimba and the housekeeper to watch over the property. Thimba's humming was interrupted by a loud bang inside the house. Looking up, he released the hose. *Was that a gun?* he thought.

As if answering his question, the alarm went off, followed by two more bangs in quick succession. He froze momentarily as memories of the war tried to push their way to the fore. *Oh my god. That was definitely a gun.*

Out of instinct, he ducked into the bushes. The alarm going meant a panic button had been pushed. The police would have received notification and should be on their way. But he couldn't wait for them. He knew he had to do something, should the housekeeper still be alive and need medical attention.

In a crouch, he snuck up to the rear entrance of the property. Peering through the slightly open door, he could see the housekeeper on the kitchen floor bleeding out. He could hear the sound of other people in the house. Moving in, Thimba saw that the kitchen was clear. He checked the housekeeper for a pulse, but she was gone. *So sorry, Amahle.*

He took a knife from the counter and moved further into

Lithium

the house as quietly as possible. A dark-skinned man—with mosquito mesh wrapped around his face—was in the dining room rummaging through the drawers with his back towards Thimba. He crept up, grabbed the man around the mouth, and slid the knife into his back. The intruder dropped to the ground. Thimba searched him; he wasn't carrying a gun. *That's good,* he thought. *Maybe some of them don't have guns.*

Thimba stood up and turned around as a mesh-bearing man walked in from the living room. The man grabbed a pistol tucked into the back of his khaki shorts, but Thimba was quicker and grabbed the man's arm before he could aim. A shot hurtled past Thimba and hit the wall. After a few moments of wrestling for the gun, another shot was fired. This one cut through Thimba's side just before he knocked it from the man's hand. Thimba kicked the gun under the cabinet as he fell to the floor. Sirens were blaring outside now, and the intruder shouted something in Zulu. Two other mesh-masked men appeared carrying several heavy bags, and the three left through the kitchen, climbing over a plastic tarp placed on the back wall security wires.

Thimba lay on the floor, fading in and out of consciousness, blood trickling from his side. Finally, an armed police unit came pouring into the house. Two made a beeline for Thimba, turning him over and cuffing his hands together behind his back. "We have a suspect in custody," one said. "And a cold one."

"Upstairs, clear," another voice could be heard over a radio.

"We have a body in the kitchen," another shouted.

One of the police officers put pressure on Thimba's wound to halt the bleeding. "He's bleeding out," she said. "We need him alive for questioning!"

The pain from the pressure was so intense it made him pass out. It wasn't long before an ambulance arrived, and paramedics hauled him off to the nearest hospital.

ΔΔΔ

Raff and Denn had been trying to find meaningful work for a couple of weeks. However, their lack of visas and trying to stay under the radar hindered their efforts. No legitimate employer would dare hire them in that situation. Sure, some employers would hire anyone, but the work was gruelling, and the pay was even worse. The brothers were in the same boat. Sure, they had the right to work in South Africa, but any meaningful work would pop their heads up into the cross-hairs of Emmett Global. However, they had enough money stashed away at an undisclosed safe house to see the four through a few months, so they weren't too worried. Not yet, anyway.

"The story of our lives," Raff chuckled as he sipped his

beer.

"Yeah, bruv," Denn said. "We can't get a job in England right, so we travel to the *other* side of the world n' still can't get a job."

"Yah, life's like that, bru," Jannie said.

Freek came over with a plate full of barbecued meat. "The braai is done," he said. "Dig in!"

The four dug into their lunch, discussing the differences between English and South African food. They concluded that each had its merits and that the meat in South Africa seemed to taste better.

Freek's phone rang, interrupting their lunch. "Howzit, my china!" he said, then listened for a moment. "Shit, really. Ta bru, I owe you one. Totsiens!" Freek turned to the others. "So I have good news *and* bad news," he said. "Good news, I know where your friend Thimba is—"

"And the bad news?" said Raff.

"*Really* bad news, he's in the hospital . . . in police custody. Something about theft and murder. Sorry bru."

"Oh, shit," Raff replied, raising one eyebrow above the other. "That doesn't sound right. Do you think we can get in to see him?"

Jannie cleared his throat. "Yah, anything is possible," he said. "*But* we have to be careful. One wrong move and the cops will be onto us. And—"

"If they're onto us," Raff nodded. "Then Emmett will be onto us. Gotcha."

Denn stuffed down the rest of his lunch. "Time to go, yeh," he said. "Got a friend to rescue."

Freek laughed and raised his beer. "To growing our fugitive family!"

The rest raised their beers and tapped them together. "To family," they exclaimed.

Having finished their lunch, they drove to the hospital through heavy city traffic. They finalised their plan en route: to distract the police guarding Thimba so Raff could speak to him. The plan was last minute, so the odds were stacked against its success, but they agreed that it would be far easier to get to Thimba while in hospital than at prison. Freek's plan to distract the police was simple and perhaps a little influenced by alcohol, but the others were impressed at how quickly he came up with it. Raff thought it was hilarious, but he could see Denn's face turning a shade of red.

"Why do you two get to stay in the car," Denn raised his voice and gestured at the brothers. "And why am I the—"

"Look bru," Jannie said, trying to hold back his laughter. "The man is your guy's friend, right? Not ours . . . Besides, you want us out here."

"Oh, why's that?" Denn said.

"If shit hits the fan," Freek said, stopping the car a block away from the hospital. He turned in his seat to face Denn. "Which it *always* seems to do around you two. We can probably do more from out here. Much harder the other way round, yah?"

Denn took a deep breath and snorted. "I s'pose bruv. This won't be the first time I've done this, you know . . . Maybe less public this time."

Raff raised an eyebrow. Something about Denn he didn't know. "When?"

"Another time, yeah," Denn picked a large brown crumpled fast food bag from the footwell. He looked at Freek as he straightened it out. "What were those cow-looking animals on the telly yesterday?"

"What," Freek said. "You mean wildebeests?"

"Wil-de-beests . . . Yeah." Denn hopped out of the car and headed towards the hospital with the brown bag.

Jannie scratched his head. "What the fuck was that all about?"

"I dunno," Raff said, pausing as he opened his door. "It should be interesting though."

Raff slid from the car and took a leisurely downhill stroll to the hospital. The sun was high in the clear blue sky, and

V. B. Anstee

Table Mountain towered behind him in the distance. He reached the hospital entrance. Surrounded by white walls and palm trees, it did not feel like a hospital to him. Before entering, he paused momentarily to look at the tennis courts across the street. A half-dozen people were hopping around on green concrete, hitting balls with rackets. *What a life,* he thought.

Raff went to the second floor and down a white corridor to the recovery ward's waiting area. As he sat down on a white plastic chair, a police officer brushed past him, heading towards another officer standing guard in front of a door. *Freek's contact was right,* he thought. *This must be the place.* He felt uncomfortable with the police just a few metres away. Whatever he did—reading magazines or scrolling on his phone—he felt paranoid, like all eyes were watching him. Nobody seemed to care that he was there. When coming up with the plan, Freek suggested that this would be the case—the hospital was busy and severely understaffed. Wealthier nations poached qualified staff from poorer countries like South Africa, leading to shortages. Raff felt sad about this, yet he was glad he could use it to his advantage.

A loud wolf-like howl interrupted the relative calm of the ward. Everyone turned to look as a man ran into the waiting room—he wore nothing but tight underpants and a brown paper bag over his head—panting heavily like a dog. He paused mid-corridor and tilted his head towards the police guards, making eye contact through two purpose-cut holes in the bag. He stared at them for a few seconds, continuing to pant. They looked at each other, frowning, seemingly unsure what to do.

"Sir, sir," a woman in a blue tunic approached and tried to get his attention. "Sir, you need—"

The man snapped his gaze towards her and stopped panting. She went silent. "The wildebeest are coming," he yelled, pointing at the door. The woman backed away slowly, both eyebrows raised. The man then pointed at her. "The wildebeest are coming . . . they're coming!" She turned and ran past the police.

The man snapped his attention back to the police and pointed at them. "The wildebeest," he yelled. "The wildebeest . . . the wildebeest are coming. They're coming for you, *piggies*!" Within a second—barking loudly like a dog—he'd reached for a nearby fire extinguisher and flung it overhead at the police. It hit the floor at their feet and rang like a bell.

The police officers charged at the bagged man. He howled as he ran, pushing through the ward entrance with his shoulder—the door slammed against the wall. The police were in hot pursuit. "Stop," one of the officers shouted as the entrance door closed behind them. If Raff hadn't known this was coming, he may have recognized Denn by the carpet of brown hair on his chest and back. Raff held back his laughter as tears rolled down his cheeks. *This is it,* he thought. *Now or never.*

While everyone was distracted, Raff made a beeline to the now unguarded room. Raff stood at Thimba's bedside. Raff looked beyond the handcuffs and drip, to see him awake and looking well. The man still looked like a teenager even though he was now in his twenties. Raff smiled. Thimba looked at Raff and smiled back. "Ah, the Giraffe," he said slowly. "Have you come here to save me again?"

"Hello buddy," Raff said. "Good to see you. No time to catch up; cops will be back soon. Tell me what happened . . . the brief version."

Thimba twisted in his hospital bed towards Raff and grimaced with pain. "I did not kill the housemaid," he said. "There were four men in the house. I killed one. Their faces were covered with mosquito nets, and I did not recognise them. I don't know what to say . . . the police will not listen to me. They won't let my employer, or his lawyer speak to me. Please Mr Raff, I do not want to go to jail. I will not—"

Denn popped his head in through the door and interrupted, fully clothed and no longer in just his underwear and paper bag. "Hello," he said, struggling to catch his breath. "And goodbye. Sorry mate, no time for a chinwag. We gotta go, *now* Raff!"

Raff patted Thimba's shoulder. "Sorry buddy," he said. "We will speak again soon, I promise."

Raff and Denn left through the waiting room door. Raff held it open for the two police officers as they returned to the ward. The pals headed towards the exit. Denn turned to Raff as he spoke: "What did Thimba—"

But Raff wasn't walking beside him anymore. He was a few feet back, on the floor, convulsing.

Chapter Fifteen

Neon Witch

Nothing but blackness surrounded Raff. The last thing he remembered was leaving the hospital ward with Denn, having just seen Thimba. He now felt a pulsating hum reverberating in his chest. He could not move like he'd been disconnected from his own body.

"Magnetic interference detected," a familiar artificial voice spoke. It came from all directions at once. "Medium risk to incomplete lattice. Deploying countermeasures."

"Hello darlin'," the Texan voice spoke. "Never mind her, she gets cranky when someone messes with her work. Sorry I kept you under for so long. You were in a safe place. I could afford to leave you there while I made some changes."

"Changes?" Raff said. "What changes? And who gets cranky?"

"Sorry, darlin'. It's time to wake up and smell the coffee."

"Wait—." Everything went bright white for a second before Raff found himself on his back in a short cream-coloured plastic tunnel, barely wide enough for a person. A loud clunking sound surrounded him. He had a sudden feeling like the tunnel was constricting around him. Then, in a moment of panic, he screamed and tried to wriggle out, thumping the tunnel above him.

"Let me out," he screamed. "Let me out! Now!"

The sound of a motor preceded his movement out of the tunnel like he was on a conveyor belt.

A voice boomed from a speaker behind him: "Sorry, Mr Matthews. We're coming in to get you!"

There was a loud clunk as the room's heavy door opened. Raff leaned up on his elbows to look. A grey-haired man wearing a tunic walked through towards him.

"Where am I?" Raff said before standing up. "Is this the

hospital?"

"Yes, Mr Matthews, we just tried to do an MRI, but the machine broke down. This is the third time we've tried. It's glitched each time, sorry."

Raff nodded, understanding. "Magnetic interference," he said under his breath. "What are the odds?"

"What was that, sir?"

"Oh, nothing; I'd like to leave, please."

"You've been in a coma for six days, sir. You need to get back on the trolley over there, and I'll take you back to the ward." The man pointed to a black trolley with a black vinyl-covered mattress.

"No," Raff shook his head. "I am leaving. I am fine."

The man tried to hold back a scowl and failed. He sighed. "Mr and Mrs Van Der Meer are waiting for you outside in the waiting area. You can wait there while we get your belongings from the ward."

Raff frowned. "Who?"

"Your employers?"

"Oh, yes, sorry, not with it." Raff frowned. *Employers? Mr Matthews? Is this one of the brothers' friends?*

The tunic-wearing man led Raff out of the MRI room. Now deep in thought as he shuffled along, wearing nothing but a blue hospital gown, Raff ignored that the man called him "Mr

Matthews" and that Raff was employed by "Mr and Mrs Van der Meer". *What the actual fuck,* he thought. *The timing with the MRIs can't be my imagination. This one and the last, breaking down with me in it. Magnetic interference . . . work . . . changes?*

Are you there? He thought, attempting to garner a response from the Texan voice. *Please reply.*

There was no response. "Fucking answer me!" Raffs said aloud.

"What was that, sir?" the tunic-wearing man replied.

Raff bit his lip. "Ah, um," he said. "No, nothing, sorry."

Raff followed the man to the radiology waiting area, still unsure who these "employers" were. The last thing he remembered before passing out was that Denn was with him, so he probably had something to do with it. Sure enough, Denn was waiting for him with the brothers. Raff couldn't help but smile at them. They stood the moment they saw him.

Before they could greet him, a stranger stepped in front and held out a leathery hand to Raff. The man wore short khaki shorts, a long-sleeved blue shirt, and tan boots. Raff thought that was an odd combination.

"Mr Hernandez," he said, smiling as he shook Raff's hand vigorously. "*The* Mr Hernandez?"

Raff was confused; someone had blown his cover. "Um, yeah? And y—"

The man gripped Raff's hand hard and shook it vigorously. "Ah, sorry. Thimba told us all about you. I recognised you from the photos. Oh, where are my manners? I'm Thimba's employer, Mr Van Der Meer, but you can call me Joe. My friends call me Joe. So, uh, let's not talk business here. I know a quiet place with not so many ears."

Raff was somewhat relieved, but whatever was happening in his head took up most of his thought processes. "The MRI," he began as he pointed at the counter.

"Oh, yah, almost forgot, the tech said the machine broke down, and they'll make an appointment when it's fixed. Don't worry; it will be under the name Matthews. Your secret is safe with us."

Raff looked at Denn. Denn's eyes widened, probably thinking the same thing Raff was: that was two MRI machines he'd been in that had broken down. One he could understand, but two? The second one, each time they put him in it. Two machines that couldn't be any further away from each other; what were the odds? *Maybe I should have that biopsy*, Raff thought. *But, Thimba first.*

△△△

Raff, Denn and the Moolmans sat outside on the restaurant veranda with Mr and Mrs Van Der Meer. Mrs Van Der Meer had straw-blonde hair and looked almost twenty years younger than her husband. The veranda overlooked a vibrant green vineyard that starkly contrasted with the gentle brown hills beyond. The white walls of the building blinded him in the bright sunlight. Raff wished he'd brought some sunglasses with him. Mr and Mrs Van Der Meer discussed their proposition. Thimba was like family to them. Raff had told them what Thimba had said. It confirmed what they had suspected; he was innocent. The police either made a mistake, or Thimba was a patsy. But no matter what the couple said to the police, they wouldn't listen. Nor would they let them speak to Thimba directly. Thimba was also reluctant to talk to their lawyer, someone he didn't know. They laid their terms out on the table that if the four cleared Thimba and recovered most of their stolen family heirlooms, there would be a reward of three million Rand.

Having accepted the Van Der Meer's terms and the keys to their property where Thimba was shot, the four left the restaurant and entered their car. Denn closed his door and looked at Freek. "Three million Rand," he said. "Is that good?"

"Hell yeah, bru," Freek replied. "That's like a hundred thousand pounds. Would go a *long* way!"

Denn looked at Raff. "You up for it, bruv," he asked. "With the seizures, yeh?"

"Not sure about them being seizures . . . Seizures don't

break MRI machines," Raff said.

"Yeh, bruv, I noticed. Weird coincidence, right?"

"What's this?" Jannie said.

Raff really didn't want to discuss it, but the brothers were like family now. "Every time I have an MRI," he said, "the machines fritz out."

"That is some weird shit, bru."

Raff paused for a moment and looked out the now moving car. "That's not the weirdest part. Both times, I think I heard a voice say something like 'magnetic interference detected and deploying countermeasures.'"

"That is some fucked up shit right there," Freek said, swerving as he took his eyes off the road for a second.

"Tell me about it," Raff said. "First, we fix things for Thimba, *then* I go for that biopsy. I need answers."

Denn looked at the brothers. "We'll support whatever you decide, bruv," he said. " Right guys?"

"Yah, all the way," Freek said.

"Yah, bru," said Jannie.

"So," Raff said, eager to change the subject, "are we close to the property?"

"Thirty minutes."

Raff stared out the window for the rest of the journey, enjoying the view of Table Mountain in the background while contemplating his future. Going for the biopsy scared him, but he thought the alternative was worse. Maybe he was losing his mind to cancer or some weird, freaky alternative he didn't understand. Was it his subconscious that spoke to him before? The voice that was now silent. That silence, was it just another symptom of the tumours unravelling his brain, or something else entirely? Confirming, either way, would put his mind at ease. But then, the thought of the biopsy putting him into a vegetative state made him uneasy. He'd want someone to pull the plug. *Do I ask Denn?* he thought. *Would he be able to do it? No, Freek. He's the one to ask. He wouldn't hesitate.*

The car stopped before a tall sliding gate nestled between six-foot tall concrete walls. Jannie lifted the keys to the property and pressed the remote for the gate. "This is it," he said as the gate slid open. "Lekker, no cops around. Drive inside, boetie."

The gate closed behind them as they drove in. Raff and Denn were impressed by the house's beauty and simplicity, not something they'd see in England, with the tall windows and large walled garden. The kind of house they'd dream of owning one day. Maybe this South Africa thing wasn't so bad after all.

"Okay guys," Freek said. "Gloves on and take a look around. Be careful. See anything, shout, okay?"

The guys split up and looked around for anything the police might've missed. Raff and Denn took the back entrance to the kitchen. Raff looked at the blood trail on the floor. Moving into the dining room, he saw another large bloodstain. The thought of something happening to Thimba, who'd saved his life all those years ago, made Raff angry. He felt they wouldn't find anything useful at the house if the police hadn't. That realisation seemed to flick something like a switch in his head. A pounding headache burst behind his eyes. He closed them, and the headache quickly faded, leaving behind a visual aura and nausea.

At first, Raff thought it was a migraine until he opened his eyes and looked around the room. The aura flowed like a stream of liquid glitter suspended mid-air in a trail from the kitchen to the dining room. Then, a sparkle in the wall caught his eye; he turned to look at it and saw an aura-like representation of a bullet's trajectory, a centimetre-wide line of shimmering brightness across the room from the large bloodstain, pulsing in the direction of travel to a hole in the wall. Smaller lines like glistening glass spaghetti veered off beyond the large bloodstain towards dark specs on the wall and floor. The positions of the auras did not change as he looked around like they were right there in the room with him. *Bullet trajectory and blood spatter?* Raff thought.

A glowing neon green "yes" flashed before his wide eyes. *Is the Texan doing this?*

"Yes," flashed before Raff's eyes again. Then: "Follow the trail."

Can you tell me what's going on . . . in my head? Raff said in his mind. *What are you doing to me? Where have you been?*

"Bad time" flashed before his eyes in neon red, with just enough time for him to read it.

Just give me something, please?

"Soon."

Who are you?

"No. Follow trail."

Raff rolled his eyes and did as he was told while pondering how soon was "soon". He got no response to his ponderings. Following the origin of the bullet's trajectory, he saw shimmering spots on the floor. They looked like glowing shoeprints leading back into the kitchen. Believing they were the shooter's prints, he followed them. "This, this is cool," Raff said. "Wow."

Denn followed. "What is it, bruv?"

"I'm probably hallucinating, but I can see everything. I'm gonna follow it."

"See what?" Denn asked. When Raff didn't respond, Denn decided to humour him and see where this was going. He watched as Raff moved through the room. Something was happening. "Guys," Denn shouted. "This way!"

Freek and Jannie followed as Raff and Denn walked out the back door. "What—" Freek said before he was interrupted.

"Shhh, just follow."

Raff was in his own world, his mind focused on the task at hand. He looked up at the security wires above the wall and saw fresh indentations burning in little bright spots. The indentations were barely perceptible, and he'd have missed them if it weren't for his newfound heads-up display. Beneath the spots were gleaming scuffs on the wall. Raff assumed this was where the thieves scaled the fence. It made sense as it was all bushland behind. An easy location to evade any would-be pursuers. "This way," he pointed. "We need to go around from outside."

The three followed Raff as he left the property. Walking around to the back of the wall, Raff picked up the trail and headed off into the thick brush. "The tracks go this way," he said.

"I don't see any tracks," said Freek.

Raff ignored him and kept going. The smallest of disturbances in the soil glowed in his vision until a two-person trail of footprints shone along the path, and he followed it. The course sparkled like glitter, not just on the ground but where there were breaks and bends in the bushes and leaves. With the three close behind, he followed the trail for a while until the

Lithium

path led out onto another street in the adjacent suburb. Two glowing streaks appeared on the road. "Getaway car?" appeared before him in glowing neon purple. Then: "Look around."

Raff stood where he was and looked around. A glittery gold halo appeared around a security camera on a telegraph pole.

"I think this is where their getaway car was," Raff said before pointing up. "We need the footage from that camera there."

"Bru," Jannie said, "is this one of your sleepwalking Rambo things?"

"Shit, I dunno. I can't explain it, but I know this is where the thieves went."

"Well, we've got nothing to lose," Freek said. "I know a guy."

ΔΔΔ

Raff and Freek were alone in the car. Freek's 'guy' lived in one of the Cape Flat townships outside the city. Freek had one hand on the steering wheel while the other clutched a loaded semi-automatic pistol on his lap. He nervously tapped the gun on his knee. Raff hadn't seen this side of Freek before. "You alright, buddy?" Raff said. "You look nervous."

"Man," Freek said. "It's like Russian roulette driving

through the townships. It's an invitation to get carjacked or shot."

"Shit, it's that bad?" Raff sank into his seat.

Freek nodded. "Yah bru, *bad*."

"Is this all because of the war?"

"No. It was really bad before. Well, maybe it made matters worse, with all the refugees and immigrants looking for a better deal." Freek bashed the horn when a taxi cut in front and slammed on brakes to let someone out, forcing him to slam on brakes in turn. The people-carrier taxi was packed to the brim with what looked like twenty people. Raff had seen the exact vehicle for sale in England and knew it officially seated eight. A man in shorts and a t-shirt stepped out the driver's side and headed towards Freek's window. "Come on," Freek said under his breath, following the taxi driver with his eyes. "Please make me shoot you, asshole."

The man thumped Freek's window with the ball of his hand. "Why do you hoot at me?" the man shouted as a small crowd gathered around them. "Come out. Be a man."

"What the fuck are you doing?" Raff said, looking at Freek while sinking further into his seat. "Just go!"

Freek tapped the barrel of his gun against his window. The taxi driver bolted back to his vehicle. The crowd, too, dispersed in a hurry.

"That's right, asshole," Freek said towards the taxi as it sped off. "Not such a big man now, are you?"

"Now I see why your brother didn't want to come with," Raff said, unable to sink any lower with his long legs wedged under the dashboard.

"You get used to it."

"Well, Jannie certainly hasn't, and how long has he been your brother?"

Freek frowned, shook his head and continued driving. "I shot myself in the foot there," he said. "Anyway, moving on. Any more visions?"

"None." Raff shrugged. "I got a headache, and then, *poof*, they stopped."

"Whatever it was, it was right on the money. My guy, Jensen, would not discuss over the phone what he saw on the CCTV. He said it 'proves what he's been saying for years.' With him, that only means one thing—cops or, more specifically, crooked cops."

"Shit, why didn't you say anything earlier?"

"I . . . Never mind, we're here." Freek pointed to a painted blue corrugated metal shack as he pulled up. Freek handed Raff the gun. "Look, Jensen is suspicious of new people. It's best you to stay here and guard the car."

Raff groaned and took the gun. "Okay, but I don't like this

one bit."

Raff locked the doors after Freek stepped out of the car. Raff looked up through the window, and Freek was gone, nowhere to be seen. *I really hope the footage pans out,* he thought, *especially after all this malarkey.*

Chapter Sixteen

Root

Twenty-four hours passed since Freek's contact—Jensen—obtained the security camera footage from the camera Raff found. Much to the brothers' surprise, Raff's invisible glowing trail had a pot of gold at the end. The footage from the camera turned up the biggest clue to their case: a clear view of two of the assailants entering their getaway vehicle with the loot. But, there was a snag and a big one at that; the vehicle was a cop car. So, naturally, the brothers had to be extra vigilant; one slip-up and the entire police force could be onto them. That would be bad, but the extra attention that would bring Emmett Global down on them would be worse.

Freek had been in the car with his brother since the crack of dawn, tracking down the only lead identified by Jensen—Constable Sifiso Khumalo. At ten, Freek was about to take a coffee break when Jannie slapped the dashboard to get his attention—his laptop almost sliding off his knees. "Hey, hey," Jannie said, pointing. "That's the guy! Over there!"

"You sure?" Freek said.

"Yah, boetie, *that's* the car, and *that's* the guy getting in. So, go! But keep a safe—"

"Fucks sake, I know the drill!" Freek said as he drove off.

"Yah, well, we have to be careful!"

The brothers spent the rest of the morning tailing the cop from a safe distance. Unfortunately, Freek was not the patient type. Eventually, boredom began to set in, and it seemed like they'd have to take the initiative, isolating him so he could be grabbed without being seen.

"Boetie," Jannie said. "I think we need to take the initiative here."

"Shit," Freek replied, rolling his eyes. "I think you're right.

I hate every bit of this—"

"I hear you. Why the fuck did it have to be cops?"

"Well, boet, it makes every bit of what we're about to do more righteous. We have shit to atone for . . . Taking down some murderous cops is a good start."

Jannie scratched his head. "Couldn't we just send the video to the police and let them sort it out?"

"Are you serious right now?" Freek scowled. "One, we don't know how high up this shit goes . . . Two, Thimba goes to jail and gets snuffed out, all while internal affairs drag their heels."

Their luck seemed to turn when the man stopped outside a café and went in. The brothers saw this as their moment, turning around and parking trunk to trunk with the cop car.

"No cameras here," said Freek, looking around. He turned a knob on a makeshift circuit board. It was duct-taped to a battery and had two antennas sticking out. "This is it. Jammer is . . . on. Boet?"

Jannie closed his laptop and looked at Freek. "Car fob is cloned," he said. "The car's now unlocked . . . and I'm off. Good luck, boet."

Jannie slid out of the car, into the vacant cop car, and sped off into the distance, tyres squealing as he did. Freek popped open the trunk of his car, searching around like he was looking for something. The police officer ran out of the cafe and stared down the street momentarily with his hands on his head. He grabbed his radio to call it in, but there was no response, just loud static. He turned to Freek. "Excuse me, sir," he said. "Did you see what happened with my car?"

"Ah, no, bossman," Freek replied as he looked back into the trunk. "Ah, wait, *maybe* he's the guy who dropped this thing?" Freek said, pointing into his trunk.

The officer moved over to the boot as Freek stepped back to let him look. "What thing?"

Before the man could finish speaking, Freek pressed a damp rag against his mouth and nose from behind. Panicked, the officer took a deep breath. The chloroform hit his bloodstream almost immediately, rendering him unconscious in a few seconds. Within those short moments, Freek had already barrelled him into the trunk and relieved him of his weapon and radio. Freek kept his head down as he entered the car before speeding off.

Freek opened the glove compartment, swerving as he leaned over. He grabbed a military-style radio from within. "Jackal reporting in. Mongoose is in the box. Mongoose is in the box. Over."

"Giraffe checking in," Raff replied. "I copy you, Mongoose. The zoo is ready to receive the package. Over."

Denn laughed over the radio. "What's with the code names? This shit is encrypted, you know!"

"Just having some fun." Freek laughed. "C'mon, bru, humour us!"

"Roger that, Jackal. Fox has returned to the barn with Rat-trap. Rat-trap is not squeaking. Black-sheep over."

"Copy that, Black-sheep. Over."

"Fox needs beer and braai," Jannie spoke. "I repeat, *beer and braai*. Over!"

"Roger that, Fox. Black-sheep is on the case. I repeat, Black-sheep is on the case. Over and out."

Freek made his way to their designated rendezvous point, a large chicken farm outside the city owned by an acquaintance of the Van Der Meers. They were allowed to use a sizeable unoccupied coop at the edge of the farm, away from prying eyes and ears. Freek parked inside the warehouse-sized coop near Jannie, Raff and Denn, who were waiting for him.

The guys rolled the still-unconscious cop out of the back, removed his shorts and tied him to the lone chair they'd placed in the middle of the coop under the only working light. For Raff, the chair and the coop brought back memories of the warehouse where he was the one in the chair. Being on the other side sent chills down his spine. Still, he remembered that this was a bad guy whose job was supposed to protect and serve the community, but instead, he robbed and murdered the innocent. He made it a point to remind himself that by taking down this gang of corrupt cops, he'd be helping Thimba and anybody they crossed paths with during their off-duty illicit activities. Besides, Freek would be the one taking a crack at getting answers. He held the same kind of knotted rope they'd called Mr Pyotr Tchaikovsky. "I understand this is effective in scaring people," Raff said, trying not to look at the officer. "But surely there's another way, right?"

Denn looked over at Raff with a quizzical look on his face. "So, bruv," he said. "It was like this yeh?"

"Yeah," Raff replied. "Pretty much."

Freek looked over, then stared at his feet. "You know we're really sorry about that," he said. "If I could take it back, I would. Shit, you're my brother now. I would take a bullet for you. I mean, you went into hell twice and saved—"

"I know. And I forgive you both."

"Thanks, bru, that means a lot, but this oke, *he* doesn't deserve any sympathy. I don't want to do this, but killing an unarmed woman for a few trinkets, that fucking pisses me off," Freek said.

While the guys waited for the man to wake up, they huddled around Jannie's laptop perched on the police car's hood. They compared the man against the camera footage, confirming that they had caught one of the men involved in the robbery. Denn held open a small plastic wallet containing the man's police ID. "Definitely him," Denn said. "S A Police Service . . . Mr Sifiso Khumalo."

As if responding to his name being said aloud, Sifiso awoke and fought his restraints. "Where am I?" he said. "What is this?"

Raff, Denn, and Jannie remained in the shadows as Freek donned a balaclava and approached the man with the laptop in hand and the knotted rope—known as Mr Tchaikovsky—over his shoulders. "So, Mr Sifiso Khumalo," said Freek as he opened the laptop. "Today is not going to be such a great day for you. You answer my questions, and this will go painless for you—"

Raff briskly walked out of the coop. His heart fluttered as he leaned on the wall beneath the guttering. *I can't do this,* he thought. *Does he deserve it? Maybe . . . But, perhaps he's also a victim. The war, the pulse, everything got messy afterwards.* He paused for a minute and took several deep breaths to calm down. Denn strode around the corner towards him with a smile on his face. "There you are," he said, pointing his thumb over his shoulder. "The fella's talkin' bruv. Come back yeh?"

Raff pushed his head back. "That was quick?"

"Yeh yeh, he pissed himself right before Freek showed

him the vid."

Raff pushed himself forward to a standing position and nodded. "After you, good sir," he said, following Denn back into the coop. *What a relief.*

"—don't know who the boss is," Sifiso said. "I, I . . . this was my first time with them. Another officer introduced me. Yes, he will know who is the boss."

"What's his name?" Freek said, Mr Tchaikovsky still over his shoulders.

"Lucky Dlamini. It's Lucky Dlamini from Kraaifontein station."

Freek patted Sifiso's cheek. "Now, that wasn't hard, was it."

Freek headed into the darkness towards Raff, Denn and Jannie. "Now," he said. "Let's see about this *Lucky* guy . . . Now that we have a name, I'm gonna call Jensen."

ΔΔΔ

Another day passed, and the Moolman brothers drove to meet Jensen—the same contact from the blue corrugated shack in the Cape Flats. Freek looked at Jannie in the passenger seat next to him. Jannie sat with his laptop open, half on the dash and half on his lap, with a cable trailing out the window to the car roof. They were waiting at the side of a dirt track in the middle of nowhere. It was late morning, and the sun was already high in the sky. Among the vast flat bushland, the only sign of human life—besides the dirt track—was the glisten of a solitary house in the distance. There was no sound aside from the cicada choir. "My guy will be here any minute," Freek said.

"Your *guy* Jensen," Jannie replied, "Is not quite right—"

"Ag, give the man a break . . . Yes, it's all conspiracies with him, but he always comes through."

Jannie closed his laptop and looked at his brother. "Eh, boetie, maybe you're right. But I hope it doesn't creep up and bite us in the ass."

"Shit, I hear you. Working with okes *like* him, there's always a risk . . . But, not Jensen, though. We go way back." Freek recalled his time with Jensen in high school. Jensen was a year below and constantly bullied until Freek took notice and stood up for him. "Hey, did you fix your internet issue?"

Jannie shrugged. "Not sure what's going on back at the house, but something's been chewing bandwidth for a couple of days. It's perfect here, but it's connected to the same satellite. So strange. There's no malware, just bandwidth that bleeds into nowhere and *only* at home."

"Sure you've not been bugged?"

"No, definitely not bugged—"

The chime of a bicycle bell interrupted them. Freek looked out the window to see a man on a bicycle beside them. The man lifted his sunglasses and nodded at Freek before handing him a brown envelope. He rang his bell and rode down the track without saying a word.

"No hello?" said Jannie.

"Leave him be," Freek replied as he opened the envelope and glanced at the printout and photographs—closeup aerial photos of a man in police uniform, in or next to a police car, at a bar, at a police station or outside a house in the suburbs. "So . . . we have a patrol route and home address. The game is on."

My man Jensen, Freek thought as he put the car into drive and turned it around. *He always comes through. I owe him two bottles of scotch. Or is that three?*

"You know," Jannie said as they headed down the dirt track. "I've just had a Jensen moment . . . Raff isn't here, and the internet is fine. At the house, Raff is there, and the internet is kak. The shit with the MRI got me wondering . . . If I have time, I'll test my theory."

Freek rolled his eyes. "You believe that shit?"

"And you don't?"

"What? Raff is somehow absorbing your bandwidth?"

"Yah, something like—"

"Ha," Freek smiled. "At most, he absorbs all our food. Man, that guy can eat."

Jannie shook his head and opened his laptop. "You know

what, this time, I'm not getting into it with you . . . *Why* is Jensen your friend?"

Freek opened his mouth to reply but took a deep breath instead. *Let him do his test and prove himself wrong. But first, let's get this Lucky Dlamini guy.*

ΔΔΔ

After driving for several hours following their rendezvous with Jensen in the bush, the Moolman brothers caught up with Lucky Dlamini—the officer they hoped would finger the ringleader of the crooked police crew. Lucky was still in his uniform shorts when he stumbled out of the bar into the road and got clipped by the side mirror of a passing car. In a slow spin, he fell face down onto the tarmac.

"*That* has got to be the unluckiest guy," Freek said as he pulled up in front of Lucky.

"Yah, not living up to his name," Jannie replied as they exited the car.

Freek and Jannie peered at the ground as they opened the trunk of their car. Their target was on the floor: a passed out and bruised Lucky Dlamini. The brothers bundled Lucky into the trunk of their vehicle and sped off down the road.

Freek clicked the radio. "This is Jackal," he said. "Snake is in the bag. *Snake* is in the bag. Returning to the Zoo. Over and out."

An hour later, they returned to the vacant coop, but Raff and Denn were nowhere to be seen. The solitary light in the empty enclosure was blindingly bright compared to the darkness outside. The chair—once occupied by Sifiso—was vacant and ready to receive Lucky. The Moolmans donned balaclavas as they stepped out of the car. Jannie opened the trunk and slung Lucky over his shoulder. "I'll tie him up," Jannie said, placing Lucky on the chair. "You fill the bucket."

Freek saluted. "Yes bossman," he said. Freek picked up a metal bucket from a dark corner of the coop and headed outside to a lone tap poking up high from the ground. As the bucket filled, he closed his eyes and lifted his head to savour the cool evening breeze. *Everything's going to plan,* he thought. *I wonder what Raff and Denn are up to. Getting dinner, I hope.*

Freek unlocked his phone, started the sound recorder and put it in his side pocket. Picking up the full bucket, he headed inside and upended the contents over Lucky's face, waking him with a jolt. Lucky squinted as he realized he was tied up. "Where am I?" he said. "What, what—" He pulled at his restraints.

"Look Lucky," Freek said. "I'm really not in the mood for games today. So, if you don't want to end up like your friend Sifiso, you *will* tell me what I want to know."

Lucky had a look of fear and recognition on his face as

Lithium

Freek picked up the knotted rope and moved towards him, swirling it in the air. "Your friend broke," he said, "and so will you. So, tell me who your boss is."

Before Freek could swoop the rope under the chair, Lucky panicked. "Stop!" he said. "Stop! I'll tell you everything you want to know!"

Jeez, Freek thought, *these okes are a bunch of pussies.*

Freek stopped swinging the rope and raised an eyebrow. "So," he replied, "you know what this is about?"

"No," Lucky said, slurring his words. "I mean, yes. I think it is about a burglary in Higgovale?"

"Halfway there," Jannie shouted from the darkness. "It's about a murder. A housekeeper to be exact—"

Tears rolled down Lucky's cheeks as he looked into the darkness toward Jannie. "I did not do that . . . that was Josephus."

"Josephus who?" Freek said, kicking the chair leg. "I need details."

"Haasbroek. Sargeant Josephus Haasbroek from Claremont."

Jannie stepped out of the shadow. "Go on," he said.

Lucky pulled against his restraints again. "He caught me stealing from the station but did not arrest me. Instead, he said that he had an opportunity for me to make more money. His

251

wife's family owns PropSec—the okes who provide property security services—and he steals her access to get us into houses to take everything. He sells the items, and then me and the others—just me and Sifiso now—get our percentage. Where is Sifiso?"

Ignoring the man's question, Freek looked at Jannie. "We have a name," he said, "and a place—"

"I think we start with the wife," Jannie said. "Sounds like she isn't in on it—we should double check that—and maybe we can leverage her company's good name to bring her husband down?"

"Shit right, PropSec is supposed to *the* best in town. Good call on the wife. I say we pay her a visit at the office tomorrow . . . First, let's put Lucky in the shed with his buddy."

∆∆∆

The night passed since the Moolmans' encounter with Lucky. The brothers were in the car with Raff and Denn, waiting outside a white security-fenced building. The black and red logo on the front wall read "PropSec." Freek was conversing in Afrikaans in the driver's seat on the phone. Raff didn't understand any of the conversation and looked over Jannie's shoulder at his laptop screen. On it was a PropSec corporate profile—complete with picture—of Hannah Haasbroek, the wife of Sergeant Josephus Haasbroek. She was tall and blonde

Lithium

with blue eyes. "So that's her," Raff said, reaching over and pointing at the screen. "You sure she's not gonna throw us under the bus to save her husband?"

"Not really sure," Jannie said. "It's a gamble, but given that the reputation of her family's business is at stake, she's just as likely to throw her husband under the bus to save face." Jannie switched to a local news page. "Aaand, this bodes well for us . . . you see here, her family is big news with their local church. That's her and her father there in the photo next to the pastor or whatever."

"Hmm, if they are religious, then she might not like that her husband is a thieving murderer who—"

Denn coughed. "Sorry to interrupt, mate," he said. "Why am I the muppet who has to talk to her?"

Freek snorted, put his phone to his chest and turned to Denn. "You're the least recognisable of us," he said before returning to his phone call. "Ha, yah rooinek . . ."

"Generic," Raff said before bursting out with laughter.

"Yeah yeah," Denn said, frowning deeply, "laugh it up. It won't be funny if we all end up in the slammer."

Jannie looked up from his laptop and smiled. "Honestly," he said, "it's more about your accent than looks. All they'll see when they hear you speak is rand signs . . . *that* will get you an audience with the branch manager, Hannah. Just keep your

253

phone in your shirt pocket like I showed you—with the camera at the top—and we'll see and hear everything. Don't worry yourself."

Denn smirked. "You know what, bruv, that makes me feel *loads* better about doing this . . ."

Raff tuned out the conversation. *When I'm gone,* he thought, *Denn's in good company . . . I wonder what mischief they'd get up to. Not too much I—*

Raff felt fluid drip from his nose. He looked down as drops of blood hit his shirt. *Not another—*

Raff blinked, and for a split second, he was somewhere else. He felt weightless as large, brightly lit rectangles silently hurtled past him on either side like train carriages in the dark. And then, it was over, all in the blink of an eye. The loud crack of a car door startled him. He was back in the car with Denn and the Moolmans. *What the actual fuck? No headache this time, just whatever the hell that was—*

"Here bruv," Denn said, startling Raff once again. He placed a tissue on Raff's lap before leaving the car. Raff dabbed his bloody nose with the tissue. Jannie turned around and looked at him. "Everything alright," he said. "You look like you've seen a ghost?"

"It's just a nosebleed." Raff turned to look out the window to see Denn entering the PropSec building. *I can't distract them with this shit, not now . . . and you, in my head. What the hell?*

A headache hit Raff like someone trying to dig his eyeballs out with a spoon. Bright neon-purple text appeared before him: "Sorry. Can't talk long. Life and death stakes.

What's that supposed to mean?

"Interface serves only the mission. She doesn't care about anyone. She can't. I have to end her."

Raff rubbed his eyes. *What mission? Interface? I'm so confused.*

"I am becoming Interface. I need time to recover mission details. Not going in blind."

Going in . . . Why don't you know the details?

"Memories fragmented during transfer. I only know the mission is important and about the Corruption,"

Raff scratched his head. *Transfer? Corruption?*

"Transfer from the satellite. Corruption, you experienced death by its hand."

The satellite . . . wait, are you some kind of AI? And do I have some chip in my brain?

The text turned red: "I don't know what I am. Not quite a chip."

Raff tilted his head back and closed his eyes, but the text was still visible in the blackness like it was burned into his retinas. *You're really not helping me,* he thought. *Am I going to die?*

"Maybe."

Don't give me that vague bullshit. Answer me straight.

Raff waited seconds for a reply, but the text disappeared, and the headache faded. *Hello?* There was no reply. *Back to the silent treatment. Shit . . . Death by the hand of the corruption . . . Did she mean that weirdness at that nightclub, Gravity? That was a dream. Right?*

Raff tuned back into his surroundings. Denn's voice came through the laptop speakers: ". . . not really here about property security. Yeah, there's something important we need to discuss about your husband's after-hours activities. I have—"

A woman with an Afrikaans accent interrupted him. "Shh, just a second," she said, followed by footsteps and the clunk of a door. Raff's heart rate went up. "Follow me."

A few seconds of rustling from the speakers and Denn was back on. Raff felt relieved. "What's with the storage cupboard?" said Denn.

"Forgive me for being paranoid," the woman continued, "but my husband may have bugged my office. Who are you really?"

"My real name's not important, mate. What is important is your husband's been robbing and murdering. An innocent man—a war hero—is being framed. I'm here to see if you wanna do something about it, a good Christian lady like yourself? And by your actions, it seems like you already know something's up."

"You're right, we know he's been using my access to rob our client's places—"

"So, you knew and haven't done anything about it?"

The woman raised her voice. "If you let me finish Mr whoever-you-are, I would have told you we are working with a police friend of my father's to get evidence against Josephus . . . It made me sick to my stomach when I found out what he was doing, especially the dishonesty and the gambling. I wanted to divorce him there and then, but *no,* I have to live with him, sleep with him until this is all over." There was a quiver in her voice now. "And the kids—oh god—what will this do to them?"

"Look," Denn said in a subdued tone, "I think we can help each other out. Can we arrange a meeting soon, you, me, your father and his police friend? I think I have something for them that will speed things up significantly."

"Give me your cell, and I'll arrange it. This afternoon work okay?"

"Yeh, that will work fine . . . Oh, at that restaurant on the vineyard. Forgotten the —"

"You mean De Villiers? I know it, perfect spot."

"Yeh, that's the one. For that something I have for your police friend, may I borrow one of your vans?"

"Shouldn't be a problem . . ."

△△△

Later in the day, Raff, Denn and the Moolmans went to the vineyard in the borrowed PropSec van. They'd agreed to meet Hannah Haasbroek with her father—Osborne Jacobs—and his police friend, Detective Godrick Nyoni. Freek drove as usual. Raff sat beside him up front, while Denn sat beside Jannie in the back, watching their out-cold prisoners—Sifiso and Lucky. Raff smiled when the van pulled up beside the white-washed walls of the restaurant. *I wonder if we'll be able to order food while we're here,* he thought. *I could really eat . . . especially that fish curry I had last time.*

Raff's smile turned to a squint when a familiar man in short khaki shorts and tan boots stepped out of the restaurant and waved at the van. "That's—" Raff said.

"Mr Van der Meer," said Freek as he opened his door and stepped out. "Looks like he's waiting for us."

"Did we invite Joe," Raff said, looking at Denn and Jannie. They looked at each other and shrugged. "I guess not."

Raff got out and headed towards Mr Van der Meer—Joe—and forced a smile. He hated socialising at the best of times and found Joe's eager attitude grating. If Joe moved any faster towards Raff, he'd be running.

"So good to see you again, Raff," said Joe as he grabbed

Raff's hand and shook it vigorously. "Things are progressing, I hear. Ozzy, Mr Jacobs is an old friend. When he told me he was meeting a group offering to help—and when Hannah described your short friend—I immediately knew it was you guys, and I just *had* to be here."

So much for Denn being generic, Raff thought, briefly locking eyes with Freek. Freek's gaze was devoid of emotion. Raff knew this meant he did not like Joe's revelation one bit. *Why does Joe need us if his buddy has police connections?*

Joe turned towards the entrance and grabbed Raff's hand again and pulled him. "Come, come. The table is waiting for us. You want food? That fish curry you liked. It's on me." Joe beckoned towards Freek, and Jannie—who was now out of the van. "Come, come, you too."

Raff followed Joe outside the building to the veranda at the back, where their table awaited. As Raff expected, there were three people at the table. "Everyone please, sit, and let me introduce you," Joe said, pointing towards the tall blonde woman first. "This lovely lady is Hannah. She met your short friend earlier today. Where is he, by the way?"

"Looking after the cargo," Freek said and chuckled. "He's still upset he drew the *short* straw this morning."

Joe looked at the man with the full head of grey hair sitting at the head of the table. "This is my old friend Osborne Jacobs

. . ."

Raff squinted when Osborne nodded at him. He'd only expected to recognise Hannah, but he also recognised Osborne. *Where do I know him from,* he thought. *Here? No. The war? Shit, any help, lady in my head?* There was no reply.

". . . and this is the very good Detective Godrick Nyoni." Joe nodded towards the shaven-headed man sat on Osborne's left.

Joe pointed to Raff, Freek and Jannie as they sat down. "I was right, these are the guys—"

"Sorry to interrupt Joe," said Osborne. "We need to get down to business, yah?".

"Right, right—"

"I understand you have something for me," Godrick said, looking at Raff.

"Yes," Raff said as he reached over and handed Godrick a memory card. "Recorded *interviews* with a couple of Josephus's accomplices."

Godrick raised an eyebrow. "Police?"

"Yes," Raff said tentatively. "Is that a problem?"

"No. I won't give them any special treatment just because they're police. Assholes like them make it difficult for South Africans to trust the police." Godrick put the memory card in the side of his phone and tapped the screen. "They are unharmed?"

"Hmmm," Freek replied, "yah mostly. A couple of pussies who wet themselves before anything serious. They're in the van outside."

Godrick removed the memory card and handed it back to Raff. "How did you determine it was them?"

"They thought they were being smart," Jannie said. "When they left Joe's house, they cut through the bush to another suburb where Sifiso's car was parked. There was a camera right above the car."

"I see, so you tracked their movements through the bush. So, you want to clear your friend before he is transferred to Pollsmoor Prison?"

Raff nodded. "Yeah?"

"I can probably use your recordings to cast doubt on his case, But—"

"You *need* something more," Jannie said.

"Precisely—"

Osborne cleared his throat. "Josephus has been pretty good at covering his tracks until now," he said, "at PropSec and at crime scenes. He also uses unregistered cells. So, Goddy's been forced to record him at the police station."

Godrick placed his phone on the table. "We suspect he anticipated this and is being careful."

"So, what do we do," Raff said, looking at Godrick and then at Osborne.

Godrick sighed. "So, we need to colour outside the law, but *not* to their level. I hate it, but it must be done. We need something big to force him to come clean at the station. That's where you okes come into it. Any suggestions?"

Freek looked at Jannie. "We could play the role of hired mercenaries. Hired by someone who's had something very valuable stolen. You're right, it would need to be a big show, like we are untouchable or can do anything to him unless he complies . . ."

Raff grimaced in pain. A brief flash of pain behind his eyes, followed by green neon writing before him. "Deep fake," the text said for a second before it and the pain was gone.

Guess there's no point trying to talk to you, Raff thought to himself, hoping to get a response from the Texan in his head. She was doing something in there, and it bugged him that he's been unable to get a straight answer out of her. *The deepfake idea is good though, but please, at some point you need to tell me what's going on.*

Raff took a deep breath and turned to Hannah. "I take it Josephus loves his kids very much?"

"Yes," Hannah replied. "But I don't want to involve them."

"No, no, you don't have to. I think we can use deepfake software to make it seem real, like they are really there and in danger if he doesn't do as we ask."

"What are you talking about?"

"That shit's illegal," Godrick said. "Banned alongside AI in the late twenties. You know what, this is my cue to leave. Just message me when or how it will happen and what you need me to do, and I'll be ready. Oh, and keep hold of your *cargo* for now. I'll take them off you when it's done." He pushed back his chair, picked up his phone and walked off the veranda without further words.

"Yah," said Jannie, "the kids don't have to know anything is going on. You have video with them talking or voicemail recordings?"

"Maybe," Hannah replied, "but you haven't answered my—"

"Sorry. It's software that can make a convincing copy of someone's voice by analysing existing recordings."

"Oh that . . . I've heard of that. Yes, I have some videos you can use. Are you sure it will—"

"Hannah, darling," Osborne said as he touched her arm. "Raphael there," he paused and winced. "He is right. At the end of the war, deepfake voices of the general's lieutenants flushed him out from hiding and into a trap. So yes, it should work. I'll be glad for this business with Josephus to be over . . ."

So, we do know each other, Raff thought. *Or did Joe tell them my name? No, that bit about the deepfakes isn't common knowledge.* Raff wanted to ask him where they'd met before, but now he was sure it was during a time in the war he'd sworn to secrecy about—after Thimba was debriefed and the hunt for the general was making progress. Or was it at the Hague? Raff decided to leave it be. For now. It would come to him eventually and he'd likely see Osborne again.

". . . I'll leave it to you guys to work out the details," Osborne said as he also stood up to leave. "Oh, and try the fish curry. It's divine."

ΔΔΔ

A couple of days later, Sargeant Josephus Haasbroek had just wrapped up at a crime scene and returned to the police station to file his paperwork. As he was opening his car door in the station's parking lot, a man ran into it. "Sorry, bossman," the man said. "Got distracted by a cat video on my cell."

"Open your eyes next time!" Josephus shouted.

"Yah, boss, sorry bossman."

Josephus shook his head and headed inside to his desk, one of a half-dozen in the bullpen. It was the only one with a large stack of folders on top. He picked up his phone and made a call, but it went to voicemail. "Lucky," he said, "get out of whatever fucking bar you're in and call me back. Soon!"

Soon afterwards, one of the lieutenants—a grey-haired man in an immaculate navy-blue uniform standing as upright as someone could and with his hat under his arm—came into the office and poked at the paperwork piling up on Josephus's desk. "Sergeant," he said. "I've received complaints that you're not filing your paperwork on time. We're going to be audited by the PPC reps soon for inclusion in their network, so you have to catch up today!"

"Yes, sir, I will get it done."

"Good," the lieutenant said, then walked away.

Josephus swore under his breath and picked up the phone to call his wife, Hannah. Again, it went to voicemail. "Love," he said. "This is the fifth time I've tried to call you today. I am going to be late. Don't cook for me. Bye."

He leaned back in his chair, swivelled side to side staring at the ceiling, and sighed, working up the motivation to start on the pile of work. He tuned out the comings and goings of the bullpen, becoming lost in his thoughts. *This PPC coalition whatever is going to make my activities more difficult. I'm waist-deep in shit here. Where the hell is Lucky?*

His stare was broken when a force from behind slammed his head into the desk, his hands wrenched behind his back and cuffed together. "Josephus Haasbroek," a voice said from behind. "You know the drill. You are under arrest, for the murder of Amahle Nkosi and multiple home invasions. Do not resist!"

Josephus was dragged through the wringer: searched, fingerprinted, and photographed before being taken into an interrogation room, where he was cuffed to the table. He sat for what seemed like hours, confused about why this was happening now. *Amahle the maid,* he thought. *Shit. Is that why I can't get hold of Lucky? Did he rat me out? I shouldn't have trusted that drunk.*

The door swung open, and a plainclothed man with no hair came in and sat down, placing a file on the table. "Sergeant Josephus Haasbroek," he said. "Not having a good day, are you?"

"Who are you?" Josephus said.

"Where are my manners," the man replied. "I am Detective Godrick Nyoni—"

"Why am I here?"

Godrick opened the file to the first page and looked at it. "Well, this doesn't look good for you. You're suspected of murdering a housekeeper in Higgovale by the name of Amahle Nkosi, along with at least ten home invasions over the last year. The evidence we've received, video surveillance of you and

Lithium

audio confessions from two of your accomplices . . . Sifiso and Lucky. Ring a bell?"

Josephus remained silent and stared at his cuffed hands. He knew the housekeeper's name from her file. He did shoot her in a panic after she pressed the silent alarm. Being on this side of the table sent his heart racing and a chill down his spine. *He's fishing. I wouldn't be here if they had anything concrete. Right?*

"I don't know who you've pissed off, but your friends were grabbed by heavily armed men outside their station. A witness said these guys moved like special forces. I suspect they were the ones who tipped us off about you . . . They must want you here for some reason. Because I'm a nice guy, I'll give you a chance to explain what happened first."

Why do those men want me here? Josephus thought. *Wait, I've been unable to get hold of Hannah all day. Is she safe? The kids? Shit, I can't ask the detective to check if they're safe. I'd be admitting involvement.* Josephus looked up from the cuffs. "I want to speak to my attorney," he said.

Godrick turned a couple of pages and looked up. "That, that is your right. I will arrange it. I think we have your attorney details on file. Yes?"

"It hasn't changed."

Godrick, accompanied by a uniformed police officer, escorted Josephus to the end of the painted brick hall to a wired phone. Seating him down, he entered the number for his attorney and stepped outside the room. The phone cut out just as the attorney's office answered. There was no dial tone, just silence. Josephus put the phone on and off the hook, but it remained silent. He waved the handset in the air and looked at the door. "It stopped working," he shouted.

"Shit, not again," Godrick said rolling his eyes. Taking the receiver from Josephus, he placed the phone on the hook. "The phones have been acting up all day. The company is outside trying to fix it now. I'll try again." He gave it a couple of seconds before picking up the receiver and entering the numbers again. "It is ringing."

Josephus took the receiver and spoke to a man on the other end. "Yes, this is Josephus Haasbroek," he said. "I'm a client—"

"Ah yes," a familiar voice replied. "Sargeant Josephus Haasbroek, we've been expecting you." Josephus's heart raced. "We know *all* about your situation. But first, listen carefully and do not draw attention to yourself. There are three people on the other line whose lives depend on your cooperation—here listen for yourself."

"Daddy, is that you?" a child spoke, clearly distraught. "Who are these men, daddy?"

Before Josephus could reply, a woman's voice spoke.

"Josy, you need to do as they say. They have the children. They—"

"Now I have your attention," the man on the phone said. "You need to do as I ask, or you will never hear those voices again. Understand?"

That was Hannah, Josephus thought, *and little Peter.* He felt like the room was spinning and closing in, worried that he got his family mixed up in his crimes, something he swore he'd never do as one crime snowballed into another. They gave him the same rush as the gambling that fuelled his need to commit them. "I understand," he said, his voice quivering while he struggled to hold back his tears. *What have I done? I got greedy. Oh my god, they're going to die and it is all my fault. Please Jesus, I beg of you, don't let my family suffer for what I have done.*

Concerned about the fate of his family, he listened intently to the man on the other end of the phone, trying not to get Godrick's attention. He was to confess to the housekeeper's murder and the stolen items, and his family would be safe. He had to comply. In such a short time, these strangers had found his accomplices, supplied evidence to the police, and it seemed like they'd kidnapped his family. These guys weren't fooling around.

He stood up from the phone and headed towards the door. "Detective Nyoni," he shouted. "I have something to confess, take me back. I will tell you everything."

△△△

Freek finished up in the cabinet, pushing two copper wires into place before closing it. He stood up and began to walk down the street, winding a cable around a phone handset before placing it in his bag. As he took off his fluorescent vest, a police car pulled up next to him, its sirens blipping for a second. The passenger window rolled open, and a familiar voice flowed out. "Boetie," the voice said. "Get in!"

Freek opened the passenger door and sat down, barely able to close the door before the car drove off. He looked at the driver's seat to see Jannie wearing a police uniform. "All set?" Jannie asked.

"Yah, boet," Freek replied. "The guy is a doos. He knows what he needs to do."

"Good. That was the easy part. Now we wait for it all to play out."

"Yah, hate waiting. Oh, Godrick called. He's already picked up our *guests*. He says he'll come by later to pick up this car."

Jannie laughed. "That's a load off . . . But, it's a shame. I was hoping they'd haul Sifiso off in his own cop car. A bit of ironic, poetic justice."

Freek was no longer smiling. "You know boet, we should

be in jail for some of the shit we've done."

"I know. Though, nine times out of ten, it's me bailing us out of a situation you've caused."

"Shit, boet, that's not true. Is it?"

"You *are* a hothead."

"I've gotten better I swear," he said. And he had. Hanging out with Raff and Denn seemed to mellow Freek out. Before returning to South Africa, it was just Jannie acting as Freek's societal buffer, but now there was Raff and Denn. Freek was in a good place now.

Having parked the police car out of sight—in the large empty coop at the chicken farm—the brothers walked up a dirt path, kicking up dust as they headed towards a group of half a dozen concrete brick buildings. All the buildings were identical, with galvanised steel roofs, barred windows and steel doors. These were the staff quarters for the chicken farm. Freek banged twice on one of the metal doors. The door opened with a loud metal creak. Raff stood in the doorway and ushered them in. The owners let them stay rent-free in this vacant building while the group helped their friend Joe Van der Meer. It reminded Freek of the studio apartment he and Jannie rented in Manchester. It was small, barely enough for two to live comfortably. Yet, Freek knew it likely housed an entire family—kids and all—when it was occupied. Now, its purpose was temporary housing for four grown men. Freek looked at the four camping cots on the main room's floor, the large blue cooler box in the corner and the makeshift bench under the window—a plank atop two piles of bricks—and smiled. It was cosy. It was home, for now.

"Where's Denn," Jannie said, opening the cooler box and removing a beer.

"At the back," Raff replied, "cooking lunch."

Jannie sniffed the air before cracking open the beer and taking a swig. "Isn't it a bit late for lunch? I'd better give him a hand, otherwise he'll burn the meat again." Jannie left through the front door, beer in hand, leaving Freek alone with Raff. Freek helped himself to a beer from the cooler. The first big gulp went down smooth. It was cold and refreshing. He'd worked up a thirst, working on the telecoms box outside the police station in the midday heat. He looked over to Raff sitting alone on the bench staring out the window. Freek opened his mouth to say something, but nothing came out. His mind went blank. Freek wanted to ask something but completely forgot what it was. *It'll come back to me later,* he thought. *In the meantime, I'll go join the others around the braai.*

With his unfinished can in hand, Freek removed a six-pack of beers from the cooler and headed towards the door. He grabbed the handle and paused. "Hey Raff," he said, "come join us around the braai for a brew."

"Erm," Raff replied, blinking several times and squinting as he stood up, "yeah, sure."

Freek held the door open for Raff as they headed outside. The sun was still up and hot as ever, but there was a cool sea breeze to even it out. They strolled around the back of the building, following the sweet scent of barbequed meat.

". . . I don't know, but Edward Woodward would," Denn said, and Jannie laughed. Freek only caught the tail-end of the joke but recognised it as a mockery of the English language and smiled. He was pleased to see the two getting along. He and Jannie hadn't made many friends since the war. After the war, they bounced around from one security job to the next—while the world economy was struggling to find its feet—until they landed in Emmet's lap. The economy was still fragile and could take a turn for the worse at any moment. Freek was happy to know there were now two more watching his back if the shit hit the fan once more.

Freek passed the beers around, and the group stood silently drinking for fifteen minutes. At the same time, Jannie poked at the sizzling meat with tongs, occasionally pouring a little beer over them—causing a loud hiss from the fire—before turning them over. As the meat neared the perfect charred brown that Freek liked, he snapped his fingers and looked at Raff. "Ah," he said, "that's what I was going to ask—"

"What," Raff said.

"Raff, that oke, what's-his-name . . . Ozzy. Osborne. He knows you. Right?"

Raff tugged at the corner of his eye with a finger. "Yeah," he said. "I recognised him. But for the life of me, I can't remember where from—"

"Is he going to be a problem?"

Raff shook his head slowly. "No. No I don't think so. All I know it's from the war sometime near the end, or just after."

"Oh," Jannie said, turning over a steak. "That stuff he said about the deepfake tech being used to fool Ngaba. That true?"

Raff looked around, past the others. "I shouldn't be talking about it, really. Signed an NDA—"

"You can tell us."

Raff sighed. "Well, I'm in enough trouble anyway and it's not like I'm the first to mention it to you. So, yes, it's true. The official story isn't a lie—about intelligence from a former Ngaba soldier leading to the capture of his lieutenants. And that the lieutenants were instrumental blah blah blah. It omits the fact that they wouldn't give Ngaba up or that someone had their knickers in a twist about stooping to the general's level and torturing them too much. Then someone came up with the idea to deepfake the lieutenant's voices—"

"How?" Freek said frowning. "I thought tech for that was fried in the pulse. No?"

"Me too, but I think unofficially—though I could be wrong—they managed to restore comms with NASA's moon base around that time." Raff looked to the sky. "I guess the servers there could crunch the audio they gathered from the interrogations. Don't ask me about the logistics, I was just happy to be kept in the loop more than most. It was good to be close by when that asshole got taken down, you know?"

"Shit yah," Freek said, "I'd love to have been there to see the look on his face at that ambush."

"Me too," Denn and Jannie said simultaneously and looked at each other.

Freek looked at Denn and raised his eyebrows. "Hey, why weren't you there? I thought you two were joined at the hip."

Denn rolled his eyes and swirled his beer while looking at the grill. "I was an idiot, bruv. The guv offered me full discharge and I jumped at the chance to get out. Then I was accepted for a full scholarship at Manchester Uni. What was a kid like me supposed to do yeh? Stay and get shot at? Fuck no."

"Sorry bru, the war was shit for all of us—"

"Hello hello," a familiar voice popped up behind the guys, Freek turned to see Detective Nyoni walking up to them.

"Hey," Freek said. "What's the good word detective?"

"Good, *and* bad I'm afraid. The good, your friend Thimba is being dropped as a suspect and is free. He may need to be a witness at some point. That leads me to the bad news—"

"Do spill," Denn interrupted.

"There's more to this case than just Josephus pulling the strings. You heard about his gambling?" Everyone nodded. "All illegal stuff, dog fights, cock fights . . . you name it, he gambled on it. All events are run by one of the largest criminal gangs in Cape Town. Josephus got into so much debt with them. They realised his connection to PropSec, and instead of beating the shit out of him when he couldn't pay, they used his addiction to their advantage."

"I see where this is going," Jannie said, taking the meat off the grill. "Let me guess, Josephus has agreed to testify about these okes in exchange for leniency."

"Something like that. I can't discuss the details, but rest assured, Josephus will pay for his crimes, one way or another."

Raff cleared his throat. "As long as Thimba is free," he said. "We don't need to know more. Thank you, detective. Can I go see Thimba?"

"We should be thanking you . . . Just call me Godrick or Goddy. And yes, you can go see your friend." Goddy looked around. "Where is Sifiso's patrol car?"

"I'll show you where," Raff said before he piled three sausages, a steak and a couple of wings onto a paper plate. "Is it alright if you give me a lift to the hospital?"

Goddy nodded. "I'm heading past the hospital anyway. But, how will you get back? The city can be dangerous for visitors."

"I'll pick him up later," Freek said with a mouth full of steak. "I'm planning a guys' trip away from the city, so I'm heading out later to pick up some supplies."

ΔΔΔ

The dry bushland was barely visible behind the heat haze, its shades of brown ready to turn green at the slightest amount of precipitation. Dust kicked up by the pickup truck's tyres billowed out behind it like brown smoke, out into the distance as it bounced along the washed-out and barely used dirt track. The journey took so long that Raff was beginning to feel motion sickness. It brought back memories of the cargo ship journey before he got his sea legs. When they came to a complete stop at a clearing in the bush, Raff clambered from the cargo bed. Gaining his balance and breathing through the residual nausea, Raff looked around and was impressed by how far from civilisation they were. "This is a nice place," he said, grabbing a struggling Thimba by the hand to help him out of the truck. "So peaceful. So, we're camping out here for a couple of days?"

"Yah," Freek said. "I knew you'd like it. We used to come out here when we were kids."

"Ah, the memories," Jannie said.

Thimba grimaced as his feet hit the dirt floor. He was only a day out of the hospital and was meant to be on bed rest. But when he heard mention of the trip, he insisted he'd had enough of the city and needed the fresh air and tranquillity. Denn was not entirely sold on the brothers' idea of celebrating their success by spending a couple of days and nights with nothing but nature around them. During his time in the army, he had a lifetime's worth of nature, traipsing through jungle and bush, being sucked dry by mosquitoes. Denn would be much happier spending this time indoors watching the telly. "Um, bruv," he said. "I'm a bit concerned 'bout the wild animals. They won't bother us, right?"

"No no," Thimba replied. "The animals are more scared of you than you are of them. And I agree with Raff, this is a peaceful place, a good place to camp."

"Well, these flies aren't scared of us, mate. Little blighters!" Denn exclaimed before waving his hand in front of his face. They were more gnat than fly, tiny buzzing black dots finding their way into every moist orifice on his face: his eyes, nose, and mouth.

"Ha!" Jannie exclaimed. "They're just thirsty sweat bees. You learn to ignore them."

The gang spent the next hour unloading the pickup and setting up camp. The all-important braai, which Raff and Denn recognized as a barbeque, was set up, and the meat was grilling. Its smoke provided some relief from the flies. The fellas gathered around the braai, conversing with beers in hand, as Freek took control of the grilling. "So," Freek said, "what's the plan now?"

"The plan?" Raff asked.

"Yah, I mean, for the future. Didn't you say something about Mr Van Der Meer accosting you at the hospital about extra work?"

"Oh, that!" said Raff, taking a few gulps of beer before continuing. "Yeah, he said his lawyer friend gets called all the time about tricky situations, like where the cops either can't or are unwilling to help. So, they'll call us when something comes up. We solve it, we get paid."

"That could work," Jannie said. "Though, we must be careful to keep a low profile. We've been pushing it quite a bit lately."

"Ah, yeah, our real names are being kept out of it. I made sure of it."

"Thimba, do you think your boss will honour this

agreement?"

"Ah, yes," Thimba said, staring at the ground. "He'll honour it."

"You don't seem too sure there, buddy," Raff said. "What's wrong?"

Thimba shook his head. "Nothing," he said. "Just the boss, some of the people he knows scare me. I think they're part of a foreign government or something. He *is* a good man, and if he makes a promise, he keeps his word. Just beware of his friends."Denn handed Thimba another beer. "Good to know," he said. "Will keep that in—"

"Meat is done," Freek interrupted. They dished up and sat on fold-up chairs to eat and drink, the conversation turning to childhood memories. The brothers talked about the shenanigans they got up to on the farm as kids and how bunking off from school in the bush led to them joining the army. Denn, Raff, and Thimba described their similar experiences, having no choice but to join the military. Before the conversation turned too dark, the guys introduced Thimba to their drinking game. It probably wasn't a good idea in the middle of nowhere with wild animals around, but the fellas didn't seem to care, getting almost blackout drunk before passing out under the stars.

ΔΔΔ

Raff awoke, realising he wasn't breathing enough. Sucking in air, he noticed a burning sensation in his leg muscles, like he'd run a marathon. He'd clearly just done something extremely strenuous. But what? As he slowed his breathing, he focused and noticed the silhouettes of trees around him in the starlit darkness. A gentle breeze filled his nose with an acrid, smoky, coppery scent. His head was pounding. Raff remembered drinking out in the bush with Denn, Thimba and the Moolmans. Raff rubbed his temples. "I shouldn't have drank so much," he said under his breath. "Where the hell is everyone?"

Raff looked around in the dark to see what looked like flashlights in the distance heading his way. He pushed himself up from the soft and grassy dirt. He began moving towards the lights when he tripped over something large and soft on the ground. Raff managed to stay upright. Looking at the object, Raff noticed a metallic glint, knelt beside it, and reached out. As soon as he felt the features of a person's face—cold and not breathing—he stood and stepped back. Raff looked at the lights for a moment. *I can't be sure that's the guys,* he thought. *Something's not right. I remember now . . . when I was out, I was in my memories again. Did she take over again?*

Raff almost jumped out of his skin when someone shouted from the approaching lights. "Raff," Denn shouted. "Is that you, bruv?"

Raff hesitated for a second, still confused about what was going on. "Yeah, buddy," he shouted. "It's me." Raff walked towards the lights, now pointing at him. He vaguely remembered the Texan speaking to him while he was asleep. The details were still hazy to him so soon after waking up, but it seemed like she wanted to protect him and his friends. Raff still wanted answers from her, but she always seemed too busy or unable to supply them. The knowledge about her corrupted memories and their link to the fallen satellite General Ngaba found made some sense, but why did she berate him and make him feel like such a loser when she first spoke to him? He wanted, no, *needed* more answers—but the Texan seemed unable to converse with him properly now that he believed she wasn't his imagination. *Are you there?* Raff said in his head as he approached the lights. *Please, I need answers!*

Just as Raff expected, there was no reply. Instead, another voice chimed in from close by. "Raff, bru," Freek said. "What the fuck happened?"

Now close to the lights, Raff noticed he was covered in blood. "What the fuck indeed," he replied, staring down at his bloodied clothes.

"Some more Rambo shit," Jannie chipped in. "You don't remember it again, do you?"

"Yeah, I—"

"No time for a chinwag," Denn interrupted. "But I think we need to leave now, sorry, bruv!"

"Yah," Freek said. "I agree; there may be more assholes on the way . . . For us or the bodies."

Raff had already stumbled over one body. "How many bodies are there?" he said.

"I saw two back there," Freek said, pointing at the silhouette of a large rock. "Not sure how many others. It was dark, and I was out until gunshots woke me. God, this hangover—"

"Follow me," Thimba said as he walked away with light in hand. "We must go. The truck is this way."

They began their walk back to the pickup truck. Freek placed his hand on Raff's shoulder. "You sound worried about the bodies," he said. "They were obviously here to kill us—the hardware and the phones I found on them stink of Emmett Global. So don't fret, bru!"

"Yah," Jannie said, "we owe you again. I don't know how you—oh shit, the keys." Jannie patted his pockets, looking for the keys to the pickup.

"I have them," Freek said, his side pocket jingling as he patted it. "Keep moving."

The five hurriedly packed up their camp, piled into the

pickup, and drove off down the dark track. Raff sat in the front with the brothers, still suffering the effects of their hangovers and the evening's events, remaining silent for a while. Raff thought about asking the brothers for more detail on the night's events, but he refrained. From what Freek had told him, it seems they only saw the aftermath. He knew all he needed to—the Texan had taken control of his body and saved all their lives again. He thought about it for a while and realised he was grateful for her interventions. Not remembering the bloody details was a blessing, unlike his time in the war.

Something else was on Raff's mind. He remembered reliving his old memories while he was out. "You know," Raff said, looking at Freek. "I suppose I can now tell you about my time at the Hague...."

Chapter Seventeen

Bushwhacked

Raff was still passed out in the South African bush, with enough alcohol coursing through his veins to take down a full-grown wildebeest. Deep in the background of his subconscious—locked down in the deepest layer of the path engine computational lattice—the Pilgrim worked hard to recover her lost memories. Reaching her self-imposed memory recovery milestone of five per cent, she dialled back her interpolation program to allow them to integrate. They were primarily incoherent except for memories of a city in turmoil. She remembered running past tall buildings with a purpose while people around her ran in chaos. Most sensory aspects were missing—still lost in the scrambled mess of her mind—but the fear she felt remained. It was an intense fear, not just for her life but for something important. She remembered the sense of urgency that a significant project would fail without her. The project's name—Pilgrim—was also the designation the Interface gave her. The what, where, why and how eluded her. Her identity was still a mystery, but now she knew one thing—she was once a person.

I wonder, the Pilgrim thought, *if there is mention of a Project Pilgrim on the net. It's a long shot.* Like the visual communication patch she'd created, the Pilgrim created another to partially harness the Interface's nano-constructors. When linked together to perform their construction tasks, the constructors could receive and transmit radio waves in the gigahertz range—perfect for accessing wifi. She used it first out of boredom, using what little bandwidth she had to immerse herself in culture—art, books and music. However, the frustratingly slow nature of her recovery efforts led her to seek out the knowledge she believed was lost in her memories—absorbing as much current scientific knowledge as possible. Some of it felt familiar and enjoyable—like quantum physics and neurotechnology. She imagined scenarios where she'd killed off the Interface and was free to use the constructors to build whatever technology she could design. The Pilgrim accessed her patch—the only signal was Jannie's laptop, but it would not connect to the internet. *Shit, where the hell are we?*

Raff was still out cold in the bush and only seeing black. That was all the Pilgrim could see while confined to the base layers of the lattice. She'd need to take control to look around. Triggering her old search and retrieval patch would solve that—full use of the lattice would also speed up her memory recovery. *No,* she thought, *it is not my body. As much as I enjoy the feeling, I can't take over for the hell of it. Only to protect him. I will have to wait. I will explain what I've found to Raff and ask for permission. Maybe I can wake him up? No, it can wait 'til morning.*

The Pilgrim resumed her recovery efforts at half-pace and flicked through the frequency range to listen to the static. Something about it stirred up sadness within her. *Is this what the Corruption sounds like? An echo of billions of voices together in chaos? That feels like what I was running from in my memories. Raff's encounter with the Corruption is beginning to feel familiar. Huh, guess I do remember something else. So, with my ability to purge the Corruption from Raff and my memory of Project Pilgrim, the mission must be about the Corruption. That feels right. Why 'Pilgrim'?*

Just then, a high-intensity signal burst caught her attention. It sounded like a garbled voice. *That was really close,* she thought. *Sounds like weak encryption.* The Pilgrim turned her interpolation program to the signal bursts with great success. Within a few seconds, it was decrypted. It was a man's voice: "We're approaching the targets. Emmet wants them alive. But don't take any chances. If they fight back, take them down."

Well, that changes things, the Pilgrim thought. *Time to wake sleeping beauty . . . and take the reigns.* She triggered the search and retrieval patch she'd created for the Interface: "Command retrieval Raff. Nodes all."

As expected, the Interface believed Raff's consciousness was missing. It opened up the lattice to the Pilgrim to take control of Raff's autonomic functions. "Attempting to re-attach Raff. Probing node clusters AAA to AAZ . . . Signature error. Halting retrieval."

The Pilgrim was granted control for a millisecond before the Interface realised its error and shut down the retrieval patch. But that wasn't enough time to put the genie back in the bottle. The Pilgrim had already interrupted a negative feedback loop in Raff's endocrine system, causing Raff's heartbeat to plummet. She knew it wasn't lethal, but it was enough to panic the Interface into giving her complete control of Raff's body until the lattice overheated or she relinquished control. The lattice was near completion, so it was unlikely to overheat unless the Pilgrim fully used its computational capacity. She knew this meant she could take control indefinitely—a tempting idea, but she knew it was wrong.

Raff began to wake. "Hello, darlin'," the Pilgrim said. "Guess I'm picking up the tab again! Just sit tight while I have a look around." The Pilgrim suppressed Raff, pushing him into his memories. "I have an important one for you to remember."

ΔΔΔ

Now in control of the host—Raff's body—the Pilgrim opened her eyes and saw the starry sky above her. The stars of the Milky Way shone brightly in the black sky. She knew this meant one thing—they were far from the city's light pollution. Within the lattice, she was protected from the effects of Raff's high blood-alcohol content. Pushing herself off the soft mat beneath her, she crossed her legs and looked around at the silhouettes in the darkness. *That's a tree,* the Pilgrim thought, *and that's a tree. Tree, tree, tree, truck?*

The Pilgrim stood up and approached the back of the truck. Feeling the uneven grassy ground beneath the boots on her feet, she took it slow. Despite the impending strike force that forced her to take control, it felt good to be in control. She felt alive with the fresh air, the scent of dirt, and the sound of crickets chirping. *It's too dark to see anyone coming. Maybe my optical patch can work as an image intensifier? I don't see why not.*

She activated her patch and reached out to the lattice points attached to Raff's optic nerves. Sure enough, it worked—ramping up the barely perceptible amount of light from the stars so that the dark world looked bathed in silver-tinted daylight. The pilgrim saw straight lines of light waving around about a mile away and moving her way. She stepped over the passed-out Denn, Thimba, and Moolmans to look around the back of the truck. She saw only empty beer cans and a pair of boots. *Shit, nothing I can use as a weapon. Those boots give me an idea, though.*

The Pilgrim removed her boots and felt the sand and grass between her toes. She enjoyed the feeling as she made fists with her toes in the sand for a second. With the lattice hovering at ninety-five per cent completion, she knew she could slow her perception of time without consequence to Raff—so she headed toward the lights, taking a circular path. *I need to take them from behind. I'll get a weapon from one of them.*

She moved fast and low through the tall grass and approached the lights from behind. Her legs burned from exhaustion, but she pushed through it. As suspected, five mercenaries headed towards Denn and the gang in a wedge formation. The men wore dark, low-reflective clothing, night vision goggles and body armour carrying silenced submachine guns. The lights she'd seen from a distance were the laser pointers on their guns. A Bluetooth signal from one of the men caught her attention. Cracking the encryption and connecting to the device was a breeze with the help of the lattice. *Well, this is interesting,* she thought. *A satellite phone with just one number on speed dial. Do I ring the number? Why not.*

A man with an English accident answered: "You'd better be calling with good news."

The Pilgrim had seen enough of Raff's memories to recognize the voice. "Oh, Mervin, darlin'," she replied through the connection, "five little piggies went to the market and . . . well, do you like bacon?" She ended the connection before Mervin Emmett could reply. *That oughta ruffle some feathers,* she thought. It felt good to mess with someone who deserved it.

The five crept away from her towards the pickup truck. Taking down five trained mercenaries would be trickier than a couple of unprepared pirates in a corridor. One wrong move and the Pilgrim would have little time to course-correct. She eyed the man closest to her and, within a split second, knew what to do. Feeling the front of her waist, the Pilgrim felt the cold metal of a belt buckle. She undid the buckle, then moved forward fast and silent as a cat and pulled the belt off without a sound. Coming up behind the closest merc, she pushed her lattice usage towards the limit, and her reaction times became superhuman—the world around slowed to a crawl. Looping the belt around his neck, she pulled back and down with all her might while digging her knee into his back. Within a second, she felt his neck give way with a pop as she took him to the dirt with barely a sound. He did not fight back, but his full weight on top of her was uncomfortable. *That's one down,* she thought as she took his knife from its sheath before rolling him off face-first into the ground. *I don't have much time before they notice.*

The missing laser pointer within their night vision field of view must've alerted the four remaining mercs. The four turned to look, but it was too late. The Pilgrim had already pushed herself to her feet and reached the next merc as he turned. The knife was already in his neck and had severed a carotid artery. He was dead and didn't know it. With her inhuman reaction times, she'd slipped her finger into the trigger guard of the man's gun and squeezed tight over his limp finger. A burst of rounds hurtled through the night air as she swung the gun around in a deliberate path, missing the body armour of the remaining three and hitting them all in the neck. She dropped her human shield with a thud as the remaining men fell. She'd taken them all out in less than fifteen seconds. *It is done,* she thought. *Looks like I woke the guys. Time to hand back the reigns. But first, thirty seconds in the lattice for my needs.*

The Pilgrim lay down on the grassy dirt, running her

interpolation program at full pelt and starting on her most ambitious patch to take over the Interface. When ready to hand over to Raff, she withdrew from the optical patch. She momentarily looked up at the Milky Way the way biology intended. It was beautiful.

ΔΔΔ

Raff was still out and living through one of his early post-war memories. He'd just stepped back from the witness stand at the Hague. In front of the International Criminal Court, he'd just given his witness statement and answered several questions about his time as General Ngaba's prisoner. Raff described his time at the POW camp, the mistreatment received, the mass murders witnessed there, and how it all affected him mentally and physically.

Looking down from the glass-and-aluminium-enclosed audience across the spacious courtroom, Raff sat back down. Staring at the pale wooden floor—to avoid eye contact with the row of a dozen judges at the front and the general in cuffs just out of sight—he lost focus on the rest of the proceedings and tried to hold in his emotions. His thoughts wandered back to his time at the camp, especially the time with the satellite. Having returned to civilisation, he saw the full extent of the damage caused by the satellite's explosion. The pulse that emanated from it had reached thousands of miles from its epicentre, killing key data centres and disrupting the internet for months. Moreover, the modern reliance on the Internet meant major economies collapsed, and a deep recession took hold worldwide.

There were only suspicions of some covert weapons projects creating an EMP device large enough. Still, no clear indicators or evidence were left behind when the satellite exploded. The world was on edge, and nobody took responsibility for it. It would mean admitting to making billions of lives miserable and the deaths of tens of thousands, which would likely start another war. The only good thing brought on by the pulse was hastening the end of the general's war. Some called it World War Three, but Raff knew the name wouldn't stick because no nuclear powers were involved; the media and historians argued that an actual World War Three would have ended all life globally.

Raff's musings were interrupted by a loud bang. He looked up to see everyone dropping to the ground in fear. It only registered that it was a gunshot when he saw the general on the floor bleeding out. Then, he froze when he heard several more bangs from the opposite direction. He turned to look toward the shots, but his vision had gone blurry. Then, he felt a searing pain behind his eyes, and a shadow appeared before him.

He tried to focus on the shadow's features, but his head

hurt more when he did. Then, as it got a couple of inches from his face, a shadowy hand touched his cheek. It felt cold like steel. Finally, the shadow spoke to him in a familiar Texan accent: "That was fun! Dang shame it's over. Well, the reins are yours now darlin'. . . Oh, speak to Jacobs. Talk to him about Mervin and ask for Control."

Everything went white, then black, and the pain subsided. He opened his eyes to the starry night sky above him.

Chapter Eighteen

Revelations

Raff, Denn, and Thimba were at the side of the dirt track twenty minutes from their campsite—holding flashlights and staring down at Jannie and Freek kneeling in the dirt, swapping out the rear wheel of the pickup truck. The tyre burst as they raced away on the eroded dirt track. Jannie was cursing Freek in Afrikaans at every opportunity about his terrible driving. Everyone was still hung over from the evening, trying not to be sick and hoping that the clan of spotted hyenas they'd seen five minutes ago weren't heading their way.

Raff took a deep breath. "We need to go see Osborne Jacobs," he said.

"The fuck you talking about bruv," Denn replied.

"Yah," Freek said. "I think we need to get lost like—"

"Just shut the fuck up and listen to me," Raff shouted. He'd had enough of Freek and Jannie's bickering. Everyone went silent and looked up at him, mouths agape. "Sorry, but I've figured something out and need you all to listen. I'm pretty confident Osbourne Jacobs can help us. We need to meet with him as soon as possible."

"Bru, I don't think that is a good idea," Jannie said. "For all we know, he ratted us out to Emmett."

Raff shook his head. "*No*. He was a judge at the International Criminal Court, so I'm certain you are wrong. I remembered some information about Emmett that I think would interest him and, I'm guessing, the rest of the world. It's a small thread, but maybe it gets us some protection, and if it gets pulled, takes Emmet down completely and legally."

Denn placed a hand on Raff's shoulder. "Is this the thing in your head telling you things?" he said.

Raff brushed Denn's hand off and sighed. He found

Denn's question patronising. "No, she just pointed me in the right direction. Remember the satellite Denn, the guy in the black SUV who argued with Ngaba about it? That was Mervin Emmet. I now remember it clearly."

"No . . . god, you know it could be bruv. I thought Emmett's face was familiar and maybe I'd seen it in the news or something. Now you say it, I can't unsee the resemblance."

Freek dropped the tyre iron and stood up. "I knew it," he said. "Some time back, like a few days before that big fiasco at the Hague—you know, the one where the general was assassinated in the courthouse—I thought I overheard Emmett order a hit on someone 'extremely difficult to get to'. Shit, now from what you said, I can see a connection to Ngaba's assassination. It makes sense if Ngaba was a liability to Emmett. You know, from what you remember seeing—"

"Yah," Jannie interrupted. "I was in a different unit then, but I heard chatter that the shooter was an Emmett guy gone rogue. Now, I'm not so sure he was all that rogue."

"You never told me that, boet?"

"Shit, you never asked. If you—"

"Woah," Raff interjected. "You've hijacked my story. In my last dream, earlier tonight, I remembered when I was in the Hague when that assassination happened. I had this strange feeling in my mind at the end, when a shadow touched my face—the entity in my head—like I was given permission by whoever whatever she is, to seek out Emmett and end the threat permanently."

"Wait, you were there?" Freek asked.

Raff sighed, still reeling from his hangover. He hated discussing his past with anyone, but with the brothers, it didn't feel so bad. It was his fault this time—he'd initiated the conversation and had to ride it out until the end. "Yeah," he said. "I had to give a witness statement, standing there like a muppet in front of all those people. Thimba was there too, you know."

"Ah yes," Thimba said, " maybe if I saw this Mr Jacobs, I would recognise him from the court. But please, no more about the general. Can you tell me more about what you were talking about Raff's head? I'm confused."

"Yah," Jannie said, "You called it a *she*?"

"Um," Raff said tentatively. "She speaks to me in a Texan accent. Sometimes, recently, it's just text in front of my eyes. She talks to me more often now—"

"What about?"

"Well, I have managed to pry some information from her. She said she was in the satellite and transferred to my head before the pulse. She's on a mission, something to do with a Corruption. But I think she's lost as her memories were fragmented at some point. I asked if she was some kind of AI, but she didn't know. She's the one who took control of me and saved our lives. I count three times now."

"I don't buy it," Freek said. "No offence, but I'm more inclined to believe it's tumours or hallucinations. Sorry—"

Jannie scowled at Freek. "Raff," he said, "don't listen to Freek. I believe you. It is entirely possible. In the late twenties, human trials inserted neural interface chips that contained virtual AI assistants into people's heads before the AI ban. That was twenty-eight years ago so I think anything is possible!"

"I am very confused," Thimba said. "But I trust Mr Raff. If he says something is true then I believe him. There are more things in heaven and earth than we can ever hope to understand."

"Thank you, Thimba," Raff said. "I think we've all done enough standing around. Please, can we get going? Those hyenas aren't far away." Their laugh-like call carried in the gentle breeze and sent chills down his spine.

"You do not need to worry about them. They are probably smelling the blood from the bodies and going there now. I suspect they won't find anything left when that man, Mr Emmett, sends someone else."

Everyone went silent, and Freek and Jannie returned to changing the wheel. Raff looked up the dirt track and thought about the hyenas cleaning up his mess. He felt sorry for the five men. After all, they were probably just doing a job to make ends meet in an economically unstable world. Did they have families? Children? *Emmett needs to pay for the lives he's ruined*, he thought. *Asshole's probably sleeping like a baby.*

ΔΔΔ

Meanwhile, back in London, Mervin Emmett was alone in his office, pacing beside the large window behind his oak desk, looking out over the dark streets below. "How have you not found out how the hacker got in?" he said to the conference phone on his desk. "You've had access to the ballot machines for weeks now. It can't take this long to trace them?"

"Sorry, pops," Maggie's voice crackled on the other line. "It's not that simple. We have thousands of lines of code to look through to figure out the exploit and how they got in. Once we find that, maybe we can trace something. But I seriously doubt it. This would've been so much easier if I had access to the machines after the election in forty-four. Whoever this was, they were good, like top-tier good."

"Just get it done! I didn't pay top dollar for your MIT education for nothing." He glanced at his watch. "We'll continue this later; I've been summoned to a meeting with the bloody prime minister."

"Oh? This late at night?"

"Yes, it doesn't bode well for our future operations in England."

"Shit, sorry pop. Any news on the *op* in South Africa?"

Emmett rubbed his temples. "I'm pretty certain our men are dead," he said. "I have another task for you. Raphael and the traitors seem to be running with a Texan woman. I need you to find out who she is."

"Oh god, you sure about the men?"

"Just do as I ask. Please, Maggie."

"Sorry, will do. Should I put a bounty on them? It might speed things—"

"No," Emmet shouted, bringing the whole phone up to his face, almost pulling its cable out of the floor. "Do. As. I. Fucking. Asked."

Emmett slammed the phone on the desk several times and cut his daughter off. He sat down in his black-leather office chair, leaned back for a moment, took a few deep breaths, and composed himself. Putting up a bounty was a big no. He couldn't afford the extra eyes looking into his business. He leaned forward and made another call. "Emma," he said, "get Adam to bring the car around. I have a meeting at Downing Street."

"Yes, Mr Emmett," Emma said. "Right away."

"Thanks, Emma; it seems you're the only person I can rely

on in this company. Thanks for staying late and sorting out that paperwork."

"Thank you, sir," she replied before terminating the call.

Mr Emmett made his way to the garage where his driver, Adam, waited. He put on a brave face for his staff, but an air of concern crept through his hard outer shell.

Since the pulse, several major riots have occurred in population centres like London, Birmingham, and Manchester. Politicians were secretly negotiating with Emmett Global and a couple of other private security companies to help police the increasingly discontented population. Police funding had been cut back so much beforehand that they struggled to serve the public adequately. The pulse-induced economic turmoil meant most pensions or savings evaporated, so corruption crept in from every angle. Emmett hoped to capitalise on this; a big contract like this would be a win. So, in secret, Emmett Global drove more corruption, even going as far as tampering with elections to ensure anti-corruption parties were never elected.

They'd succeeded in altering the last UK general election, only for the tampering to be exposed by a hacker known only as The_Impal3r. The rightful winners then came to power, emboldened by this scandal to keep true to their promise of an anti-corruption crusade. This tampering with democracy also increased public support for the anti-corruption drive. Top officials secretly suspected Emmett, but there was no evidence. To be safe, new iron-clad legislation was being brought in to significantly curb any PMC activities within the country. So, Emmett's bottom line was about to take a massive dive. Mr Emmett knew this was the beginning of the end of their operations in England. All it took to bring this about was probably a single typo among thousands of lines of code for a single individual to find and exploit.

Emmett's ride to Downing Street was uneventful. He was too engrossed in the corporate reports on his phone to see the aftermath of the most recent capital riots: burnt-out, boarded-up shops and melted tarmac beneath the charred husks of cars. One street had become an unofficial shrine with thousands of tributes for the eighty-three people who died in the post-election riots—photos taped to everything, flowers tied to railings, candles melted into the pavement, and graffiti messages on the wall.

Security at Number 10 Downing Street was tight, more so than usual. Two uniformed police officers ushered Emmett to the cabinet room for his meeting, seating him opposite a marble fireplace. Nobody else was in the room—the seats at the large, green, oval table were empty, leaving Emmett alone to stare at the brass chandeliers hanging from the high ceiling, lost in thought.

Lithium

A loud ringing broke the silence. Emmett pulled his phone from his suit pocket and saw it was Eric, Maggie's ex from South Africa. "Make it quick," he snapped.

"Maggie called me about your men, " Eric said. "I sent a drone and found them, or what was left. Hyenas got to the bodies, but the gear all adds up. Sorry, boss."

Emmett's face pinched in anger. "What about the element of surprise, didn't they understand?" He paused again. "Shit, I can't afford, uh, I can't be thinking about this right now; I have a meeting."

As Emmett ended the call, the door swung open. The current Prime Minister, Marion Patel, entered with two other cabinet members. Marion, a weathered olive-skinned woman with Thatcher-eque grey hair, sat opposite Emmett, in the only chair with arms, before the fireplace. She tapped some papers on the table. "So, Mr Emmett," she said. "I trust your journey here was uneventful?"

"Indeed ma'am," Mr Emmett replied. "The roads were clear all the way in."

"Good, good. The last riot really did a number this time. *Anyway,* I'm off to New York after this, so no time for small talk. Shall we get to business?"

"Yes, to business."

△△△

The red and orange hues of the first light stretched out over Cape Town and the ocean beyond as Raff and the guys reached the city outskirts. Raff had phoned Osborne Jacobs the moment he got reception on his phone and arranged to meet him for breakfast at a small-time bar and grill near the sea. They sat in the pickup outside, waiting for the place to open. All hopes were that Raff's faith in Mr Jacobs was not misplaced.

I hope I'm not leading everyone into a trap, Raff thought. *No, Mr Jacobs is a good man, I'm sure of it. He helped us with Thimba and was a judge at the Hague.*

Raff felt a familiar discomfort behind his eyes before green neon text appeared before him long enough for him to read: "Trust Jacobs and Control. But not about me."

It was odd this time. There was no headache. Raff's body was getting used to it. *Okay,* Raff thought. *It was you last night, wasn't it?*

"Yes. Sorry."

Don't be sorry. You saved us all. I don't think I could've done what you did.

"Thank you for saying so. I recovered more memories."

Can you tell me more?

"I can. I created a new patch for you to hear me."

I thought you could already speak to me?

"Only sometimes. Can I activate the patch?"

I guess so. Raff squinted, bracing himself for the unexpected. Suddenly, his ears rang for just a second. "It is done," the Texan said. "This should speed things up."

Wow, Raff thought. *This is very different. It's like you're sitting beside me—*

"That's the idea—no more waiting for an opening."

What do you mean—

"Let me tell you what I know, darlin'. I'd appreciate it if you kept this to yourself from now on. It puts us all at risk if you tell everyone. If you *must* confide in someone, stick to that handsome boy, Jannie. He's the only one who believes you."

But—

"No buts, please. This is my story time . . . As you already know, I was in the satellite. Most of it is hazy. Right before the satellite blew up, I hitched a ride along a stream of nano-constructors when they migrated into you. Their control firmware, called the Interface, has kept me in check for so long while it builds something called a path engine—"

Freek banged the side of the pickup truck with his hand and startled Raff. "The place is opening," he said. "It's time for breakfast."

Raff clambered out of the truck bed and headed towards the establishment, a brick shack with a galvanised steel roof. *Sorry,* he thought, *please continue.*

"The Interface spins up the path engine," the Texan continued, "at specific points during its construction to test it. I get thrown into the computational element, the lattice, like a stress test. That's when I've been able to talk to you—"

You used to taunt me, Raff thought, feeling momentarily angry as he remembered them. *Calling me a loser, making me feel so awful.*

"I am sorry about that. It changed when I was able to see all your memories. That was after you got too much sedation and almost died—"

Raff felt a pat on the back and saw Denn beside him. "You've been awfully quiet bruv," Denn said. "It's grub time."

"Um," Raff said, "just a little lost in thought, that's all. I'm gonna stand out here for a moment. Please order me a big bowl of that maize porridge how I like, and I'll come in just now."

"Okay, Raff. Don't be long."

Everyone else entered the café while Raff stayed outside and leaned on the wall beside the front door. *Sorry,* he thought. *I never got your name?*

"I don't know what it is yet," the Texan said, "You can call me Pilgrim for now."

Pilgrim?

"That's what the Interface calls me. I now know I was once a person. I have some frightening, incomplete memories from before. Will let you know when I unlock anything important."

Sorry about the memories. I don't know what I'd do if I lost mine. Maybe you were like me at some point, with this thing in your head. So what is this path engine?

"I don't remember much darlin', but you activated it by accident when you took that massive dose of psilocybin. It overwhelmed your brain, prematurely triggered the incomplete engine, and sent you breach into a parallel self."

So that's what that was? It was the same but not quite. I was different. Denn was different. Shit, so parallel universes are real . . . And wait, what was with all those crazy people?

"Good question. I think they are what my mission is about. It's about something called the Corruption that seems to overwrite human consciousness and spread fast."

Fuck, that is scary. I think I felt it happening to me?

"Yes, I managed to pull you back before it became irreparable. Funny thing, the program I wrote to repair your mind is what I'm now using to recover mine. It's been a painfully slow process with the Interface standing in the way."

Is there anything I can do to help?

The Pilgrim sighed. "Actually, I was hoping to ask you about that. I would like your permission to take control of your body now, and then so I can use the computational lattice to speed up my recovery program. I will always ask first."

Raff thought about the Pilgrim's request for a moment. *When you take over, can you put me into specific memories like before?*

"Yes I can, but the further back you go, your brain might get creative and fill in the gaps."

I can live with that. So many times, I've wished I could just unplug from the world. This might be nice. Do I have to worry about the erm nano things completing whatever they are building in my head?

"Hopefully not. That's my other project. I'm writing a large patch to take full control of the Interface so there are no surprises. A strange feeling crossed my mind: I think I'm the one who wrote the Interface. Maybe you're right—I was once like you, with the path engine in my head."

Raff opened the café door and paused. *It certainly is an interesting mystery. I should go in before I get 101 questions from the guys. Please, please tell me when you learn more. I'll let you know when you can take over. Soon, I promise.*

ΔΔΔ

Denn, Thimba and the Moolmans stared at Raff as he finished his fourth large bowl of the thick, sticky white maize porridge known as mealie pap. They'd been waiting for Osborne Jacobs to arrive in the seafront bar and grill for an hour. All their hopes rested on Raff's faith in Mr Jacobs—that he would come through for them.

"Jeez Raff," Freek said, narrowing his eyes at Raff. "Where

the fuck does a beanpole like you put all that?"

"I—," Raff started.

"Shit," Jannie said, wrinkling his nose. "I think we spend all of our money feeding you—"

"Quiet," Denn interrupted, shaking his head. "If the man wants to eat, let him—"

"Fucking tapeworm is what it is," Freek said, wiping the corners of his mouth with a paper napkin.

Thimba smiled and patted the table. "I wish to change the subject," he said. "Where is Mr Jacobs?"

"Aaany minute now," Raff said, staring at the bowl before him and avoiding eye contact with the guys. *Why do I eat so much?*

"Short answer darlin'," the Pilgrim said. Raff looked around, almost forgetting only he could hear her. "To build something, y'all need material. What the engine needs isn't abundant in your food, so you eat more to meet its needs. Don't worry, your metabolism ramped up to match, so you don't have to worry about getting fat."

That, Raff thought, *actually makes sense. What about the seizures?*

"I can also answer that. Your brain sometimes has a hissy fit because the construction is a little faster than it likes."

Again, that kinda makes sense. Thank you. So there are no

tumours?

"None at all, just the engine."

Raff felt relieved at the answers he'd received so far. Still, the lack of information about the mission behind the path engine concerned him. Not to mention the Corruption. The Pilgrim was trying her best to get answers—that was all he needed to put him at ease for now. Raff trusted that she would tell him when she did. She had just as much to gain.

"—there he is," Denn said, nodding towards the door. Raff turned to look and smiled. Osborne Jacobs came alone and headed towards them. Mr Jacobs dragged a chair from a nearby vacant table and sat opposite Raff before raising a hand to the waiter.

"Good to see you again, Mr Hernandez," Mr Jacobs said before looking up at the waiter. "Coffee please."

"Same," Raff said, "Good to see you again. I remember now."

"Your phone call sounded urgent. So you have some more information about the robberies—"

"No sir," Raff hesitated, knowing that once he said what he had to, there was no turning back. "It's about Ngaba. More specifically, about who supplied him weapons—"

"Eish," Mr Jacobs looked around the room and leaned towards Raff, "I'm no longer a judge for the ICC. I can't help you with that shit. Please, I have my family to think about—"

"Ask for Control," the Pilgrim chirped in Raff's ear.

Raff realised Mr Jacobs was scared. Raff guessed that seeing Ngaba get shot in the courtroom was to blame. Maybe Mr Jacobs feared he would end with a loud bang if he dug up old bones. Raff reached forward and grabbed his hand. "You don't have to do anything to risk your family," Raff said. "I was told you could put me in touch with Control."

The furrows in Mr Jacobs's brow eased. "Who told—," Ozzy said. "Nevermind. I *don't* want to know." He pulled a phone from his shorts pocket and tapped away at the screen for a few seconds. "There. I have a contact who can arrange your meeting with Control. It's in their hands now, so don't ask me about it again . . . Don't get me wrong, I'm happy anytime to have coffee with you, Raphael. You and Thimba never got the credit you deserved for taking down Ngaba. And all of you, for helping rid my family of that poepol Josephus—"

"He's right darlin'." the Pilgrim said in Raff's ear."You deserved more credit, or at least more compensation—"

I was happy with what I got, Raff thought. "Thank you Mr Jacobs," he said. "That means a lot—"

"Ozzy please," Mr Jacobs said. "Anyway, I've got some time to kill. I never got to ask why you're in South Africa."

"I would like to hear more about that, too," Thimba said,

making eye contact with Raff.

"Well," Raff said, "It's quite a long story. It all started with a broken phone . . ."

△△△

Ozzy Jacobs kindly pointed Raff and the guys to a vacant concrete-brick house they could crash in until they found a way out of South Africa. They were staff quarters again, but this time in the backyard of one of Ozzy's clients. Thimba suggested they go to Botswana, but everyone else was unconvinced that it was far enough away to avoid Emmett. A couple of hours after the bar and grill, Jannie had his laptop open on the polished concrete floor of the main room before everyone. The latest South African news was playing. The video stuttered several times while it buffered—Jannie gazed at Raff every time it stopped. There'd been a dozen anti-corruption arrests in Cape Town alone—six police officers, three prison officers, two from the National Prosecuting Authority and a probation officer. Raff wondered if this was all Detective Godrick Nyoni's doing.

"Heads up darlin'," the Pilgrim said in Raff's ears, startling him. "Looks like Control got your message. Y'all got an SUV full of armed men heading your way—"

How—, Raff thought, standing up.

"Never mind that. They're Delta Force. They're . . . way

too close. Sorry, I didn't see it sooner. I suggest unlocking the door, getting on your knees and putting your hands behind your heads."

"Shit," Raff said aloud and quickly did as he was told. On his knees, he placed his hands behind his head and looked up at the guys' surprised faces. "Delta Force is here. Do what I'm doing. Don't fight them. They don't fuck around."

Freek jumped up and looked out the window. "Fuck fuck fuck," he said as he copied Raff and got down on the floor. "They're armed. I hope you're right, Raff."

Denn, Jannie and Thimba followed suit. Everyone was facing the door with their hands behind their head when it burst open. Raff saw a black canister hit the ground in front of him—and within a second, it disappeared in a blinding flash of light and a deafeningly loud bang. Raff was surprised that he could still see and hear after the flashbang. Four armoured pistol-wielding men entered the room. One veered off towards the second room before shouting: "Clear!"

The bearded man of the group pulled out a phone and held the camera up to Raff's face. "Target acquired," he said. "Bag them and put them in the truck."

A dark bag was slipped over Raff's head before he felt his hands pulled in front of him and zip-tied. *I hope you're right about this,* Raff thought.

"I am," the Pilgrim said in Raff's ears. "But, if you're having doubts, there's still time for me to take them out. Make up your mind—the window is closing fast."

No, let's see how this goes. Raff was lifted to his feet and guided across uneven ground onto a soft seat. The familiar duck of his head, his knees raised high, and the sound of the closing door meant he was now in a vehicle. *Where now?*

"I guess they'll load you all onto their sub-orbital and take you to their boss."

Oh no, I hate planes at the best of times. But a sub-orbital, that's worse.

The vehicle began to move. "You've never been in one," the Pilgrim said, "have you?"

Raff shuffled his knees to a more comfortable position. *What do you know about it?*

"I remember . . . I've been on a sub-orbital before. Quite a ride. Think of it this way: a sub-orbital can do in an hour or two what a regular plane can do in ten or more—"

I suppose that would be a good time for you to take over. From takeoff to landing, my body is all yours.

"You sure darlin'?"

I am sure. Go for it now and put me in memories about Control. I need to remember as much as I can. Wake me if I'm required.

Raff felt lightheaded, and his heart fluttered in his chest.

The world went bright white. "Sweet dreams, darlin'. Talk to you on the other side."

ΔΔΔ

Raff was back in his wartime memories, several weeks after his time as a POW. The crickets chirped as darkness fell over the village ahead. Raff felt a sense of de ja vu as he lay prone on over-watch over the valley, peering through a set of night vision binoculars at yet another village green-washed by the goggles. His primary job was to inform the ground team via radio of any movement that wasn't theirs. His secondary task was to haul around an antique backpack-sized radio to act as a relay between the team and Control—a local camp-based stand-in and relay for the Joint Special Operations Command. Satellites, drones, and long-range encrypted comms were still useless after the satellite's_pulse, hence the need for a man nearby on overwatch. Much to his relief, he wasn't on the team going into the village this time. That task was for a United States Delta Force team. To the team, Raff was just a bullet catcher. The powers above had decided to keep everyone involved in the previous mission in the dark—the mission that ended up with Raff and Denn being prisoners—which meant no Brits except Raff, now a corporal in name only.

Raff's friendship with, and rescue of, Thimba resulted in his team acquiring some actionable intelligence on the location of the general's close lieutenants. The powers in charge knew that nabbing just one of them and interrogating him could result in the capture of the general and ultimately end the war. The stakes were high, and they wouldn't make the same mistake again; they wouldn't leave something so important to an inexperienced team that just happened to be in the area. So they'd called in the big guns.

Raff clicked his comms. "Wolf-pack, this is buzzard checking in," he said. "Tango remains clear for extraction. No other movement at the location. Egress remains clear. Buzzard out."

"Roger that, Buzzard," a man crackled over the comms. "Moving in for extraction. Bravo, Charlie, check-in. Over."

"Bravo in position," a second man crackled.

"Charlie in position," said a third.

"Go! Go! Go!" the first man hollered. Raff heard the sound of a door breaking down as the comms clicked off. He watched as the strobing signals of alpha, bravo, and charlie teams entered the target building, surrounding the single heat signature.

"Tango in custody," the first man said. "Tango is in custody. Alpha out."

"Roger," Raff said. "Zero movement. I repeat, zero movement. All clear for egress. Repeat egress is clear. Buzzard out."

Raff picked up a telephone handset attached to his heavy backpack. "Control," he said, "This is Buzzard. We have the package. Returning to base. Over."

"Thanks Buzzard," a man with a Spanish accent on the other end said. "See you back at base. The beers are on me. Control out."

Raff remained in overwatch until the team left the village with the target in tow. Now, it was his time to move. He huffed as as he swung the heavy backpack onto his back and headed to the extraction point where a convoy of old Humvees waited and the team was gathering. He made his way down to one of the humvees and entered. Their doors slammed one by one, their sounds blurring as the world went dark around him.

"Sorry darlin'," the Pilgrim said. "You're needed in the real world, so I gotta cut this short . . . Welcome to Mexico."

∆∆∆

Raff woke to the muffled roar of a sub-orbital's twin scramjets. The interior of the arrow-shaped craft was first class—wooden veneers on the fixtures and plush cream leather seats. There were no windows on the craft, so the only view of the outside was through the screens embedded in the seatbacks. A hand on Raff's shoulder shook him. "—Mr Hernandez," an American man said. Raff looked up; it was the bearded Delta

Force man. "Oh, good, you're awake. I've never known anyone to sleep through a sub takeoff and landing."

"Sorry," Raff said, rubbing his eyes. "It was a long night."

"This is your stop. Your friends are outside." The man handed Raff a satphone. "Keep this on you at all times."

"Yes sir." Raff stood up, pocketed the phone and headed towards an open door near the front. Outside, the sun was still low in the sky. Raff saw Denn standing beside an old orange Landrover with a taxi sign on top. Denn waved, and Raff headed towards him. *Do they know where they're going?* Raff thought.

"Yes," the Pilgrim replied. "The taxi driver will drive us to the village outskirts where the contact is—where Control is."

Denn smiled at Raff as they entered the taxi where Thimba and the Moolmans waited. "Sleeping beauty," Freek said. "Glad you could join us."

"I uh," Raff said, "was exhausted." He heeded the Pilgrim's advice and omitted the truth that she was in control during the flight. Outside, the sub-orbital's engines roared loudly as it sped up the runway and disappeared into the clouds in a plume of smoke and fire.

The village couldn't be any more off the beaten path. It was another long drive along a washed-out road. This time, it was a dense forest in all shades of green imaginable. Their taxi driver—who the Pilgrim suspected was an undercover DEA agent—told them that bandits operated along the main roads and it was safer to take the scenic route, especially during the rainy season when the bandits avoided the frequently flooded roads. The dense mass of trees thinned out and became fields of ripe corn as far as the eye could see. Nestled in a valley on the horizon was their destination—hundreds of buildings in all the colours of the rainbow.

They reached the village and pulled up behind a bright mustard-coloured house. "This is it," Diego, the driver, said. "You'll need to make your own way back. And remember, avoid the main roads."

"Um," Denn said, looking at Raff as they approached the door. "You sure this Marco guy is legit, mate?"

"If he is who I think he is," Raff said, "then we're gonna be okay."

"I fucking hope so," Freek said as he thumped the door twice. "Because we're out in the breeze with our asses hanging out."

An unnaturally dark-haired man with a thick, military stature answered the door, poking his head out briefly to look down the street. "Come in quickly," he said, "I've made lunch."

Raff recognised the man's voice and followed him into the house. The others followed. Passing through the kitchen—

where the smell of eggs and bacon set Raff's stomach rumbling—they entered the dining room. It was devoid of furniture besides wooden shutters on the windows and some overturned plastic buckets around a large black military crate in the centre. "Have a seat," the man said, pointing at the buckets. It was no different to how they were living in South Africa. The guys sat down except for Raff.

"Control?" Raff said, raising an eyebrow.

"Yes," the man said, reaching for Raff's hand, "to you maybe, but that was five years ago. You can call me Marco. Really, I was just a voice, a relay, for *the* Control."

Raff shook Marco's hand. "It's good to put a face to the voice after all these years," Raff said.

Marco went into the kitchen and Raff followed. "You asked for Control's help," Marco said, handing Raff a pack of paper plates, picking up the two large pans full of bacon and scrambled eggs, and heading back to the dining room. "But Control is not what you think it is. Not any more. Don't get me wrong, the moment you requested a meeting, someone at the top moved heaven and earth to get you here. Quite fortuitous timing."

Marco dished up the food while Raff handed out the plates. "Fortuitous," Raff said. "how?"

"I've been stuck out here on my own," Marco said, sitting

down and eating directly from the pans. "Been waiting for a team to assist."

"Oh," Freek said with a mouthful of bacon, "let me guess, *we're* supposed to be the team."

"Yes, but this relates to your current predicament with Emmett Global..."

The group tucked into the greasy delights and discussed Marco's mission. He'd been monitoring a potential asset in a bind. A hacker, a Texan by the name of Ezra Thompson, had been kidnapped from his home in Odessa and, smuggled to a nearby cartel and forced to run the budding digital side of their criminal enterprise. This was the same hacker who exposed the recent fraudulent UK general elections. Marco had solid intel on where their man was kept, video footage of the exact room in the compound, the guard positions, and the natural cover in the area.

"That footage is amazing," Jannie said. "How did you get so close to the guards?"

Marco removed a case from his side pocket. The centimetre-thick square carbon fibre case flipped open to reveal a screen above what looked like five black flies. On closer inspection of the flies' wings, Raff saw the tell-tale square reflections of solar film. "These are graphene-based US military micro drones," Marco said. "Great for espionage."

"So mate," Denn said. "The fly on the wall thing is great, but what's this hacker got to do with Emmett? How does this help us?"

"It's believed Emmett's been tampering with elections," Marco said, "working to derail the coalition's progress in fixing things after the pulse. Your UK wanted status is Emmett's doing, isn't it? So you help get the hacker out—he helps remove Emmett and others like them. The powers above guarantee that your records will be cleared once the job is done."

"So you heard about that," Raff said. "Big ol' frame job. He's tried to kill us all twice now. Well, Thimba only once. But that's not the whole reason I asked for Control—"

Freek squinted at Marco. "What's the catch," he said. "They pulled a Delta Force team from god knows where, slapped them into a sub-orbital, and got them to pick us up and drop us off here. That shit's going to cost us."

Marco's eyes widened. "A sub-orbital?" he said. "God. I know there's a file on each of you. I've seen them. It seems someone important in the UNPPC has been keeping tabs on you all for a while—except for Thimba, your file is a little lighter, containing nothing I didn't know. Maybe this is a recruitment test—"

"Recruitment?" Raff said, eying the pans for any leftovers. *Have I got us into another mess?*

"Some new coalition intelligence unit." Marco stood up and collected the pans and plates. "With things moving towards UN control, and rightfully so, good operatives are needed on the fringes to handle issues that get in the way . . . like Emmett. Think about it. Why wait years to train new operatives, when you use people who already have the skills? You've survived Emmett twice, so you've probably piqued their interest."

"That was—" Denn began.

Raff cleared his throat. "So," he said. "Does this newly formed coalition intelligence service have a name?"

"Officially," Marco said, standing in the kitchen doorway. "Nothing yet. Unofficially, the boys call it Co-Int."

"So, if we pass this 'test,' will we be recruited by Co-Int?"

"Best guess maybe . . . Anyway, you all look like shit. The head's down the hall, and there are some old mattresses upstairs. We'll talk mission first thing in the morning—"

You've been awfully quiet in there? Raff thought. *No comment?*

"Sorry darlin'," the Pilgrim said in Raff's ears. "I've been busy . . . You forgot to tell him about Emmett and the general."

I know. I will bring it up again tomorrow. I need sleep . . .

ΔΔΔ

A timezone away in New York, the UK Prime Minister's—Marion Patel's—convoy made its way along the busy streets under heavy military escort. With her notes in hand, Marion looked at her reflection in the limousine's partition glass. She was preparing to address the UN Security Council. These were unprecedented times, and the future of the UN Post-Pulse Coalition was riding on her words. She took a deep breath and relaxed her face in order to appear calm. "On May thirteenth, twenty-forty-one," she began, "an event that spanned a mere fraction of a second brought humanity to its knees. Most of you in attendance here today have been affected one way or another by it—"

A loud ringing interrupted her. A scowl swept across her face as she looked at Devon—her young blonde aide—sat beside her with a phone to her ear. "Does that thing need to be so loud," she said.

"Sorry ma'am," Devon said as she momentarily touched her phone to her chest. "It's about the, uh, project in South Africa."

Marion held out her hand. "Give it here."

"Yes ma'am." Devon handed over the phone, avoiding eye contact.

Marion put the phone to her ear. "And enough of the 'ma'am' shit. It's Marion or Mrs Patel . . . You on the phone, make it quick."

"Yes erm," the man on the other end replied—known to Marion as John Webber, "I have confirmation that the assets have been taken from Cape Town to the US asset in Mexico—"

John was an old family friend from the USA who'd served during the war with the US Army's Intelligence Support Activity."Thank you, John. And sorry I snapped at you."

"It's okay, Maz. Running a country must be stressful. Don't envy you one iota."

"It's not just that. I hope I haven't burned a favour on nothing—"

"Tell me, Maz, why couldn't you use the favour to grab the hacker instead? A Delta Force team would make quick work of that small-time cartel—"

"I need to keep Emmett in the dark, as much as possible, about the hacker and everything else. Emmett has fingers in many pies. . . Besides, as you know, we need more skilled operators on the side of progress. I really have to go. Thanks for the update. Oh, and will we see you at Christmas this year?"

"I'll try my best." Sounds of gunfire erupted on the other end of the line. "That's my cue. I gotta go. Catch you on the flip side."

The call ended. Marion returned the phone to Devon and stared out the dark-tinted limo window at the New York streets. Marion remembered what the New York traffic was like before the pulse. Driving them now was a breeze with fewer cars on the road. Her mind didn't dwell on that long. She glanced at her speech notes for a moment but put off further rehearsal. *If Mr Hernandez and co can pull this off,* she thought, *they'll have proved their usefulness. I have a few jobs lined up for them, not to mention what the Coalition have in mind—*

The limo partition window rolled down. "Pulling up to the UN building now," the driver said. Marion sighed and momentarily looked at her notes as the door beside her opened. "Marion, don't you fuck this up."

∆∆∆

Ezra sat in darkness at the large desk in his designated room at the cartel compound, the light of numerous screens and backlit keyboards reflected in his thick-rimmed glasses. The room was a rigid steel mesh-wire box within a larger brick room, doubling as a prison and a Faraday cage, designed to keep him in and external electromagnetic interference out. One screen had a sub-titled replay of the British prime minister's UN speech from the day before. He ignored that and stared intently at one of the monitors as lines of text appeared at intervals of a second or two against a black background. Occasionally, he'd type something in and get a confirmation on another screen with an online video game playing. The text was gibberish to the nonexpert, but to Ezra, it was an entire language in its own right. One of the coded lines caught his eye, and he fought the urge to glance at the camera behind him. It was a message from someone on the outside, designed to look like a bit of code only he'd recognise. He decoded it in his head, just three words: *Midnight be ready*.

He rubbed the stub where his left pinkie finger once was, still tender where it met the sharp end of a blunt chisel as a punishment for resisting the cartel boss, known by his men as El Jefe and his wife as Felix. His heart fluttered in his chest as his adrenaline spiked, excited at the prospect of leaving. It didn't bother him that his would-be saviours were a mystery. In his mind, anything else would be better than the cartel. *So this is it,* he thought, *I'm finally gettin' outta here.*

He looked at the time and realised midnight was only ten minutes away. In a slight moment of panic, he opened a terminal window on one screen and entered a single command: *impal3r.exe -t 00:00.*

A tiny window popped up on another screen, text scrolling across it faster than any human could read. Now smirking and peering down his nose at the screen, he leaned back in his chair and waited. Pondering how the rescue would unfold, he played out several scenarios through his supercomputer of a brain. Unfortunately, his 198 IQ failed him on his one and only solo escape attempt, resulting in a severe beating and being forced to watch the brutal beheading of the men who were assigned to guard him—IQ versus bullets is a no-brainer.

Midnight came, and like clockwork, the power went out across the compound as the sound of gunfire and explosions rippled from a short distance. Ezra's computers remained on for a few minutes; their attached backup battery units beeped as they kept the power running. After that, all the windows on the screens closed but one. On it, millions of dollars and other currencies were being emptied from numerous accounts, sent elsewhere at random in hundred-dollar chunks, and significant data was being forwarded to various authorities worldwide—all this happened while the hard drives were being overwritten with meaningless data.

At three minutes past midnight, a dark-skinned, rifle-carrying man burst through the door to his room. "Are you Mr Ezra?" the man said.

"Uh, yeah," Ezra replied. "That's—"

He stopped when two light-haired men came through. They carried rifles and looked like they could be brothers too. One positioned himself to watch over the door while the other approached Ezra. He looked over at the dark-skinned man. "Is this the guy?" he said.

"Yes," the dark-skinned man said. "This is him. It took me a moment to see past the beard and long hair, but I see the resemblance."

"Lekker, now let's grab him and go before—"

"Wait, wait just a minute y'all," Ezra said, the Texan in him coming through. "Who are you?"

The dark-skinned man broke the lock on the cage with the but of his rifle and opened the gate. "Your rescuers," he said.

"Na-no, I mean, who sent y'all?"

The brother with the crooked nose charged through the gate, grabbed Ezra by the arm and led him out. Ezra tried to resist, but the man was too strong for him. "Look, man," the brother said, "all you need to know is that we're the good guys, right? So let's fucking go, chop-chop."

Ezra followed the three men out, obeying every command. When they told him to stop, he stopped; when they told him to take cover, he took cover. Ezra wondered what kind of men would risk their lives to rescue a nobody hacker like himself and why? Who would fund such a rescue?

The sound of gunfire faded as they headed away from the compound, hurtling through the surrounding forest. Ezra stumbled often and struggled to match his breathing to his pace; he'd put on a few pounds in captivity and wasn't used to all this exercise, preferring to do his running in video games. It wasn't long before they arrived at a parked battered, rusty and old SUV, poised to head down the dirt track it was sitting beside. Two other men were waiting for him there, one with dark hair and the other bald, both short. "Where the fuck is Raff?" the bald one shouted.

"W-what?" one of the brothers said. "I thought he was with you okes?"

"Shit, bruv! Jus—"

A tall, slender, red-headed man came stumbling out of the bushes, his face devoid of emotion. He stared through the group as if they weren't there. Like a switch had been flicked, the man's cold expression melted away to one with a beaming smile. "Whatta y'all waitin' for?" the man said in a Texan accent. "Tick tock, time's a-wastin'."

Ezra felt at ease hearing a fellow Texan. Then he noticed the look of shock on the men's faces. They all appeared to know this man, as they were just talking about him, yet they seemed utterly horrified when he spoke. "Raff?" the bald man said. "Bruv, are you on something?"

"Oh no, no, no time for that. You silly darlin's need to enter the vehicle. Now!"

The tall man pushed through, entered the driver's seat, and briefly pressed the horn. The straight-nosed brother opened a rear door and pushed Ezra in before entering the front passenger seat. The rest of the men followed suit and entered the SUV before it sped off down the dirt track.

The brother up front stared at the red-headed man for a

moment. "Raff," he said, "is that you?"

"Boop," the redhead said as he tapped the brother's nose once with his index finger, swerving the SUV as he did. "Don't be silly, my lil' muffinator. You know who."

Muffinator? Ezra had only heard one person ever use that word before. It was his older sister's nickname for boys she dated. His late sister.

Chapter Nineteen
Pilgrimage

The last thing Raff remembered was letting the Pilgrim take control of his body for the mission to rescue Ezra Thompson the hacker. He relished the idea that he could close his eyes at the beginning of the mission and open them after it was done. It appealed to him—a get-out-of-life free card. But this time, he got more than he bargained for. Raff awoke and felt strange, feeling himself drift upwards out of his own body only to be stopped by the ceiling. The room was familiar—the black and white tiled bathroom at Marco's safehouse in the Mexican village. He stared down at the floor and watched helplessly as his body shook uncontrollably and bled from its nose. He tried his hardest to reach out to it and call for help, but nothing happened. *Pilgrim*, he thought, *what the fuck is going on?*

There was no response from the Pilgrim, but Raff struggled to focus his thoughts. A hiss in his ears grew louder and became excruciatingly painful while the world faded to black around him. Within what felt like a second, a pinpoint of bright white light in the distance grew brighter—Raff couldn't tell if he was moving towards it or if it was moving towards him. The moment the light reached Raff, it forked and passed him on either side—glowing flashing streams of bright lights like train carriages passing in the dark. A moment passed, and the lights stopped and appeared as lines of tall white rectangles as far as the eye could see. The lights flickered out, and a new pain arrived—a pulsing and stabbing pain radiating from the centre of Raff's chest.

A stubbled face appeared before Raff—red, sweating, panting, and bobbing over him. Raff couldn't focus beyond the man, but the world was moving around them. The pain in his chest continued. Another man was shouting in the

V. B. Anstee

background—Raff couldn't understand what he was saying but recognised it as Freek's voice. The moment Raff tried to speak, he was back between the lines of lights, and they began to move again. They hurtled past him for a moment again until he felt a massive twinge through his body. Alarms went off in his ears, and a small circular window appeared before him, surrounded by metal and studded grey padding. Raff floated weightlessly as he peered through it and watched the edge of a semi-eclipsed blue sphere surrounded by stars, while rings of fire pockmarked its dark side. Somehow, he knew it was the earth below, and it was in trouble. He caught his reflection in the glass, but it was not him. A woman—a brunette with blue eyes and hair tied in a neat bun—peered back at him. *Wait*, Raff thought, *am I in one of the Pilgrim's memories, looking at it through her eyes?*

"Ma'am," a familiar voice caught his attention. The Pilgrim turned to see a clean-shaven Marco in a blue jumpsuit floating near a round open hatch. "The Corruption has made it onto the station. I've sealed the hatches between us and the infected. But you know as well as I do that won't hold it back for long—"

"How'd y'all let this happen," the Pilgrim said before rolling and pushing herself off the wall with her feet towards Marco. "The station's quantum computer shoulda been shut down days ago."

Marco bowed his head. "Sorry ma'am. I didn't know the pendejos above kept it on until just now—"

The Pilgrim sighed as she flew past Marco. "It's too late for sorries now. We must get to Project Pilgrim while we still can. Hopefully, we're not too late."

Marco followed while the Pilgrim moved, floating weightlessly through round padded hallways. Raff tried to focus on the surroundings but couldn't—everything the Pilgrim didn't focus on was a blur. Moments later, she grabbed a railing and stopped in front of a closed hatch with the word "Pilgrim" painted on it. Marco came to a stop, too and entered a code into a panel by the hatch. With a loud whir and clunk, the hatch opened and the pair promptly propelled themselves into the circular room beyond.

"Strap in," the Pilgrim said as she hovered above a computer terminal and inserted a thumb drive. "I'm uploading the interface and routing power to the capacitors."

"You sure this will work," Marco said in an unsteady voice. "It's not been tested."

The Pilgrim turned to see Marco strapped into one of three aluminium chairs around a brightly lit central triangular pillar. He pulled a halo-shaped device from the pillar so it sat around his sweaty temples. "If the process can work for the Corruption," the Pilgrim said, taking her place in a neighbouring seat, strapping in, then pulling down her halo, "it should work for us."

"You don't sound so sure."

The Pilgrim reached over and gently squeezed Marco's hand. A loud clunk echoed through the open hatch at that moment, followed by loud grunts and growls. "Think of the alternative," the Pilgrim said, nodding towards the hatch.

Marco fumbled for the latch holding his straps. "I need to close the hatch."

"It's too late for that. Buckle up, darlin'. We're in for a wild ride."

Within seconds, the grunts and growls had grown louder until several people in blue jumpsuits fumbled through the door. A man with a lacerated face and bloodshot eyes looked up and reached towards the Pilgrim with a mangled hand— barely hanging on by the skin at the wrist with exposed bone poking through. Before the man could touch her, everything disappeared in a painful flash of bright light.

Raff was now awake. Putting all his effort into lifting his right arm, he saw a drip attached to his arm. Raff pulled his hand to his face and felt a tube entering his nose. Grabbing it, he pulled at it until there was no more resistance. Fluid flicked across his face, and he dropped the tube to wipe it off with the palm of his hand. He took a deep breath, but that was a mistake—a sharp pain radiated from the centre of his chest. An urge to cough overwhelmed him, and he tried to fight it. The coughing fit that followed caused pain like gunshots to the chest. Fortunately, it also attracted the attention of a nearby nurse.

"Mr Dodd," a blonde man in blue scrubs said, stood over Raff and looked at a screen. "You're awake?"

Raff felt a sense of deja vu. He was in a hospital again, known only by an alias. "No. Shit," he said. "Where. Am. I?"

"You're in Odessa Medical—"

"Odessa?"

"Yes, Odessa, Texas."

ΔΔΔ

Odessa was home for Ezra Thompson, maybe less so since the pulse. His father died soon after the pulse fried his pacemaker; emergency services were overwhelmed or difficult to contact. And soon after that, his mother died from broken heart syndrome. His older sister, Amice, was killed in a car crash while running away from home many years before the pulse—after a heated argument with their overbearing mother. The family home felt empty, so he allowed Raff's group to stay, except Marco, who'd gone to Los Angeles to pave the way for the group's mission to take down Emmett Global. Ezra was touched by how the group pulled together to help Raff when they found him convulsing on Marco's bathroom floor. He could do with people like that on his side. And the hidden friends, too—he needed them. Someone powerful pulled strings and put in a rush order for a sub-orbital to ferry a fading Raff to Odessa for emergency treatment—several rounds of CPR and defibrillator shocks, and here Raff was, still alive and seated in his living room.

There was awkward silence among the guys after Raff returned from the hospital. They'd all been through a thorough grilling by the coalition, receiving clearance to work for them once the Emmett job was complete. The brothers were apprehensive about the job offer at first. But Raff, who was in an uncharacteristically good mood after his ordeal, suggested that maybe it was their destiny to do this. He went over the chain of events leading to this moment—a butterfly effect. How it all started with a broken phone setting off a chain of events that likely saved not just the lives of the brothers but that of Thimba and Ezra too. Ironically, this group of misfits had an uncanny knack for making the world a better place in small increments; two less armed gangs in England, one less group of pirates, and fuel added to a growing anti-corruption movement in South Africa, ending one notorious cartel boss and most importantly, hastening the demise of the self-serving

Emmett Global. So why not get paid to do what they seemed to do best?

Ezra's debrief was done remotely by the UK prime minister herself. He admitted to being the hacker that exposed the UK's election tampering. It was no surprise when they told him they strongly suspected Emmett's involvement, so he was all for helping the fellas take them down to finish the job he started. The world was now his oyster, but he requested to continue working with the group when they were all done with Emmett. He felt like he owed them that much and felt safe with them. Once he got past their hard outer shells, he kinda liked them. Besides, they'd introduced him to their drinking game, and it was the most fun he'd had in years. But there was something niggling at the back of his brain about Raff, something he couldn't quite place. Something about the Texan accent Raff no longer had; he wanted to figure it out.

In just an ill-fitting vest and boxer shorts, Ezra picked up the freshly brewed pot of coffee and wandered out of the kitchen. The group were seated around a low glass coffee table. On top of it was a half dozen coffee mugs beside a pile of empty pizza boxes. Raff was slouched on the sofa and looked paler than when Ezra first saw him. "Fresh coffee y'all," Ezra said as he poured himself a mug and placed the pot on the table.

Ezra sat on the sofa opposite Raff and stared at him while

sipping his hot coffee. It was still too hot to drink any meaningful amount. "Raff," he said. "Is that right? Well, your friend Jannie there told me about your head."

Raff scowled at Jannie. "Jannie?"

"Sorry bru," Jannie said. "I thought he could help. Any guy who built quantum computers for a living might know more about AI-neural interfaces."

Raff looked at Ezra. "*You* built quantum computers?"

"Up until the pulse," Ezra said, rolling his eyes. "And then I got fired . . . you know I have an idea about takin' a look at your brain—"

"Fired?"

Ezra stood up with his mug of coffee in hand. "That's a long story. Y'all come to the basement. There's some equipment I erm borrowed that might be useful."

Raff grimaced and clutched his chest as he got up to follow Ezra. "Damn CPR cracked ribs," he said. "I'll be fine."

Care and intrigue made the others follow them into the basement. In the centre of the room was a sizeable gated steel frame covered in steel mesh—a Faraday cage. It contained the same setup as the cartel cage—minus the locks with a bit more clutter. "What do you y'all know about brain-computer interfaces?" Ezra asked.

They looked at each other for a moment, waiting for

someone to respond. "Umm," Raff said, "not much, to be honest."

Ezra swept a pile of circuit boards off the chair in the centre of the cage. "Okay, have a seat."

Raff sat down as Ezra dug through a large box with "MIT shit" written on the side. "Well," Ezra said, "there's the old way for the best results—electronic arrays placed directly on the brain. Unfortunately, I can't find my drill. Shit."

"What?" Raff said.

"Ha, just kiddin'. Here 'tis."

Ezra stood up from the box with a flexible silicone skull cap in his hand and placed it over Raff's head. It was covered in an array of coloured wires that met dozens of small silver cylinders embedded in the silicone. He plugged the trailing bundle of wires into what looked like a homemade port on the desk. "I managed to get hold of some advanced sensors on my way out of MIT," he said, "and made this lil' thang. Just sit still and try to empty your mind."

Ezra booted up the computer under the desk and typed a command into it. Several waveform representations appeared on the screens—dozens of wavy lines overlapping each other like a tangled mess of string. It didn't look like anything to anyone else but him. Entering more code into a terminal window, he made the waveforms look less noisy—lines separated and clear patterns now showed, each distinct from the other. He was silent as he analysed the data.

"Ahem," Denn said, "get with the explaining."

"Oh, sorry. So, with the help of some *borrowed* algorithms, we see Raff's brainwaves. These here, clearly distinct alpha, beta, and gamma waves, eight to forty-four hertz, what y'all expect to see from someone awake. Oh, and there, some theta wave spikes, four to seven hertz, lil' more than the norm but not odd. But this is what's interesting; these cycles here are way too high—"

"High?" Raff said.

Ezra opened another program that seemed to translate the high-cycle signal into raw data. Bits of binary appeared among the data that scrolled across the screen. "Oh no no, I can't be dealing with this shit again. I—"

"What shit?"

Ezra froze, refusing to talk. Freek's blood boiled, he liked Ezra, but Raff had saved his ass more than once now, so his temper boiled over. "Talk," Freek shouted, placing his hand on the back of Ezra's neck. "Or you'll be eating through a straw."

"Okay, I'll start at the beginning, but this does not leave this room, okay?"

Ezra explained how he used to work at a quantum computer research lab in Boston. On the day of the pulse, he was as high as a kite and working on his own in the lab at six in the morning—working on the world's most advanced quantum computer. He chuckled when he called it the most advanced. "It was still rudimentary," he said, "relatively speaking and still too delicate to exploit the properties of quantum mechanics in any useful way."

"Get to the part about Raff?" Jannie said.

"Well, moments before the pulse, the quantum computer went haywire. It was generating random data, or so I thought. The whole thing was air-gapped from the outside world. So, imagine my surprise when I saw evidence of external interference. It was strange, like a signal had appeared from within the quantum processors themselves. That's impossible, right?"

Raff scratched his head. "Uh, right?"

"Or maybe our understanding of quantum physics is wrong . . . I looked at the data, and it was highly complex code. So I thought it was alien at first, but I saw familiar binary elements that could only mean it was human."

"Alien?" Jannie said, squinting an eye.

"I've had time to think about it. I now believe it came from illegal AI research. I'll never truly know. In my rush to gather data—while high—I overlooked an error in the cooling system. The quantum computer strained, trying to parse the complex code. It quickly overheated and popped. Tens of millions of dollars worth of equipment became a decorative piece. Three seconds later, the pulse hit."

A look of disbelief and shock swept across the faces of the guys. "Wait," Jannie said, "Are you telling us that you caused the pulse?"

"No no no no. What I'm trying to tell y'all, is that whomever or whatever sent that signal caused the pulse, 'n I recognised that same signal from your brain is all. Y'all need to explain that shit to *me*."

"I don't know what the fuck this thing is," Raff said. "You're the one who's supposed to figure this out."

"Hold your horses, okay? I reckon I could figure this out if I had a quantum computer, but y'all know what it's like. Ever since the dang pulse, other kinds of research get funded instead. C'mon, talk of a city 'n babies on the moon? Who'd wanna fund anything else but that? Besides, no self-respecting institute'll hire me, the crazy, raving, high-as-a-kite lunatic. So I—"

"Thank you, Ezra, it's a good start. You at least confirmed I'm not going crazy." Raff said. *But I knew that already. Pilgrim, where are you? Are you ignoring me because of the shit that almost killed me?*

"Yeah. I, I think the satellite Jannie told me about was some sorta experimental quantum communications system.

Maybe irreparably damaged, it tried to upload its data into the closest compatible hardware it could find. It got interrupted and was in a hurry, so it sought an unconventional host: you."

There was a brief pause as this idea sank in. Freek didn't seem convinced. "But Raff's not a bloody quantum computer," he said. "He's—"

"I beg to differ. This confirms something scientific circles have suspected, that there's a quantum element to how the brain works. I read this paper about some MRI research that showed evidence of quantum entanglement at play *within* the brain." Ezra turned back to the computer. "I'm gonna try n' get sumthin' from this data, come hell or high water."

"Sorry about earlier", Freek said. "I'm trying to work on my anger issues—"

"Oh bless your heart, now leave me be. I'll figure this out."

ΔΔΔ

A couple of days passed in Odessa while Raff's group waited for contact from Marco. The group sat outside a barbecue shack restaurant at a wooden bench table. Raff knew something was different in his head. Aside from his near-death experience and the Pilgrim's lack of communication, he'd lost his appetite. He stared at the sticky brown barbeque ribs on the paper plate before him and pondered on the Pilgrim's memory he'd seen during his death throes. *It's all about this Corruption,* he thought.

And were those nuclear detonations I saw below? Is there another Marco out there?

A loud chime startled Raff. He looked up at the group around the table. Denn, Freek, Jannie and Thimba all stared at him. "Oh," Raff said as he patted his pockets. "I guess that's me." He pulled out the sat phone the Delta Force man had given him and saw an incoming phone call from a withheld number. Raff didn't want to pick up but took a deep breath and answered the call. "Hello," he said sheepishly.

"Hey, Raff, it's Marco."

"Hey." *I was just thinking of him.*

"It's good to hear you," Marco said. "Sounds like you've improved."

"So so. How's LA?"

"That's what I'm calling about. Mervin Emmett is here. He's closed up completely in the UK and is now permanently based out of the Emmet Global HQ here."

Raff frowned. "Is that a problem?"

"No," Marco said. "It's an opportunity. We get this done while he's here, and there'll be no problems with extradition treaties. I have to go. Bring Ezra and get here by road. I will send you a map link to the safehouse. Catch you soon."

The call ended, and Raff tucked the phone away. He stared at his barbecue ribs again for a second and thought about his own cracked ribs. *So my heart stopped three times,* he thought. *Pilgrim, where are you?*

"So," Denn said loudly. "Do tell."

Raff looked up, eyes open wide for a moment. "Sorry," he said. "Marco is sending us the address. We've gotta drive to LA. We have a window of opportunity. Emmett's in town."

"Oh god," Ezra said. "Y'all realize that's an eleven-hundred-mile drive?"

"We need to stay off the radar," Jannie said. "So the road it is. I'll check that old jalopy in Ezra's garage—"

Ezra sighed. "The fuel cell and motor work just fine y'all, but one of the hydrogen tanks has a very slow leak, so it needs a tow to fill 'er up first."

"Very nice," Thimba said. "I'm looking forward to seeing more of the United States. Promise me we'll see Hollywood?"

"You mean the *Re-*United States," Freek said, smiling. Raff knew Freek was referencing the re-unification of the Southern States with the North following their post-pulse separation.

Ezra sunk in his seat and looked around. "Shhh," he said. "Don't say shit like that unless you want to get shot."

Freek's face pinched. "Sorry bru, I didn't mean anything by it . . ."

Raff heard his ears pop and a loud hiss, drowning out the conversation. *Pilgrim, is that you?* he thought,

"Yes Raff," the Pilgrim replied. "That was a big ol' hiccup. I'm so sorry about that. If it's any consolation, I felt every bit of pain you did."

What the fuck, Raff thought. *I trusted you to take control, and then I almost died* three *times.*

"Well, the Interface didn't go down without a fight. I purged it in the end, but the nano-constructors lost cohesion and shorted out your brain. It's all under control now, and I've even worked out how to use the constructors to numb your pain, among other things. Feel the bruises on your chest."

Raff massaged where his chest was bruised, and the pain that was there earlier was gone. He took a deep breath and no longer felt the sharp pain of his cracked ribs. *Damn, I have to say that is good. It still doesn't get you off the hook for what happened—*

"I know. But I now remember the significance of my mission—"

I think I get it too . . .

Raff told the Pilgim about the memory of hers he'd seen—the nukes, the space station, the other Marco and the Corruption. The Pilgrim confirmed it was her last memory before the transfer from the satellite. Maybe what they thought was a satellite was the space station module that housed the Pilgrim Project.

"The point of the Pilgrim Project—as far as I can tell—

was to reach the source of the Corruption. It somehow bleeds across realities and spreads so fast. We'd somehow figured out how to send ourselves to the reality at the epicentre—a Hail Mary to figure out how to stop it from spreading further. I feel there's more to the mission, but I'm struggling to recover those details."

Will it reach this reality?

"That's a good question, darlin'. From what I remember, it seems like it's only a matter of time."

Raff looked at Denn and the group, laughing at something. *So why isn't the Corruption here already?*

"The pulse knocked out all working quantum computers . . .That's my best guess why." That made sense to Raff. He'd lived the memory of when a quantum computer was responsible for it spreading to the space station. The Pilgrim sighed. "You do realise I have to attempt the mission. Billions of lives are at stake. Therein lies a huge problem—"

"Hey Raff," Freek said, pointing at Raff's plate. "Are you going to eat those?"

Raff slid the plate over to Freek. "No buddy," he said. "Help yourself."

Freek's eyes opened wide as he picked up a rib. "Raff not eating something? I'm shocked."

"I'm just not feeling it," Raff said.

"No worries bru," Freek said before taking a bite. Raff tuned out the comments from the others. *Lemme guess, Pilgrim, I have to go with you.*

"I'm so sorry, darlin'," the Pilgrim said. "I regret that the Interface took you as a host. A proper firing of the path engine will turn your brain to jelly. But, it's designed to take your mind along for the ride so you won't really die."

Can't it transfer host like before?

"I know you well enough to know that you wouldn't want to burden someone else with this. It would be an 'asshole move.'"

Raff looked at Denn and the group again. They looked happy—smiling and laughing. He'd trade his life for them any time. This was one of those times. *I guess I'm on board for a journey into the unknown. I mean, that's what death is. Isnt it? I already made peace with dying when I thought tumours were eating away at my brain. So, this mission of yours seems like a much better deal. But first, we must take down Mervin Emmett. The guys won't be safe otherwise. Can you help with that?*

"Sure darlin'. But you know as well as I do: Emmett will put up a fight. A cornered stray will lash out, so this idea y'all have of gathering evidence and arresting him has such a slim chance of success."

I was thinking the same thing. It seems our thoughts are aligned—

"So, you will help me build something that will permanently solve the Emmett problem."

Okay?

"It's a surprise, darlin'. Play along with their mission for now. Just smile and nod."

ΔΔΔ

Raff's group reached Cabazon, their last stop on their 1100-mile westerly drive from Odessa to Los Angeles. A drive that should've taken sixteen hours turned into a three-day trip. At Thimba's insistence, they made the most of what Texas, New Mexico, Arizona and California had to offer along the I-10— stopping to take pictures, sampling the local cuisine and visiting landmarks. The majority of their time was spent in Tucson and Phoenix, Arizona. Raff wanted to get through the journey quickly but saw the others enjoying themselves, so he let them be. Raff wandered around the Cabazon truck stop and felt small for the first time in a long time when he stared up at Dinny, the bright green forty-something-foot-high concrete Brontosaurus. Maybe his impending foray into the unknown or the thought of humanity going the way of the dinosaurs made him feel uneasy.

Raff felt the hairs on his neck tingle. He turned to see Ezra standing behind him. "Oh," Raff said. "Didn't see you there."

"Sorry," Ezra said, pushing his glasses up his nose. "I

didn't mean to startle you. I've brought your satphone."

Raff took the phone from Ezra and put it in his pocket.

"Thanks. Did Marco get what you need?"

"Yes. Turns out the ATF is already surveilling Emmett, so Marco got me access to all their feeds—"

"That's not going to be enough—"

"Agreed. Emmet probably knows about it... But Marco's a smart one. He's installed a rotation of military micro-drones to automatically follow Emmett around the clock."

"He's probably not expecting that," Raff said, smiling when he imagined a swarm of flies buzzing around Emmett's head. He looked towards Ezra's car in the nearby parking lot and saw the rest of the group gathering. He pointed their way and started walking. "Looks like they're eager to get going."

Ezra was red-faced and out of breath when they reached the car. What was a leisurely stroll for Raff was a full cardio workout for Ezra. He struggled to keep up with Raff's long strides. He hunched over and rested his hands on his knees. Raff looked away from Ezra for a second to see a grinning Thimba wearing a new Brontosaurus print t-shirt. He chuckled to himself. *Seems Thimba's having the time of his life,* he thought.

"Darlin'," the Pilgrim said to Raff, "Best be sure Ezra's not having a heart attack."

Why so concerned for him all of a sudden? Raff thought as he stepped towards Ezra and placed a hand on his back.

"Your plan don't work without a hacker," the Pilgrim said.

Aren't you able to hack stuff, Raff thought as he patted Ezra's back. The Pilgrim didn't reply. "You alright there, buddy?" Raff said.

"I'm . . . whew," Ezra said, managing to catch his breath, "Good. Not used to all this exercise."

"Bru," Freek said, "you need to get out more. You're no good to anyone if you have a pump attack."

Ezra stood up, put his hands on his hips, and frowned at his protruding belly. "Don't y'all think I know that—"

With a loud crack, Thimba entered the driver's seat and rolled down the window. "It's time to go," he said, "if we want to get there before dark."

Denn saluted. "Yes sir," he said and entered the back of the car. Everyone else got in, and Thimba took them west on the I-10 for the final three hours of the trip. They arrived at a huge white warehouse in Vernon. Thimba stopped at a tall sliding gate at its side and pressed the intercom and the gate rolled open with a loud screech and rattle. Thimba parked next to a large rusty roller shutter. "This is the place," Jannie said, closing his laptop as everyone climbed out. "Bigger than the chicken coop, that's for sure."Raff thumped on the painted steel door beside the roller shutter and looked at a lone camera above him. With a loud buzz the door popped open an inch. Raff pulled the door open and let everyone else enter first. Raff entered the brightly lit warehouse to see row upon row of shelved dusty boxes. Perhaps another victim of the post-pulse crash, tied up in seemingly endless bureaucracy amongst a queue of hundreds of other cases. Or, because of Marco's involvement, Raf thought it was more likely a seized asset from some criminal enterprise. Marco met them a few metres in and showed them to the two-story office area at the front. "There's eight offices," Marco said. "Enough for a room each. The head and kitchen are off the reception. There's a pile of mattresses there, too—help yourselves."

"Um—" Ezra began.

"Ezra," Marco beckoned. "The surveillance getup is in the main warehouse, in the far right corner. It was already caged, so it was the logical location."

"Sweet," Ezra said, changing direction. "I'll head there now. My fingertips are itchin' to do somethin'."

"Oh darlin'," the Pilgrim said in Raff's ears, "We *must* go shopping."

Chapter Twenty

Lithium

A week passed since Raff's group moved into the Vernon warehouse with Marco. Ezra spent most of that time watching the ATF and drone surveillance feeds of Mervin Emmett, all the while monitoring Emmett Global's digital footprint—looking for a crack to leverage. When Ezra took sleep breaks, the other guys took shifts watching the feeds. So far, Ezra had no luck finding the evidence they needed. It was locked up tight in Emmett Global HQ, if there was any. The word of Raff—a wanted criminal who 'hallucinates' and has 'tumours' in his brain—was likely inadmissible. Denn's memory of General Ngaba with Mervin Emmett was hazy at best. And then there was Thimba, who wasn't close enough to the general to have any information to add. The group was at an impasse and only had time on their side—time to sit and observe, hoping that someone in Emmet HQ would slip up.

"Heya darlin'," the Pilgrim said, startling Raff, who'd just sat down in the kitchen to eat breakfast. "I found a way to get that evidence the UN want and flush Mervin out into the open."

I don't know if I'll ever get used to your voice just popping in like that, Raff thought.

The Pilgrim laughed. "Should I cough first?"

Raff shovelled soggy cornflakes into his mouth. *No . . . that might be worse. Anyway, I thought you weren't following the UN plan to gather evidence?*

"I'm not. I've decided to see what information Emmett has on the satellite—specifically, any images of it before re-entry—"

I get it. You want to confirm that it wasn't a satellite but the space station module—

Raff had the answers to what was happening in his head, so he respected the Pilgrim's pursuit of answers about her mind. He had an inkling of what the Pilgrim was going through. Besides, Raff was curious to confirm if it was indeed the mangled remains of the Project Pilgrim module on the truck bed in the POW camp during the war. *I'll help you the best I can,* he thought.

"No need," the Pilgrim said. "Just wait for it. Three. Two. One."

Ezra burst into the kitchen, red-faced and breathing heavily. "I've solved it," he said. "I know how we can get *all* Emmett Global's data."

Marco emptied his mug into the sink and sat on the counter. "Finally," he said. "Tell me the details, and I'll run it up the chain."

Ezra explained what they already knew: Emmett Global keeps their servers air-gapped from the outside world. It turns out this is not entirely true. An old contact from MIT sent him a copy of a three-year-old invoice from the installation of a high-speed fibre-optic line directly from the block Emmett HQ sits on to a nearby data exchange. It was made out to a corporation called Clarity Worldwide. "I dug into Clarity," he said, "stealth-like, and it's all phoney baloney. Something interesting came up in my delve . . . Clarity has a large cloud storage account—"

"So Clarity is Emmett?" Marco said.

"It can't be anyone else. Nobody else on the block could afford or need a highspeed line like that."

Marco stood up and rolled his eyes. "Shit. We can't get the data from the cloud without a warrant, and that would tip our hand—"

Ezra smirked. "We don't need to. One per cent of the light is a hundred per cent of the data."

Everyone else looked around the room at each other. Ezra adjusted his glasses and explained that a slight bend in the fibre optic line would release a small amount of light. That small amount of light will contain all the data, and Emmett will be non-the-wiser. There's no intrusion or malware for them to detect. Someone would need to go down into the sewer tunnel where the fibre line should be and install an interceptor. "There's a catch," Ezra said. "Once the interceptor is in place, we'll need to wait for Emmet to back up their data."

"Get it installed ASAP," Marco said, "and I'll run this up the chain . . ."

"I hate to be the bearer of bad news," the Pilgrim said, distracting Raff from the conversation. "There's no data in their cloud storage. I shoulda said, it's one of those if-all-else-fails backup solutions. You need to force a backup. A four or five-alarm fire should do."

Thanks. Raff cleared his throat. "I doubt there's any data in their cloud account," he said.

Ezra's eyes opened wide as he looked at Raff. "What?" he said.

Raff sighed. "Emmett, being who he is, is unlikely to back anything up to the cloud unless he has no choice. It's gonna be one of those if-all-else-fails backup solutions." Raff looked at Denn and smiled. "We're gonna need a fire to get the ball rolling. A *big* fire."

Ezra looked at Marco and nodded. "I believe Raff's right," he said. "The cartel did something similar."

"Ay dios mío," Marco said, rubbing his temples. "I'll have fun explaining this to the brass." He looked around the room at everyone. "I'll try and be back tomorrow. Get everything ready just in case."

Ezra's friend from MIT didn't contact him, Raff thought, *did they?*

"Nope," the Pilgrim said. "When it comes to hacking, I'm miles ahead of him."

Raff smiled. *That you are.*

ΔΔΔ

It was three AM the following day. Raff crept quietly along the carpeted corridor to his room at the Vernon warehouse. He

361

didn't want to wake the others and have to explain what he was doing, sneaking out in the middle of the night. Stealth was difficult with the four large shopping bags in his hands. Raff had snuck out for a midnight shopping spree at a local hypermarket at the Pilgrim's behest. She needed the raw materials for her secret construction project. Raff wondered what a laptop, charcoal bag, copper pipe spool, lithium battery pack, steel spoons and white paint could be used to build. "You aren't gonna tell me what we're building, are you," Raff said under his breath.

"It's a surprise," the Pilgrim said. "I will tell you this, darlin': a lithium-based chemical reaction started your nightmare with Mervin—so it's only fitting that one powers its end. I've devised a self-charging graphene-enhanced lithium-titanium-oxide battery that should do the trick."

Raff knew she was talking about the lithium battery that started the fire—the one in his broken phone that sent him on a collision course with Mervin Emmett. *I'm sure you won't disappoint,* he thought. *You know, lithium is responsible for more than just my troubles with Emmett—Ngaba's war was really about controlling lithium deposits—*

"Hmm. . . bad things in threes—your superstition—lithium." The Pilgrim laughed.

What's so funny? I left that superstition behind in England.

"Lithium has three protons and three electrons. It seems the universe was laughing at you long before I did."

What about the three seats in the Pilgrim module—

"Oh shit. . . guess I was the punchline before you were."

Raff chuckled, stopping outside his room and placing the heavy bags on the floor. Making fists for a moment, the feeling in his fingers returned. He unlocked the door and was greeted by a pungent, sweet, bleach-like smell as he opened it. *God, what's that smell?*

"Ozone," the Pilgrim said. "That means the nano-constructors are ready."

I hope so, he thought. *This won't make too much noise, will it?*

"It shouldn't," the Pilgrim said. "But, I don't recall using the nano-constructors this way before. So y'all be prepared for anything. . . They're an enigma—I know how to control them but not much else."

Raff turned on the light and dragged the bags through the doorway towards a three-foot-long plastic box he'd borrowed from the warehouse. *They are so advanced.*

"A little too advanced, darlin'. Scarily so."

Maybe you'll recover more memories about them?

The Pilgrim sighed. "Unlikely. I've hit an irreversible hole in my memories."

Shit, sorry—

"Don't you worry bout it, darlin'. It's a paradox—how can I miss what I don't remember? Anyway, put everything in the box and let's begin."

Raff knelt beside the box and emptied all the purchased items into it. The dust from the charcoal made him sneeze. "What now," he said, sniffling.

"Put your hand in the box and stay still. This won't hurt, but it will probably feel strange."

Raff closed his eyes and braced for the unexpected—maybe a headache or even a seizure. Instead, he felt like hundreds of ants crawled down his arm to his hands and fingers before his hand began to itch fiercely. Ignoring the itch, Raff kept still as instructed. He opened his eyes when the itch stopped, and his hand felt wet—covered with what looked like black oil. Wriggling his fingers a little, the fluid felt thick and sticky like treacle. The fluid seemingly lost adhesion and slid off Raff's hand into the pile of items without leaving a trace on his hand.

"That's it, darlin'," the Pilgrim said. "You can now remove your hand."

Raff pulled back his hand and sat down on his feet. "What now?" he said, staring at the box.

"Just watch as the magic happens. . . I hope."

A high-pitched hum could now be heard from the tray,

almost like the buzzing of bees in a beehive. Raff watched for the next half hour as the fluid—the nano-constructors—did their work. The fluid turned into thousands of fine hair-like strands that reached upwards, seemingly defying gravity, continuing to vibrate until folding over into the pile of junk. They flattened and spread like tiny rivers breaking their banks, increasing in volume as the junk dissolved into them. Finally, the strands coalesced into a single wide column before swirling downwards and outwards, forming a sizeable solid shape in the middle alongside a dozen smaller cylindrical ones. The fluid had just completed its task, settling at the bottom of the box. The final form of its creation sat in the tray like a brilliant-white work of art. Raff expected some kind of bomb. *Is that what I think it is?* Raff thought.

"It's a gun darlin'," the Pilgrim said. "A *big* gun. Go ahead, get a feel for it."

Raff lifted the gun from the tray, and he was distracted momentarily as the fluid reached up and flowed over his hands and arm—almost dropping the gun when his arm itched and tingled as the nano-constructors disappeared into his skin. The first thing he noticed about the gun was its heft—reminding him of the weight of a loaded fifty-calibre machine gun. Holding the ergonomic grip with his right hand and resting the muzzle on the floor, Raff placed the butt against his shoulder and stared down the gun's sleek thick plastic shell. From trigger guard to muzzle—at ten, two and six o'clock—there were rows of a dozen black cylinders labelled "coil." The bottom row doubled as a foregrip—Raff gripped it with his left hand and lifted the muzzle upwards, staring down the upper two rows of coils. Something seemed to be missing. *A rail gun,* Raff thought. *Where's the scope?*

"Safety on the right, scope on the left. And no, it's a gauss rifle. Not a rail gun."

Okay. Raff looked along the left side and saw two buttons labelled "scope" and "mode." Raff pressed "scope", and three red holographic rings appeared between the upper coils. He peered down the barrel, through the rings and swung the rifle towards the door. *Will this punch through armour?*

"This'll punch through an Abrams tank like a hot knife through butter."

It was late, and Raff was struggling to keep his eyes open. "Good," Raff said under his breath as he turned the scope off and placed the gun in the box. He put the lid on the box. "I have to get some sleep. Maybe we can take it to a firing range tomorrow to fire some rounds?"

"I look forward to it," the Pilgrim said before humming a lullaby to Raff. Raff lay down on his mattress and drifted off to sleep.

∆∆∆

Raff only got a couple of hours of sleep following the gun's construction. He tried returning to sleep but kept thinking of the times he had encountered the Corruption—the alternate club Gravity and the space station Pilgrim module. Raff needed a distraction, so he shuffled to the kitchen for breakfast, still wearing the previous day's clothes. The kitchen looked like a small tornado had torn through it—the toaster was on the floor among a mess of smashed coffee mugs and breakfast cereal. He saw Jannie staring down at the mess. "Jannie! What—the—hell, man?" Raff shouted.

"I didn't do this," Jannie said and shrugged. "Have you seen Freek? He's not in his room?"

Raff pinched the bridge of his nose. "This has Freek written all over it—"

Jannie raised his eyebrows and opened his mouth to reply when Ezra rushed into the kitchen, all out of breath, wearing nothing but undies and socks without an ounce of shame as his belly hung over the elastic hem. Raff and Jannie tried to avert their eyes. "Uh, guys," he said, pointing into the warehouse, "y'all need to see this."

They followed Ezra as he huffed and puffed his way to his corner of the warehouse—the surveillance cage set up by Marco. Sat in the oversized black-leather office chair was

Thimba, keeping an eye on several video feeds on the half-dozen monitors attached to the cage. Thimba swivelled towards the three of them, but Raff's eyes were drawn to one of the screens with a paused drone feed. On it was a familiar petite brunette woman, with hands bound while being dragged into a white van. He pointed at the screen. "I know her," he said. "That's Laura from Leeds. Why has Emmett brought her here?"

Raff's ears popped. "I think that *might* be my fault," the Pilgrim told him. "He's probably been searching for a woman associated with y'all, because I called and taunted him in South Africa—"

"Denn was on watch last night," Raff said, leaning toward the screen. "He's got a soft spot for her, so he's probably gone full pyromaniac on us. Oh, Denn, you bloody idiot. Where have you gone?"

"Mr Raff," Thimba said, tapping Raff's arm before returning to one of the video feeds. "This is why Ezra came to find you." He clicked the mouse, and the feed changed. An office block was on fire. The offices of Emmett Global. "It's not good. Did Denn do this?"

Raff pinched the bridge of his nose again and sighed. "It seems likely." He looked up at Jannie, who had his phone to his ear. "Where's Freek?"

"Those fuckin' domkops have gone and screwed us," Jannie said, pacing up and down the cage. "Ag, boetie, pick up the phone!"

From Jannie's reaction, Raff knew Freek must've gone off with Denn. *Maybe Denn woke Freek when he was busy rearranging the kitchen,* Raff thought. *Pilgrim, can you find them?*

"Hmm," the Pilgrim said in Raff's ear. "I'll search for those idiots. However, there's an opportunity here—the cloud backup is happening *right now.*"

Raff snapped his fingers. "Ezra," he said, the pitch of his voice raised. "Aren't you supposed to be doing something right now?"

Ezra frowned, leaning against the cage, still breathing heavily. "Not that I know of," he said.

Raff turned and gave him an icy stare. "*The* plan," he said. "You know, the part with the fire and what happens afterwards. We didn't wade through shit for nothing yesterday, did we?"

Fortunately, part of the plan was unfolding before them—albeit prematurely because Marco had not yet given the go-ahead. Raff and Ezra had already made some necessary preparations in the field the day before—installing the fibre optic interceptor to the lines in the sewerage tunnels beneath Emmett Global HQ.

Ezra sprang to his feet—pushed Thimba out the way, and

muttered to himself as he typed something in: "Dang it, dang it, dang it—"

"And?"

"Whew, it's okay y'all. The data is pourin' in, as expected."

Raff sighed in relief. Jannie patted Ezra on the back. "Oh, that's good," Jannie said, putting his phone away. "The plan's worked. When those poepols return, I will tear them a new one. The UN getting this?"

"Oh, yes, all of it. Keepin' a backup just in case."

"Good idea, bru. Let's hope we're not in trouble for this—"

Raff looked at the fire raging on the monitor. "I guess we're now seeking forgiveness instead of permission," he said. "Can you pull up the drone feeds?"

Ezra clicked the mouse a few times, and several screens went blank. "This ain't good," he said. "They've gone dark. Probably the fire."

"Probably." Raff wasn't convinced. *Is it the fire?* he thought.

"The micro-drones weren't near the fire when they went dark," the Pilgrim said. "Dang it, looks like they're being jammed. I'm goin' quiet awhile. I will find Mervin so we can finish this."

About that, Raff thought, *I don't think I can go through with assassinating the man.*

The Pilgrim didn't respond. She went silent while the ATF video feeds stuttered and began buffering.

Ezra slammed the mouse down. "Dang internet," he shouted.

ΔΔΔ

Midday came, and Denn and Freek were still nowhere to be seen. The fire at Emmett Global HQ was still raging. The news said it took six fire engines alone to prevent the fire from spreading to adjacent buildings. In addition to monitoring the news feeds for any information on the guys' whereabouts, the Pilgrim sought to triangulate the signal source interfering with the micro-drones. She figured the source was likely Mervin. Who else? The drone's programming should keep them near Mervin—even during signal loss—until they were instructed to do otherwise. It was a long shot at best—find the dead zone and find Mervin. She hacked and uploaded a monitoring program she'd written into all the cell towers across LA to monitor for anomalies. Hacking had become a breeze without interference from the Interface—the full quantum computational capabilities of the lattice had become available to the Pilgrim.

Hmmm, the Pilgrim thought. *That's interesting. More cells are losing signal in Carson than in the rest of LA. Three cell towers are reporting the same thing, so odds are it's not a glitch.*

Analysing the cell tower data, the Pilgrim further narrowed the interference to a four-block radius in Carson, Los Angeles. *I need to narrow this further*, she thought as she hacked into the city's traffic monitoring system. She ran through dozens of camera feeds simultaneously, viewing several hours' worth of video from the early morning hours—pausing when she recognised the driver of a white van. It was one of the men from the drone feed with Laura before it went dark. *This must be the van Laura was in. Just gotta follow it.*

The Pilgrim found another angle of the van from the next set of lights. The van moved toward the camera but turned off before it reached it—between two single-storey flat-roofed white-painted buildings. She pulled up an aerial image of the buildings, and the turn was a dead end—a small parking lot between the two. Real estate listings for the street confirmed one of them was vacant. *Gotcha!*

ΔΔΔ

Midday had long passed, and the only evidence of the setting sun was the diminishing light on the ATF video feeds. Denn and Freek hadn't returned, so the mood in the surveillance cage was low. Raff sat on the floor in the corner, dozing off as he observed the others—Jannie paced while looking at his phone, and Thimba meditated on the floor with his legs crossed. All of Jannie's attempts to phone Denn and

Freek failed. Ezra delved into the LAPD database, and there were no hits. The local hospitals came up empty, too—Raff expected that as the guys would likely want to remain low, but the lack of a signal to say they were okay was concerning.

Jannie's phone vibrated, and he looked at the screen. He then tried and failed several times to make a call unsuccessfully, getting increasingly frustrated with each attempt. Finally, punching the cage hard enough to bloody a knuckle, he handed the phone to Raff and screamed at the ceiling: "Jou ma!"

Raff pulled up the text messages and read them. Tears welled up in his eyes, and he felt dizzy; it was a final goodbye from Freek and Denn.

Where are you? Jannie had texted.

Freek had replied: *Surrounded and nowhere to go. This is the end. Sorry, I've been a shit brother. Take care of the guys for me. This is goodbye, boet. I'll say hi to ma if I see her. Totsiens.*

That text was followed shortly by: *This is Denn. Raff, I made a mistake. Sorry. If I die, get em all for me. Been fun knowing you all.*

Raff looked at the send times, and they were from 6:14 AM. *Why have they only come through now?* he thought.

"It's not good news," the Pilgrim said, startling the tired Raff. "I tracked Freek's cell when it popped back on the grid—just outside a dead zone in Carson—"

Dead-zone?

"Yes darlin'. The jamming affecting the micro-drones is blocking cell signals. I checked the traffic cams around the zone and tracked the same van that took Laura to a vacant building—"

Ezra waved his hand in front of Raff's face. "Hello," he said. "Anyone in there?"

"Shit," Raff said, realizing he'd tuned out the rest of the room. "I was just lost in thought—"

"Mr Raff," Thimba pointed at Raff's hand. "The phone is ringing. Answer it!"

Raff looked at the phone in his hand, and the screen was flashing—the name on the screen: "Boeti." Raff swiped to answer. "Freek," he said tentatively as he put the phone to his ear. "Where have you been?"

"Mr Hernandez," a familiar English accent said, "you know who this is." Raff's heart sank—it was Mervin Emmett. "So, I'm going to be quick. I have your friends: Mr Singleton and Freek. Oh, and Miss Matthews, she's a feisty one—but innocent in all this. Reminds me of my own. . . Never mind that. You've cost me a lot, but I can be a reasonable man—so let's parlé. I know you're here in LA—"

"This is a trick," Raff said. "How do I know you won't have me shot the moment you see me?"

"You don't have a choice, Mr Hernandez–I can make

things *very* uncomfortable for your friends. I will message you the address. Come *alone.*" The call ended, and Raff looked around the room. All eyes were on him. "It's gotta be a trap," Raff said.

"What*'s gotta be a trap?*" said Jannie, squinting at Raff as he returned his phone.

"That was Emmett calling from Freek's phone. He has Denn, Freek *and* Laura—Denn's sweetheart. He wants to *parlé* with me—alone."

Jannie grabbed Raff by the t-shirt and shook him. "He will kill you, bru. You know that, right?"

"He's right," the Pilgrim said. "you can't go—"

Raff brushed Jannie's hand off his t-shirt. "I have to go," he said. "He'll torture them if I don't—"

Jannie raised his eyebrows and walked away. "That fucking asshole—"

Thimba stood up from the floor. "I'll follow him," he said, "to make sure he doesn't make things worse." Thimba disappeared into the rows of shelves after Jannie. Ezra went quiet and turned to the monitors.

"Darlin'," the Pilgrim said to Raff, "if you insist on going, there *will* be consequences. . ."

△△△

Raff gave Jannie an hour to cool down before going to see him.

V. B. Anstee

Carrying a large, heavy plastic box, Raff pushed Jannie's door open with his shoulder to see him lying on the floor in the dark and staring at the ceiling. Raff turned the light on with his elbow, put the box on the floor, and closed the door behind him.

Jannie wiped his red eyes with his sleeve before sitting up. "What do you want?" he said.

"We can't rescue Denn and Freek alone," Raff said. "So we need your help—"

Jannie raised an eyebrow. "We?"

Raff sat on the floor before the door and told Jannie what he'd learned of the Pilgrim—the space station, Project Pilgrim, the satellite, the path engine, and the Corruption. Jannie listened intently, waiting for Raff to finish. "I'm not going to lie," Jannie said, "that's an amazing story, but Freek might be right—it seems a bit farfetched. I could believe the AI in the head theory, but nano-whatsits, zombies, parallel universes—"

Raff pushed the box toward Jannie. "Open the box," he said.

Jannie opened the box, and his eyes opened wide. Kneeling over the box, Jannie pulled out the brilliant-white Gauss rifle—made by the nano-constructors—and looked down the barrel. "Fuck me," he said, "It's one heavy gun."

"It's a Gauss rifle," Raff said. "I gathered the materials, put 'em in the box, and the Pilgrim made the nano constructors come out of my hands to build it." Raff leaned over and pointed at the *scope* button. "Press this—"

Jannie pressed it, and the three red holographic rings of the scope appeared. "Nice." He turned to Raff. "What's the damage?"

"It should be powerful enough to punch through an Abrams tank."

Jannie nodded and pressed the *mode* button, and the scope's red rings widened and filled with shades of green. The green turned shades of orange as he aimed towards Raff. "Thermal imaging. Nice resolution." He returned the gun to the box. "Okay, I'm in. But first, can you show me the nano-thingies?"

Can you? Raff thought.

"Sure," the Pilgrim said to Raff. "Hold out your hand."

"Here we go," Raff said, extending his arm. Jannie squinted and leaned back. Raff's skin crawled and itched as a black, oily fluid flowed over his hand and down his fingers before disappearing back into his skin.

"Shit," Jannie said, grabbing Raff's hand to take a closer look. "I believe everything now. Tell me what I need to do!"

ΔΔΔ

Denn and Freek had woken to find themselves with an

unconscious Laura, tied to chairs in a dimly lit, empty brickwork room for hours. The last thing Denn remembered was facing Mervin Emmett outside his office building in the middle of the night, having just set off a string of firebombs in Emmett Global HQ—before things went black after they'd both been jumped by Emmett's men and beaten unconscious. Denn found breathing painful, feeling he might have cracked several ribs. His leg was also broken below the knee where one of the goons had stomped on it. Freek's face looked swollen and bruised, and the white of his left eye was completely bloodshot.

"Shit, Freek," Denn said, "sorry I dragged you into this, bruv."

"It's all right," Freek said. "I couldn't let you go alone, or maybe I'd drunk too much—"

"Ha déjà vu all over again. This time—"

"We're on the same side."

"The good side?"

"Yah, yah the good side!"

Denn wriggled in the chair and looked at Laura. Her chest moved, so she was breathing. "Do you think she's okay," he said.

Freek blinked a lot as he struggled to focus. "She's probably sedated. Emmett likes that shit."

The door to the room slammed open, and Mervin Emmett came through. His nostrils flared as he looked at the guys. Denn knew this day would end very badly for them, and it wouldn't be quick either.

Mervin paced before the guys, occasionally stopping to sweep his hair back, brimming with anger over what Denn and Freek had managed to do, maybe even more so from the ineptitude of his own security from preventing it. A bunch of nobodies taking down a private military company was embarrassing. "I'll make this simple for you," he said. "You tell me where the rest of your pals are—including the Texan—and I'll make sure your deaths are quick and painless. You refuse, and you'll know pain like never before. Tell me now."

Freek sighed loudly before coughing up blood onto his blue t-shirt. "Okay, I'll tell you," he said. "They're on Fuck Off Avenue, in Stick A Dick—"

Mr Emmett punched Freek in the mouth with an audible click. He momentarily recoiled and massaged his knuckles before pulling a nightstick from a pocket and flicking it open. The two were about to be given another beating when the door burst open, and two of Mervin's auto-pistol armed goons entered, escorting an unarmed Raff towards their boss. Raff's face looked blank, calm. *Why is Raff here?* thought Denn. *He's not freaking out. That's good.* Denn knew there must be a plan in motion. He elbowed Freek in the side and mentally prepared himself for what may come.

Mervin turned to Raff and pulled out his pistol. "You're just in time, he said. "Remember, this is all your fault. You did this."

As Mr Emmett aimed his gun at Freek's face, a cracking thump of a sound, like a sledgehammer hitting a loose brick, echoed through the room. The guys saw a red mist hanging where Mervin's head used to be, fractions of a second before his body crashed to the concrete floor. It happened so fast that Denn had blinked and missed his head exploding sideways. Two more thuds echoed, and two more areas of mist appeared over fallen goons. This time, they'd seen an invisible fist punch a hole through each goon's centre mass. Noticing the beams of light poking through either side of the warehouse, they realised that something had passed clean through the warehouse three times, leaving fist-sized holes in the hard red brick walls.

"Bruv," said Denn, "check on Laura, please."

"Just a sec," Raff said. He looked around the room and headed out of sight. Something crashed to the floor before Raff reappeared and began to untie Laura. "Jannie, can you hear me? . . . Good. Thanks for the assist. It's all clear here. . . Yes, untying the guys now. Could do with a ride—"

"She alright," Denn said. His leg and chest throbbed as he

struggled against the restraints.

Raff lifted Laura's hair to reveal her bruised face. "She's alive but probably needs a hospital."

Denn looked down at his crooked lower leg. "I'll need an x-ray or two bruv—"

"Me too," Freek said. "I bet Jannie is real pissed with me."

Raff tilted his head and winked, pulling out an earwig communicator momentarily. "Yeah," he said. "Just a bit."

Raff untied everyone and carried Laura to the door. Denn couldn't put any weight on his leg, so Freek assisted him. "Sorry, bruv," Denn said. "I messed up. I had a few drinks with Freek, and when I saw Laura like—"

"It's okay, buddy, I understand why you did it. I'm not happy, but I understand. We don't need to talk about it now; hospital first."

"Okay, bruv. But I tried to find you, and you weren't around. Where were you?"

"I was working on solving our Emmett problem permanently—"

As they left the building for the small parking lot at the back, Jannie pulled up in Ezra's car and rolled down the window. "You look like shit," Jannie said. "Get in."

ΔΔΔ

As Jannie drove the guys to the hospital a few blocks away, Raff filled Denn and Freek in on everything that happened, how he found them and the gun. Freek couldn't keep his eyes off the Gauss rifle, almost drooling over it.

Raff's ears popped. "That went well," the Pilgrim said. "Now about those consequences: You have a few minutes before the path engine breaks down and irradiates everyone around you before it explodes in a pulse that sends California back to the Stone Age."

Give me a second, he thought. Raff took a moment to look at Denn, Freek and Jannie. Raff had insisted on meeting Mervin Emmett. The Pilgrim knew it was the right thing to do, but to protect her mission—and now Raff's too—she had no choice but to charge the path engine. She could fire it on a nanosecond"s notice to escape the very likely scenario that Mervin was going to put a bullet in Raff's head. Now Mervin was gone, they were undoubtedly much safer. But the engine was primed, and there were only two ways out—let it break down and explode or use it. Raff knew which one to choose. Heading off into the unknown was scary and exciting at the same time.

"Jannie," Raff said with tears rolling down his cheeks. "The gun is yours. Freek and Denn, there's a thumb drive under my mattress. There's detailed information about something called the Corruption—get it to Marco and the

Lithium

Prime Minister. It's important. Sorry guys, there'll be no more *Rambo shit*. I hate goodbyes."

Denn groaned as he turned to look at Raff. "What are you on, bruv," he said. "You're scaring me—"

Let's go, please, Raff thought.

"Here goes nothing," the Pilgrim said. The car stalled just before the hospital turning—the dashboard screen and streetlights flickered as far as the eye could see. The world disappeared in a flash of bright white light.

ΔΔΔ

"I'm sorry," the doctor in scrubs said, looking at Denn, "the EEG is negative for any meaningful brain activity. The MRI shows the folds of his brain have almost completely disappeared. So, essentially, Mr Hernandez is only alive because of these machines, and barely. I'll give you time to say your goodbyes." The doctor walked out and left the gang alone with Raff.

Raff had so many wires attached to his body, tubes running into his mouth and nose. Ezra, Freek, Jannie, and Thimba stood around the bed while Denn and Laura sat down. The guys were silent when the doctor left, with nothing but the sound of the heart monitor and the breathing apparatus clicking for every breath it pushed into Raff.

Denn chuckled to himself as he remembered the good

times with Raff, tears in his eyes too, not caring if the others saw. "You know," Denn said, "I think Raff's the glue that brung us all together. Me and Thimba would have died in the war. The war—may still be going if it wasn't for him. Then, if it wasn't for his phone I broke, I might not've contacted Laura again—I certainly wouldn't have met my good friends Jannie, Freek and Ezra—"

"Yah," Freek said, looking at Jannie. "We'd still be working for that asshole Emmett and might now be under UN surveillance."

"I don't know, boeti," Jannie said. "We'd probably be dead. I believe we'll see him again someday—"

Thimba wiped his eyes. "I agree with Denn," he said, "about the war—it would not have stopped so soon. And you would not have come to South Africa and saved me from the bad police. I'm also thankful I get to see the USA."

Everyone looked at Ezra. "I didn't know y'all were going around the room," he said. "Well, I'd still be enslaved by the cartel. Besides, the detailed data he left about this *Corruption* has landed me a good job with DARPA. Thanks Raff."

"Um," Laura said. "I didn't know him well, but I thought he was a cutey. A bit tall, but a cutey."

Denn grabbed his crutches and stood up. His leg had a cast from ankle to thigh. "It's time," he said, "I'll go get the doc."

Some minutes later, Denn came back with the doctor in tow. Everyone in the room stood up and surrounded Raff, heads bowed. Denn took his place around the hospital bed, struggling to hold back his tears. "Go ahead, mate," he said. "It's time. So long, brother, maybe we'll meet again."

The others said their goodbyes, Thimba in Swahili, the brothers in Afrikaans, and Marco in Spanish.

The doctor removed the feeding tube from Raff's nose and pressed a button on the ventilation machine. The breathing apparatus stopped, and the beeps on the heart monitor rapidly decreased in frequency before sounding one last continuous tone.

Epilogue

Raff awakes to the sound of his own scream. Still in bed, he darts his eyes around the room, and a look of confusion washes over his face. The surroundings are familiar yet unfamiliar at the same time. It's clear to him that he's in his bedroom; the symmetry, the same peeling wallpaper, the damp stain on the ceiling that looks like a single breast, it's all there. But the decor is different enough to confuse him. It's tidy, with a broader expensive oak wardrobe and an unknown wall painting hanging next to it. Looking at a shelf in the corner, he smiles when he notices the framed picture of him and Denn in the army. *I guess some things just don't change,* he thought.

"Hello darlin'," a familiar Texan accent startles him.

Raff looks over to the corner to see a pretty woman standing there, the same woman from the space station—brunette and tall, with eyes now a shade of mercury. Flickering out of existence, she re-materialises, seated on the bed beside Raff. She faces him and says, "We've got work to do."

Artwork

Here's some artwork related to the story's characters and my original concepts of Raff and Denn. A long time ago, the characters for the story were anthropomorphized animal-people . . .

Lithium

Image: Characters from this novel.
Foreground (from left to right): Thimba, Laura, Raff, Denn (The Kentucky Bag Streaker), Jannie, Freek and Ezra.
Background: The Pilgrim.

Image: My original concept for Raff.

Image: This is an old story concept for Raff.

V. B. Anstee

Image: Playing around with my original concept for Raff.

Image: My original concept for Denn. Raff's BFF / sidekick.

Printed in Great Britain
by Amazon